Will Kennedy Is Not Himself Today.

When Chad, the coolest kid in Shadyside Middle School, offers to switch bodies with super-dorky Will, Will thinks it *has* to be a joke. Then he goes to Chad's house on Fear Street, and realizes Chad is serious. Really serious.

Will decides to make the switch. And he loves being Chad. But he misses his old body. Too bad Chad likes being Will, too. In fact, he likes it so much, he's decided to keep Will's body.

Forever.

Also from R. L. Stine

The Beast
The Beast 2

R. L. Stine's Ghosts of Fear Street

Available from MINSTREL Books

R·L·STINE'S
GHOSTS OF FEAR STREET ®

BODY SWITCHERS FROM OUTER SPACE

A Parachute Press Book

A
MINSTREL ®
BOOK

PUBLISHED BY POCKET BOOKS

New York   London   Toronto   Sydney   Tokyo   Singapore

A MINSTREL PAPERBACK *Original*

A Minstrel Paperback published by
POCKET BOOKS, a division of Simon & Schuster Inc.
1230 Avenue of the Americas, New York, NY 10020

Copyright © 1996 by Parachute Press, Inc.

BODY SWITCHERS FROM OUTER SPACE WRITTEN BY
NINA KIRIKI HOFFMAN

All rights reserved, including the right to reproduce
this book or portions thereof in any form whatsoever.
For information address Pocket Books, 1230 Avenue
of the Americas, New York, NY 10020

ISBN: 0-671-00186-8

First Minstrel Books paperback printing November 1996

10 9 8 7 6 5 4 3 2 1

FEAR STREET is a registered trademark of
Parachute Press, Inc.

A MINSTREL BOOK and colophon are registered trademarks
of Simon & Schuster Inc.

Cover art by Broeck Steadman

Printed in the U.S.A.

R·L·STINE'S
GHOSTS of FEAR STREET®

BODY SWITCHERS
FROM OUTER SPACE

I hate spaghetti days at Shadyside Middle School.

But does anyone ask *my* opinion? No. Instead, they torture me with spaghetti every Thursday.

I was prepared. I wore my spaghetti-day clothes— a red-orange shirt with white lines. That way, stains would be less likely to show up. But this spaghetti day was worse than usual. The lunch lady glopped spaghetti *and* chocolate pudding onto everybody's lunch tray.

So when I tripped, I knew my shirt was doomed.

Okay, I admit it. It doesn't take much to trip me. A crack in the sidewalk. A piece of paper in my path. I'm really a huge klutz. My feet just don't get along with each other. But this time it wasn't my fault.

Somebody stuck out his foot as I passed by. I didn't have a chance.

Wham! I fell face-down on the floor, right on top of the tray. Yecchhhh! Hot spaghetti and cold pudding smooshed together under me. All across the front of my only slightly stained, almost clean shirt.

No matter how many times I take a flop, it still really bugs me!

"Way to go, Will the Spill!" somebody yelled. Then some kids started chanting, "Will the Spill! Will the Spill!" Yeah, that's right. I'm sort of a legend here at Shadyside Middle School. No one ever calls me by my real name, Will Kennedy. Noooo. It's always Will the Spill.

I got up. And slipped on a blob of cottage cheese someone had thrown. Down I went. I scrambled to my feet again.

I could feel heat creeping across my face. I knew I was turning beet-red all the way to my ears. I always do.

I picked up my tray and shoveled as much gunk back onto it as I could. With my head down, watching my feet, I shuffled carefully toward the window. I wasn't going to take another spill. I would stash my tray with the others on the windowsill and quietly sneak out to my locker. I was *starving,* but no way was I going through the spaghetti line again. I keep a supply of Twinkies for spaghetti-day emergencies.

"Hey, Will."

I glanced around to see who called my name. My *actual* name. Chad Miller gave me a wave from a nearby table.

Yeah, Chad Miller. The coolest kid in Shadyside Middle School. He's our star athlete. At every sport.

Chad doesn't have a mouthful of braces like me, either. His teeth are as straight and white as a TV star's. He has straight blond hair. Mine's dark and always messy.

So why was Mr. Perfect—the coolest guy in school—calling me? I really wasn't sure. The whole time he's been at Shadyside, he's never said two words to me.

Until a few weeks ago, when Chad said hi to me on my way to class. At first I thought, He can't be talking to me. I glanced all around the hallway to see who he *was* speaking to. But there was no one else around. And Chad was looking straight at me.

Then, last week, he borrowed my notes. And yesterday he asked me to shoot hoops with him. It was weird, to say the least. But it was also nice to have someone as cool as Chad paying attention to me. I felt as if I was in the middle of my favorite daydream, the one where I'm one of the cool kids and everybody likes me and envies me because I never make any mistakes and I'm not clumsy.

"Will, come here a minute," Chad called, snapping me out of my thoughts. He waved a bunch of napkins at me.

I noticed an empty chair at his table.

I sat down by Chad and took the napkins from him. I cleaned myself off as well as I could.

Chad glanced at the other kids at the table. "You guys are finished, right?" he said.

For a second nothing happened. The other kids looked at each other.

Then they nodded, picked up their trays or sack lunches, and left.

Making people go away just because you said so! Now, that's power!

How did Chad do it?

His eyes darted around. I guess he didn't want anyone to hear our conversation. No one was nearby.

He leaned toward me and said, "You ever get fed up with being yourself? You ever want to be somebody else?"

I stared at him. "Are you kidding?" I wondered if Chad could read my mind.

I *hate* being me.

My feet always trip me.

I can't throw.

I can't catch.

I can't kick.

I continued staring at Chad. I remembered watching him in gym class. Boy, could he tear up the

4

basketball court. He could hit home runs. He could pitch.

Everybody wanted to talk to him, but they wouldn't unless he talked to them first.

He was the definition of cool at Shadyside Middle School.

If I could pick anyone else to be, Chad would be number one on the list!

"No, I'm not kidding," Chad said. "Don't you wish you could be somebody else?"

I looked down at the chocolate pudding stains on my spaghetti shirt.

I didn't even have to imagine what my little sister Pepper would say when I got home. I'd heard it all before.

"I'd give *anything* to be someone else!" I finally answered.

Chad lowered his voice. "Listen," he said. "My dad's a scientist. He has a machine that can switch people's bodies." He glanced around the cafeteria again. Then his eyes locked onto mine.

"Let's do it!" he urged. "Let's switch bodies!"

2

"Huh?" I said. I must have heard wrong. He couldn't have said what I thought he said.

"Just for an hour," Chad continued.

"What are you talking about?"

"Switching bodies," he repeated.

"You're making this up!" I may be clumsy and uncool, but I'm not stupid. Chad had to be joking.

"No. It's true," he insisted. "I saw my dad do it. He put a dog in one change chamber and a cat in the other. When they came out, the cat barked, and the dog climbed trees. It really works! I've wanted to try it out for a long time. But everyone I ask is too scared. You're not scared—are you, Will?"

No way! I wasn't scared because this whole thing

absolutely could not be true. It was unbelievable! And I wasn't buying it.

"My dad's done it with people before. I know he has," Chad went on. His eyes sparkled, as if he were really excited. "I looked at his lab book where he wrote down the experiments. I know how to work the machine, Will. We could do it, just for an hour."

I stared at him. He seemed pretty serious.

This story sounded so wild it *had to* be a joke.

But boy, was I wishing it could be true!

Sometimes it seemed as if I had spent the last two years doing stupid, klutzy things. Like falling into my spaghetti. But that part didn't really bother me anymore. What really steamed me was when other people laughed at me. And when they called me things like Will the Spill.

I have my own private revenge, though. I draw cartoons. See, my dad writes stories for that cartoon show, *Judo-Jabbing Adolescent Mutated Coyotes*. I began drawing pictures of the coyotes when I was three. I started drawing pictures of everything else pretty soon after that.

In the back of my notebook I have mean, funny pictures of everybody who has ever picked on me. I have pages and pages. There were always new people to draw.

Of course, nobody knows I'm fighting back, because I almost never show my cartoons to anyone. But someday I'm going to photocopy all my pictures

7

and put them on bulletin boards all over school. Then we'll see who's laughing.

Well, I *dream* about doing that, anyway.

Almost as often as I dream about being someone like Chad.

Chad's voice interrupted my thoughts. "Come on, Will." He wasn't giving up. "What have you got to lose? One hour. We'll switch bodies for just one little hour. You said you'd do *anything* to be someone else."

"But—" Oh, man! If only!

"It really works. Honest it does. It's safe, too. The cat and dog switched back and went right back to normal."

I stared at him. I could be one of the coolest kids in school! Could it be this easy?

"Come on, Will." He held up his arm, made a muscle, looked at it for a second, then grinned at me. "You want to switch. You know you do."

Maybe this was just a dumb joke, but why should that stop me? I fall for dumb jokes all the time.

And if it wasn't? That was too awesome even to think about.

"Okay!" I told him. "I'll do it!"

He stood and smiled his bright, white, straight-toothed smile. "I knew you'd come around. Meet me in the playground after school." Then he dashed out of the cafeteria, waving at kids who called out his name.

I shook my head a few times, trying to clear it. If this wasn't a joke, it was all too good to be true.

After school, when we reached Chad's house on Fear Street, he didn't invite me inside. Instead, he signaled for me to stay back. He snuck behind a tree in the front yard and glanced at the windows. All the curtains were closed, and none of them moved.

He waved at me and I joined him behind the tree. "All clear," he whispered. We walked our bikes quickly past the side of the house. "If my mom or dad knew we were doing this, we'd be in a lot of trouble."

I couldn't even imagine what *my* parents would say!

Chad led me to a shed in the backyard. You couldn't see it from the street. The closer we got to it, the stranger it looked.

It was like no other backyard shed I had ever seen. It was shaped like a puffy mushroom, big and round and bulging. Some of the bushes and vines grew right up over it.

The shed was shiny silver and it had no windows. I couldn't even see a door. I did spot a yellow-green circle the size of a baseball stuck on the smooth wall. It had a raised black border around it.

Chad touched the yellow-green part with his thumb. *Whoosh!* A round opening appeared in the side of the shed.

My mouth dropped open. Some door! It was

totally invisible. No hinges. Not even an outline. No way to know it was there until Chad opened it. I had never seen anything like it.

I let out a little whistle. "Wow!" I was totally impressed.

Chad shrugged. "My dad invents lots of stuff." He nodded at the mushroom building.

"Cool," I said.

It was. Totally cool. Chad's dad must be one great inventor.

Did that mean Chad had been telling the truth? And there really was a body-switching machine in there?

A green light glowed from inside the shed, and I could hear a ticking noise. My heart pounded double time. I glanced down to see if it was popping out of my chest.

That's when I noticed all of today's stains down the front of my shirt. There were green grass stains from gym in addition to red spaghetti blotches and brown pudding smudges. Plus a few spots that hadn't come out in the wash from last spaghetti day.

Some things never change.

But—maybe they could.

I've wanted to be someone else for such a long time. And besides, Chad would think I was a total wimp if I backed out now.

I couldn't let a whooshing door and a weird shed stop me.

"Come on in." Chad stood in the silver mushroom doorway, waiting.

Well, here goes.

I stepped across the threshold and gave a little gasp of surprise. My foot sank deep into the floor. It was made of some kind of pink, spongy material. I bent down to examine it. The floor felt soft and warm on my hand. I poked at it in a few places before straightening up.

I watched Chad touch a yellow-green badge on an inside wall near the door. The opening whooshed shut. I glanced around the inside of the shed.

I don't think I had ever been in a round room before. A large yellow circle was painted on the floor. A pale green light glowed from the ceiling. I noticed four big dark gray boxes that reached to the ceiling and looked like closets. These had visible doors, only the knobs were square and near the bottom. Wicked-looking lockers—if that's what they were!

Shiny machines of all different shapes and sizes stood along the walls. They were made of brightly colored metal—green metal, red metal, purple metal—and they were all wrapped with thin wires and multicolored metal ribbons.

What could the machines be for? Were they more of Chad's dad's inventions? What other kinds of experiments did he do?

Two of the biggest machines in the room stood side by side. These looked like purple telephone booths without windows. Next to them was a table with a slanted top covered in shiny colored patches. I figured the table was the control panel. Those patches looked like the one Chad had touched to open and close the door to the shed.

Chad strode to the slanted table and pressed his thumb on a square blue patch.

Oval doors whooshed open on the sides of the telephone booths.

They looked dark and empty inside, and a sour smell came from them.

"Excellent," I said. I hurried over to join Chad at the slant-topped table. Well, actually, I bounced over because of the spongy floor. I wanted to check out that control panel.

Some of the slick patches on it were square, some round, some oval. One or two were squiggle-shaped. Each patch was a different color, surrounded by a black line. This was neat stuff.

"How does it work? And what are those metal things?" I asked, waving at the machines around the room.

"Never mind," Chad said. "We need to get into the change chambers." He pointed at the giant purple telephone booths. "That's how we switch bodies."

Something in the room was humming the way a refrigerator does when it's working. A lot of power was generating in the shed. These machines were plugged in and ready to go. If body switching was possible, these babies looked like just the machines to do it.

"Ready?" Chad asked. He smiled at me.

Those could be my perfect teeth. What a weird thought.

Come on, Will. Go for it. What have you got to lose?

I stumbled across the floor and tripped into one of the purple chambers.

The inner surface was shiny and dark. I touched the wall. It was warm and wet. The sour smell surrounded me.

Chad still stood by the table.

"All set?" he called.

"Aren't you getting in the other one?" I asked. My palms started to sweat. What if something went wrong?

What if it was all just a mean joke?

What if Chad shut me in here and left me?

What if he never let me out?

What if . . .? All of a sudden this didn't seem like the best idea.

"I'll pop in as soon as I program the body-switch," Chad explained. He pressed his fingers on the patches on the table.

The opening in the side of the chamber whooshed shut.

I plunged into darkness. Total, stinky darkness.

The floor started humming under my feet. My body began to vibrate, and the hum seemed to spread all through me.

I had no idea whether Chad had gotten into the other chamber.

Pink squiggly lines of light flowed over the walls. The lines turned into green swirls. Then, bursts of colored light lit up the chamber like fireworks.

Oh, man! Maybe I wasn't ready for this, after all.

Mist rose from the floor and came down from the ceiling. It made me cough. It wasn't cold and wet mist, it was more like smoke from a fire, only it tasted like perfume and it was pink.

My skin felt as if it was sizzling and popping, the way carbonation tastes on your tongue when you're not used to it. The air had become very hot. I felt as if I were flying, but I knew I wasn't going anywhere.

Something was definitely happening!

I wish I knew what was going on with Chad! Did he get into the other chamber? Was this all working the way it was supposed to?

A noise under my feet pulsed, slowly at first, then faster and faster. My body twitched to the beat. The sound pounded louder and louder, thumping like a drum or a heart. Suddenly a huge sideways lurch tossed me into the wall of the chamber. I thought I was going to throw up.

Then nothing.

No sound. No fireworks. No nothing.

14

Had it worked? Was I in Chad's body? Was he in mine?

For a minute I couldn't breathe. My lungs felt squashed.

All my muscles felt stretched out and burned.

I tried to move my head, to look around.

My neck didn't work!

I grabbed for the walls, but my arms just lay by my side. I couldn't lift a finger!

No! I thought. Something horrible must have happened! What's wrong with me? Am I paralyzed?

My heart pounded so hard my ears hurt. I couldn't move a single muscle, and I couldn't even breathe.

My body was completely frozen in place!

3

I struggled to move. My mind raced around and around. *Trapped.* Would I ever be able to move again?

The mist began to clear. The chamber cooled off. It was dark again inside the telephone booth.

Dark as a tomb.

I gasped. And this time my chest heaved and managed to pull in a huge breath.

Air! Hurray!

I realized I was really thirsty. Probably because of how hot it was in the chamber.

I licked my lips. Something was different.

But what?

My tongue pressed against the backs of my teeth.
They were the wrong shape.

I couldn't feel my braces!

Could it be . . .?

I still hadn't been able to blink or turn my head. I
tried to look down, and finally my eyelids blinked. I
thought about opening my mouth, and my head
looked down.

Every time I tried something, my body would do
the movement I tried to do the minute before! I was
always one step behind myself. Just attempting to
move was making me sweat.

Now that my head was looking down, I realized I
wasn't seeing my spaghetti shirt.

I was staring at Chad's clothes!

Oh, man!

It worked! The switch had actually worked!

I wasn't me!

I still felt like me, but I was inside Chad's body.

Chad's body! Oh man, oh man, oh man. This was
the biggest, bizarrest, most fantastic, whacked thing
that had ever happened in my life.

But I was paralyzed! I was in the most excellent
body in all of Shadyside, and I couldn't get it to work
right!

This was *worse* than being me!

What if I was stuck like this forever?

I tried to lift my hand. I blinked instead. I tried

kicking the wall and my hand lifted. I tried to make a fist, and I kicked the wall.

I couldn't live like this! I wanted my body back—and fast!

This switch was a stupid, stupid idea. Obviously, something went wrong.

Could it be made right?

With a *whoosh* a hole opened in the wall in front of me.

A tall, skinny, dark-haired dorky guy stood there grinning at me.

Spaghetti and chocolate pudding stains covered his red and white shirt.

It was me! I was looking at *me!*

Or at my body, anyway!

"Hey!" he said. In *my* voice! "Hey . . . *Chad.*" Then he grinned again.

I managed to open my mouth, but couldn't make a sound. I tried to blink, and "Hey yourself" finally popped out—in Chad's voice!

Oh, man!

"It takes a minute or two for your brain to adjust," he explained, "unless you've switched before. Come on out!" Then he turned away and did a flip.

A flip! In my clumsy body! Never in a million years could I make my body do a flip.

"So now you know," Chad said, grinning a big dorky grin. Light bounced off his—*my*—braces. "I *have* done this before. That's how I know how safe it is. You'll be okay in a couple of minutes."

By thinking one thing and doing something else, I managed to get out of the change chamber. I didn't even trip over the door sill.

"You have to open the door," Chad said, pointing to the yellow-green circle on the wall. Even though I knew there was a door there, I still couldn't see it. "It's keyed to my body's thumbprint."

"Open the door?" I protested. "I can't even walk yet!" But I *could* walk better. The lag time between my thinking of an action and doing it was getting shorter.

"It'll get easier. Just don't think too hard," he reassured me.

I wandered around, getting used to the feel of Chad's body. I checked out some of the weird machines. I was leaning over a little square yellow one with two big black patches on it when Chad yelped, "Don't touch that!"

I stepped back. "Why not?" I asked.

"It's not finished. It still malfunctions," he explained. His voice squeaked just the way mine did when I was really nervous.

"Oops," I said, and grinned.

"And keep away from the yellow circle," he instructed.

"Fine, fine, fine."

I went back to walking. Strolling. Then, okay, I admit it, skipping. Let me tell you, I was beginning to feel good. *So this is what strong feels like,* I thought. *I can definitely get used to this!*

"Come on, you've wasted ten minutes already," Chad whined. "We only have an hour."

It was weird. He was such a cool person when he was in the body I was using. But now that I was him and he was me, he sounded really irritating and uncool.

I bounded over to the wall and pressed my thumb on the yellow-green patch.

The door whooshed open.

I loved that door! I wondered if I could get Chad's dad to install one at my house.

I jumped through the door, landed perfectly, then jumped again just because it felt great.

"Yesss!" I exclaimed.

"Close the door," Chad said.

I pressed the yellow-green patch on the outside of the shed, and the door vanished.

"Listen," Chad said. "I want to look around as you. You can go do what you want for an hour. Make that fifty minutes." He checked his watch. "Let's meet back here at four-thirty so we can switch back. What time do you have?"

I glanced at my watch. "Quarter to four."

"Good. Don't be late. Otherwise—big trouble!" Then he turned and dashed off.

My eyes followed him down the driveway. He moved like an athlete. He almost made my body look good.

I sneaked away from the house. I didn't want to run into Chad's parents.

For one thing, I wouldn't recognize them.

But even worse—what if they told me to get inside and start on homework? Do chores? What a waste of my hour that would be!

I hit Fear Street running.

Now that I was used to this body, I could appreciate what a good deal I had gotten. Everything worked so well!

I ran fast and didn't get out of breath. I didn't trip over cracks in the sidewalk or fall over the curb.

I raced down Park Drive and up Hawthorne. My muscles pumped like a lean mean machine.

I cruised by Shadyside Middle School. Some kids were playing basketball in the school yard. "Hey, Chad!" they yelled. It took me a second, but then I realized they were talking to me! "Come on over and play!"

These were *cool* kids! The kind of kids who wouldn't even say hello to Will!

I ran onto the court and someone tossed me the ball. I caught it like it was part of me. I threw it and it went right through the hoop without touching the rim. *Swoosh!* Right through the net.

I wanted to stay in Chad's body forever!

We played Horse for a while. I put the ball through the basket every time. Without even trying!

I was having so much fun I never noticed the time. "Chad! Chad!"

I glanced toward the familiar voice and saw Chad in my body. His face was red. He was waving frantically at me.

"Come *on,* Chad! We're going to be late!"

"Late for what?" asked David Slater. "Where are you going with that dork?"

"Gotta go," I said. I heaved the ball at him. Hard. It caught him right in the chest and knocked the wind out of him.

That will teach him. I grinned and strode off the court.

I gazed at Chad in my body. My tall, thin, lanky body. My face was red, my mouth half-open, showing those stupid braces, and panting from running.

For a second I thought about not going back to that mushroom shed and the purple change chambers.

For a second I thought, *No way, buddy. I'm staying right here.*

I looked at my watch. It was four twenty-five.

I sighed.

I had to go back. We had made a deal. I don't back out on a promise.

I raced over to Chad.

22

"Hurry! We've got to hurry or we may be too late!" he urged.

"Too late for what?" I asked.

"If we don't change back right now," he told me, gasping for breath, "we could stay like this forever!"

4

"**C**ome on, come on, come *on,*" Chad muttered as we ran.

Amazing! I could run faster than he could. That's *never* happened before.

He sure was sweating!

We snuck around the house again. "Open the door, open the door!" he hissed at me. I pressed the yellow-green patch, and the door whooshed open.

"Close it. Hurry!"

You're pushing it, bud, I thought. *Don't forget. I'm the one with the muscles right now!* I punched the yellow-green patch inside, and the door closed.

"Now do exactly what I tell you," he said. He led me over to the control panel with the colored patches on it. He told me which ones to press and in what order.

Chad hurried over to one of the chambers and stepped in. I punched patches the way he had told me to. I tried to memorize what I was doing. It seemed like a good idea.

I hesitated for just a second before climbing into the chamber. What if I didn't go through with it? But the machine was already humming. What would happen to Chad if he made the switch and there was no body in the other chamber?

It could be horrible!

I jumped in just before the door closed.

Colored lights flashed in the slick black walls, and that weird perfumed mist flowed out again.

My skin tingled, the floor pulsed with noise, and there was a lurch in my stomach.

And then it was over.

I blinked. My eyes worked right away. I glanced down at my stained shirt, my long skinny hands.

I was me again. Will.

Bummer.

Chad must have run really hard in my body. I had trouble breathing, and I had a stitch in my side.

The wall opened and Chad peered in.

"Come on," he ordered, pulling me out by the arm. "We're really late. You okay?"

"I guess I am," I replied in my own voice.

I followed him to the door and stumbled over a

little blue box. Yep. No doubt about it. I was back in my own clumsy body.

We left the shed and snuck by the house. I got on my bike and rode as fast as I could back toward home.

I pedaled past the school yard where sinking baskets had been a breeze when I was Chad. Where kids wanted me to join their game. Those kids were still playing basketball, but nobody called out to me. One or two of them even gave me dirty looks, as if they were mad that I had dragged Chad off.

If they only knew.

After being Chad, I hated being me even more.

After dinner that night we took our regular places on the couch. Mom on the left, Dad on the right, and me and Pepper in the middle.

Pepper is nine. She has short curly brown hair and a lot of freckles, and her eyes are green. She's still short, especially compared to me, but Mom says we Kennedys are late bloomers. Pepper might turn into a giraffe sometime soon.

As usual, she clutched one of her creepy porcelain dolls. She has a lot of dolls. She collects them.

Dad had rented a couple of action-adventure videos. He was looking for ideas for the *Judo-Jabbing Coyotes.*

I usually love those movies. Only tonight I wasn't into watching them. Tonight I was thinking about how it felt to be Chad. Jumping up and dropping the ball right through the hoop.

Looking at the other kids. Seeing they wanted to be like me.

I was thinking about being Chad when I carried the stainless-steel bowl of popcorn back to the living room.

I wasn't watching where I was going.

I tripped right over our basset hound, Dumbbell, and spilled popcorn across Mom, Dad, and Pepper. Not to mention Dumbbell, who didn't mind eating it off the floor.

"Wow, Will! Takes talent!" Pepper said.

"You okay?" Dad asked, staring at me as I sprawled on the floor.

"Sure. Sure," I muttered.

He looked at me a little longer, his face concerned. Then his expression changed. His eyes sparkled the way they do when he gets an idea. He scribbled some notes on his yellow legal pad.

I knew I would be seeing another Judo-Jabbing adventure featuring Rocket Riley, the clumsy jack-rabbit who kept spilling things, tripping over things, and messing everything up for the Coyotes.

When Dad puts Pepper in a cartoon, he calls her Paprika, the super-snoopy chipmunk.

Paprika always does cute things.

Riley always does dumb things.

Sometimes I *hate* Dad's job!

I bet this kind of thing never happened to Chad.

If I could just *be* Chad again for a while, maybe I could figure out how to move without tripping.

Maybe I could practice and learn not to fall over things.

At that moment all I wanted was to be Chad one more time. . . .

The next day at school Chad seemed to be everywhere. He was always surrounded by adoring fans, or answering some teacher's question, or doing handstands in the school yard. Just for the fun of it.

I didn't have a chance to talk to him until we were on the sidelines together halfway through gym period. He was playing an awesome game of basketball. And he wasn't even sweating. Me? I was gasping for air.

"You look like you could use this," Chad said, offering me his water bottle.

The words popped out of my mouth. "Chad, can we switch again? Please? Even if it's only for another hour?"

Chad gazed at me. Then he shook his head. "I almost got in trouble yesterday. You didn't watch the time. I was late!"

"It won't happen again."

"You bet it won't, because you're not going to get the chance!"

28

He picked up a spare ball and spun it on one finger.

That could be me, I thought as I watched him.

Before I got to be Chad, I didn't realize how good I could feel. I had gone along being Will the Spill because I didn't know there was an alternative.

Now I knew. It made being me seem so much worse.

I tried to think of something to convince Chad to make the switch, just once more. Then somebody yelled something.

I turned and saw a basketball heading straight for my face.

5

The basketball zoomed toward me, getting bigger and bigger.

Yesterday, when I was in Chad's body, I could have stopped that ball from hitting me. No problem.

Today? No way. If I tried to do anything, I would either make a fool of myself or get hurt even worse. Besides, it didn't matter anyway.

So I just stared at the ball speeding toward my face.

A hand shot out in front of me.

Chad's hand. He deflected the basketball.

"Hey!" Chad yelled at someone on the court. "Watch where you're throwing that, you dope!"

Since it was Chad, the kid actually apologized.

I just stood there.

"What's the matter with you?" Chad asked me in a low voice.

I shook my head.

"You got a death wish or something? That ball almost creamed you!"

I shook my head again. How could I tell him I was too bummed about being me to bother? Instead, I muttered, "Thanks."

He squinted his eyes and gazed at me for a moment.

He turned and watched the kids running around the court, dunking, throwing, jumping. Then he looked me up and down. "It's the body-switch, isn't it?" he finally asked.

I hung my head and nodded.

Chad sighed. "Listen. If it means that much to you, we can switch again."

My head popped back up.

I was going to get to be Chad again! If I didn't think I'd fall over, I would jump for joy.

This time I was going to figure out how he moved the way he did.

This time I would remember what it felt like. And then I would take all that coordination, strength, and skill and bring it back with me to my own body.

Yes! This time everything would be different!

* * *

That afternoon Chad and I snuck around to the silver mushroom shed in his backyard. Chad stopped before the entrance and gazed at me. "Listen," he said finally. "You're not so geeky. All you need is a little more practice in a body that works better."

Then he made an incredible offer. "Do you want to switch for the weekend?"

"Awesome!" I yelled. Yes! Two whole days of being Chad!

"Shh!"

I put my hands over my mouth.

"You can't tell *anybody,* do you understand? *Nobody.*"

"I won't!"

"We switch now, then we meet back at the shed at seven-thirty Sunday night. That's after dinner at my house. When do you guys eat?"

"Six. We should be finished by then."

"Okay. We can switch then. That way we won't have to be each other at school."

"Can we really get away with this?" I blurted. "Won't your parents notice?"

"Nah," he assured me. "You're going to look exactly like me. Don't worry. It will be fine."

"So where do you live?" Chad asked.

I told him my address over on Kent Place. "My sister's name is Pepper and my dog is Dumbbell," I said. "My bedroom's the first one on the left up the stairs."

"Mom and Dad are just Mom and Dad," Chad said. "My room is the second door on the left from the top of the stairs."

We compared watches. I changed mine to match his.

Chad opened the shed door, then yanked me across the threshold. The door whooshed shut.

"I think my parents are home," he explained as he crossed to the control panel. "We have to be extra careful to not get caught."

I stepped into the purple chamber while Chad hit the colored patches. It was just like the first time. The weird stinky smell, light show, pink mist, and the pulsing noise under my feet, revving faster and faster.

When the sideways lurch came, my stomach turned over again. For a minute I felt paralyzed, but this time I was calmer. It only took me a couple of seconds to be able to move. I looked down. I was inside Chad's body again.

Oh, man! This was great!

The door whooshed open, and I jumped out, feeling how strong and springy my legs were.

This time would be even better. This time I would remember how Chad's body worked. I had a whole weekend to figure stuff out!

Chad acted strange as we headed for the shed door.

He stopped in the center of the round room. He

33

gazed at all the stuff in the shed, as if he were trying to memorize it.

He frowned for just a minute as I touched the yellow-green patch with my thumb and the opening appeared in the wall.

Then he smiled.

I wasn't used to watching my own expressions. I was especially not used to seeing my face looking like that.

His smile looked almost, well, *mean*.

That couldn't be right! Hadn't he saved my life this afternoon? Hadn't he just made a dream come true for me? He was doing me a huge favor.

I must be wrong!

We stepped out and I closed the shed door.

"Now remember," Chad said. "We'll do the switch Sunday night at seven-thirty sharp."

A wide grin spread across his, I mean, *my* face. Then he raced past the house and onto Fear Street. Even in my body Chad didn't trip over anything. He stopped on the pavement across the street, then turned around. For a moment he stared at me and the house. Then he waved and took off again. Double-time.

I thought I should be thinking about how lucky I was to be in Chad's body and not my own scrawny, clumsy one. Instead, a shiver went through me as I watched Chad disappear around the corner. I couldn't understand why.

I shook my head, to clear it. I held my hands out in front of me: Chad's strong hands. I flexed my arm. I actually had muscles. Man, oh, man! This was going to be great!

I scooted around to the back of Chad's house.

There was another one of those touch pad things on the back door. It was yellow-green, too. These door locks were awesome!

I touched the yellow-green patch and the door slid open, even though it looked like a normal door. The air coming from the house smelled funny. Sort of damp and moldy.

I hoped Chad had been wrong about his folks being home. I wanted to memorize the layout of the house before Chad's parents noticed I didn't know my way around. That would be kind of tough to explain.

The back door opened into the kitchen. I stepped across the threshold, and froze. There at the stove was a kid stirring something.

"Where have you been?" he demanded. He turned to face me.

I staggered back and almost fell back out the door.

He was blond and tall for his age. He looked about twelve years old. He had perfect white teeth.

He looked exactly like Chad!

6

Who *was* this guy?

Did Chad have a twin brother?

Why didn't he go to school, too?

And how come Chad never mentioned anything about him?

Most importantly, what was I supposed to say to this guy?

Maybe this is all a dream, I thought. *Maybe I'm still Will.* I peeked down at my hands. They were definitely Chad's strong, large hands. I looked across at this other kid. He had the same hands, too.

What was going on?

Just then a woman came through a door across from me. "Close the door, Chad-One," she said, gazing right at me. Her voice sounded kind of sticky and sweet.

Chad-One? Was she talking to me? I glanced behind me. Must be. Nobody else was there.

Chad-*One?* That's a weird nickname. How many of us were there? I stared at the woman. I knew I couldn't ask her such a dumb question.

Why hadn't Chad told me about any of this?

The woman was thin and blond. She wore a big smile, a red-and-white-checked dress, and an apron with lace around the edge. Her hair came down from the top of her head and then flipped up at the bottom, near her shoulders.

She looked a lot like the moms in the old TV shows I saw on Nick at Nite.

My dad would have taken one look at her and declared, "Sitcom damage!" That's what he always says when he sees people who look as if they're pretending they're on TV shows.

She bent her head sideways and smiled at me. "I asked you to shut the door, Chad-One. You're letting in flies."

I gulped and turned around to touch the yellow-green pad on the inside wall. The door whooshed shut. With me inside.

Oh, man! Time to face the music! I had to pull this off.

The hair on the back of my neck prickled.

37

"Did you have a nice day at school, dear?" I heard behind me.

I put a big smile on my face and turned around. "Yeah," I responded, "it was great."

A man came through the door and stood beside the woman. He was smiling, too.

A pipe stuck out the side of his mouth. It wasn't lit.

His dark hair was covered with the kind of greasy Dad stuff I saw on men's hair in old TV shows. He was wearing a blue shirt and a plaid tie and brown pants and loafers.

This was the big inventor who had made the body-switching machine? The fancy door locks? All that other excellent stuff in the shed?

He looked like a reject from "Early Television"! You know, when everything was still in black and white.

What a family!

But I figured I'd better start thinking of them as Mom and Dad. I was spending the weekend with them, after all.

He took the pipe out of his mouth. "Howdy, son," he greeted, smiling like an advertisement. He stuck the pipe back into his mouth.

This was too weird! *Nobody* had parents like this.

"Mom," whined the other Chad, "Chad-One is late again!"

"Chad-One, how many times have I told you to

come straight home after school?" Even though she was frowning and trying to sound mean, she still sounded sweet.

Chad-One! What kind of name was Chad-One? "Uh—a lot?" I ventured.

"Twenty-seven," Mom stated. "More often lately. Young man, you will have to start behaving better!"

"Yes, ma'am," I said. It seemed like the right thing to say.

"Now, help Chad-Two set the table!"

Chad-Two? I should have guessed. Boy, these were the *dumbest* twin names I had ever heard! Hey, maybe we were clones. With all the equipment in the shed, anything was possible. Maybe Chad-Three and Chad-Four would pop out of a closet any minute!

Why didn't Chad, er, Chad-*One* warn me? How did he expect me to keep up the act with all this weirdness around me?

"Hey, it's *his* turn, Mom!" Chad-Two complained. That was the first *normal* thing I'd heard so far. Pepper and I always fight over chores.

Mom just kept smiling. "Why don't you both do it? Supper's almost ready!" That kind of sounded like something my mom would say. Maybe things weren't as strange as I thought.

Muttering and griping, Chad-Two led the way into the other room, which turned out to be a dining room.

He opened cupboards and drawers, taking out

place mats, silverware, and cloth napkins. I followed him, doing exactly what he did.

The whole time we were setting the table, Chad-Two hounded me with questions. It was like the third degree. "What did you do in school today? Did any of the kids do anything interesting? What did you learn? Anything in social studies? What did Mr. Sirk make you do in gym? What about Ms. Hartman? Did you make any significant observations about students at each end of the spectrum?"

Most of these questions I could answer, but I couldn't figure out that last one.

"Significant observations about students at each end of the spectrum?" I repeated.

"Any deviations from the norm for Will Kennedy?"

"What?" I was so startled I dropped a spoon.

Of course, since I was in Chad's body, I caught the spoon before it hit the floor. Chad-Two had his back to me and didn't notice.

"He spill anything at lunch?"

"Dropped his milk," I told him. Which was true. Of course.

"What about Lance Holloway?"

Other than Chad, Lance is the coolest kid in school. He even wears sunglasses most of the time. My guess is he's sneaking in some nap time during class. Who could tell behind those shades?

40

"Nothing significant," I said, hoping that was a good enough answer.

Just then Mom came in carrying a big brown bowl with a cover on it. She set it in the middle of the table.

Dad, still sucking on the unlit pipe, came out of the kitchen carrying a covered pot. It must have been hot; he was using pot holders. He put it on the table, too.

Mom smiled and went back to the kitchen. I heard the refrigerator open and close. Then she came back in carrying a big green plastic container.

Dad went and got a pitcher of something.

Everyone smiled at everyone else.

It was so creepy! *Definite sitcom damage,* I thought.

I waited until the others picked chairs and then took the one that was left. As soon as we were all settled, Mom reached out and snapped the cover off the brown bowl.

"Everyone serve yourself," she said cheerily.

I stared into the bowl. I couldn't believe my eyes.

There in the soupy yellow liquid floated little brownish-purple creatures.

As if that weren't disgusting enough, the critters began waving their tentacles in the air.

Dinner was alive!

7

Yeecccchhh!

And that was putting it mildly. I had seen my mom and dad order snails at a restaurant. And I tried some raw fish once—but *this!* This was the grossest thing ever! I'd never seen anyone eat anything as awful as this!

It had to be some kind of joke!

Right?

Chad-Two reached in and grabbed a handful of the creatures while I sat there—stunned.

He stuffed two of them into his mouth!

For a second a couple of squirming tentacles stuck out between his lips. He sucked them in like noodles and grinned while he chewed.

Oh, man—talk about gross!

My stomach crawled up my throat!

Mom and Dad scooped out handfuls of squirming creatures. The critters slid around on their plates, wiggling their eyestalks and tentacles.

Mom popped one into her mouth. Her fingers dripped with yellow goo. She licked it off and smiled at me some more.

"What's the matter, Chad-One?" she asked. "Why aren't you eating?"

"Uh—ur—I—" *Because I have to go throw up!* "I don't feel very well! Maybe I'd better go to bed."

"Are you coming down with something, honey?" Mom asked. She laid the back of her hand against the back of my hand.

"I think . . . maybe," I said. I coughed to sound more convincing.

"You'll feel better with some food inside of you," she said. She picked up one of the purple octopuses and held it toward me. It waved a sucker-covered tentacle.

"I don't—urp—excuse me!" I jumped up and ran out of the room, through the front hall, and up the staircase.

Chad told me his room was the second one on the left. But as soon as I stepped off the top stair I knew I was going to have trouble.

There was no upstairs hall. It was like stepping inside a giant pink beach ball or a hot-air balloon.

The floor was pink and spongy, like the floor of the backyard shed. It curved up at the sides until it turned into walls. The whole place was round. I wasn't sure where the floor and walls and ceiling started or ended.

The only areas that weren't pink were two square slick orange patches on the floor. They were about two feet across, and four pairs of fat white boots sat next to them. They looked like moonboots, but puffier.

I noticed more of those circle things on the wall like the one that had made the shed door open.

Could it be? Well, I had to try *something*. Second door on the left . . . I went to the second patch on the left wall and stuck my thumb on the green-yellow surface.

A long oval door whooshed open.

I peered through the opening. There was nothing in it but some bars along the side walls, about waist high. The space was closet-sized, about two feet by four feet.

This was Chad's room? You couldn't even sit down in there, let alone lie down!

I must have opened the wrong door.

I bounced over to another colored patch on the wall. I could hear Chad's family talking at the dining room table.

"I think I'll take a plate up to Chad-One," I heard Mom say. "He may be ready to eat now."

No! No way! I was not eating creepy crawlies!

This place was way too weird for me!

I snuck down the stairs, careful not to make a sound. I pressed the patch by the front door. *Whoosh!* I shut the door behind me and took off!

I ran faster than I ever had before—faster than I ever could have in my own body.

Once I put some distance between me and Chad's house on Fear Street, I slowed down a little.

The closer I got to my own home, the better I felt.

Could I have been wrong? Maybe I hadn't seen what I thought I saw. Maybe Chad's family wasn't eating slimy, creepy, live creatures. Maybe it had just been some kind of weird noodles.

Noodles with eyes?

I still felt sick to my stomach. What kind of food was *that?*

I'd seen some disgusting food on TV, but those crawly things were the worst!

What could possibly be in the other dishes?

I didn't want to find out!

There it was! My front porch. And the shaggy lawn, which I was supposed to mow tomorrow morning. It had never looked so good.

It was great to hear the TV blaring through the living room window screens.

I charged up the front porch stairs two at a time. I didn't trip over the top step the way I always do. I rang the doorbell.

My bratty little sister, Pepper, answered the door. "Can I help you?" she asked through the screen door.

"Let me talk to Chad."

"Sorry. You have the wrong house," Pepper said. Her sneer softened as she gazed at me. She started flipping her eyelashes. It made me nervous.

That's when I remembered. I realized just in time that I wasn't me, I was still Chad-One. Or looked like him, anyway.

"No, I mean, let me talk to Will."

"You don't want to talk to Will. Will's a big dummy. I can beat him at Trivial Pursuit and Jeopardy every time."

This was a big fat lie, and I was about to tell her so, but then I remembered I wasn't exactly me.

"I don't want to play games with him," I said, irritated. "I just want to talk to him."

She looked at me for a minute, then said, "How much do you want to talk to him?"

"Huh?"

She was sharpening up into the Pepper I knew and suffered from. "Like, how much would you pay me to go get him?"

"Pay you?" I repeated.

"Is there an echo around here?" she asked, cupping her ear with her hand. "You got fifty cents?"

I reached into my pockets. I had no idea if Chad had fifty cents. There was something in the right front pocket that felt interesting, but it didn't feel like money. Then I came to my senses. "Forget it!" I shouted. I pressed the doorbell again, hoping to get Chad's attention.

He wandered down the stairs.

"Hi, Chad," he said. He stepped out onto the porch.

"Hey, tell Pepper I'm Will," I told him.

For a second he looked furious. It was almost scary. I didn't know my face could look that mean and cold.

Of course. I had promised not to tell anyone about the switch.

Then his face went back to normal. "Sure," he said. "Pepper, this is Will."

"Don't be an idiot, Will," Pepper said to Chad. "Oh. Sorry. You can't help it." She smirked.

"She's too smart for us, Chad." Chad shrugged.

"You are *soooo* dumb!" Pepper said.

She stuck out her tongue at both of us, then stomped into the house, slamming the screen door behind her.

"What do you want?" Chad asked me. That mean look came over his face again.

"We have to switch back now," I told him.

He glared at me. His jaw got really tense.

"No way!" Chad exclaimed. "We have a deal!"

"I can't stay at your house!" I cried. "Your family is weird!"

"I never said my family was normal," Chad answered. "And a deal is a deal."

If Chad wouldn't cut short the switch, at least he could explain a few things. Maybe then I'd have a shot at getting through the weekend.

"How come there's another Chad?"

Chad grinned. But it was the nastiest-looking smile I had ever seen! He never looked that way at school. "He's my brother," Chad said. "I know he's a pain, but Pepper is no picnic, either."

"What's with that weird second floor? Do you sleep in that closet?"

"It's a New-Age kind of thing," Chad explained. "My dad invented it. You'll see. It'll make you feel great!"

"But—"

Chad cut me off. "Just watch what the other Chad does," he instructed. "Copy him. Everything will be fine."

For a second he almost convinced me. But then I remembered dinner. "Chad!" I burst out. "That food . . . I can't eat that food! We *have* to switch! *Now!*"

Chad shook his head. "We had a deal. You wanted to be me. Now you *are* me! Live with it." Then his expression softened. "Come on, Will," he wheedled. "It's just two more days."

Mom's voice called from inside the house. "Will! Time for supper!"

"Get out of here," Chad said, giving me a shove. He went inside and shut the front door. I even heard him lock it.

I jumped down from the porch and stared up at my house. Some of the paint was peeling, but I didn't care. I missed my home!

I thought about all the drawers and closets in my room. I knew what was inside of them. I knew what food I'd find in the cupboards and the refrigerator. I even knew where Mom hid the cookies.

Back at Chad's house, I didn't know *what* I would

49

find. I was pretty sure I wouldn't find anything I could eat.

And my stomach was growling!

In Chad's body there was no way I could go into my own house and act as if I belonged there.

Especially if Chad didn't help me.

He could have said I was sleeping over.

But he didn't seem to want me around at all!

So now what do I do? The Division Street Mall was only two blocks away. I could go to the arcade and kill some time. I wondered if Chad had any money on him when we did the switch.

I checked my pockets.

In the front pocket I found a weird little metal thing. It was made of different pieces in shades of purple, all folded up. I couldn't get it to unlock or open. I thought it might be some kind of puzzle, or one of Chad's father's inventions.

There was a wallet in the back pocket. Four dollars in it. I could buy a burger, or play Galaxy Gremlins for six or eight hours. I'm really good at Galaxy Gremlins.

But that didn't totally solve the problem.

The mall closed at nine. Then what?

I had two friends from school I sometimes had sleepovers with. But I couldn't go over to their houses looking like Chad and expect them to let me spend the night.

It was getting dark. It was supposed to be chilly

tonight. I couldn't think of any place to go that would be safe.

I didn't want to do it, but I didn't seem to have a choice.

I had to go back to Chad's house.

The yelling started the moment I touched the door pad and walked in through the front door.

"Where have you been?"

"You know you're not supposed to leave the house without permission!"

"You know you're supposed to help with dinner cleanup!"

It was weird, all this harsh stuff coming out of people who looked like the perfect mom, pop, and son from a sitcom.

Then Mom's voice went back to being sweet. "We know you don't like the way skwiggers move," she said. "But they're better for you when they're alive! Chad-One, you have to eat!" She waved a handful of wigglies at me.

"*I* know what's wrong with him," Chad-Two shouted. "It's those slimy humans! You *like* them! You keep socializing with them instead of studying them! You're starting to *act* like a human!"

Act like a human? What did he mean?

How could I *not* act like a human?

"You know how dangerous it would be for us if the humans found out we were here!" Dad shouted.

Mom went back to yelling, too. "You were hand-picked for this mission," she scolded. "Picked because you could maintain distance from local life-forms! Do you *want* to get us all in trouble?"

I looked at Mom. I looked at the little monsters squirming in her hand.

Then it hit me. The only way you could *act* like a human was if you *weren't* human!

These people were not just weird!

They were aliens!

9

A*liens!*

I was trapped in a family of aliens!

Aliens who hate humans—who think humans are *slimy!*

What would they do to me if they found out *I* was one of the slimy humans? Would they take me back to their planet with them—whichever one that was?

Or would they do something even worse?

I had to get out of there! Faster than fast!

My palms were wet with sweat. I had trouble catching my breath. I stared at the aliens. How could I ever have thought they were humans?

I should have known. No one really looks like people on TV.

I couldn't stay here! I had to get my body back!

Then it hit me. Chad was an alien, too. There was an alien in my body!

"Eat just one, Chad-One," Mom crooned. "Come on. For Mommy. You've got to keep up your strength!" Mom picked one of the wiggling things out of her hand and held it out to me.

I almost spewed. Just looking at that thing made me sick.

But I had no choice. I had to eat it. I couldn't let them find out that I wasn't an alien! As I gagged, Mom stuffed it in my mouth. I swallowed before I could taste it much or feel it on my tongue.

I thought I could feel the skwigger move around inside my stomach. But not for very long.

The weird thing was that it stayed down, and I felt slightly better. Less hungry, anyway. And I didn't feel like throwing up anymore.

"Good boy," Mom chirped. "Now it's time for bed!"

I checked my watch. It was about a quarter to eight. Aside from everything else that was awful in this house, early curfew!

What if I made a break for it? I knew I could run fast in this body. Chad-Two could probably run just as fast, though, and Dad might be able to run faster.

"Bed!" Dad announced. He grabbed my shoulder and pushed me toward the staircase. He was really strong!

54

Maybe I could sneak out after they all went to sleep.

I followed Chad-Two upstairs.

We trudged up the stairs to the weird pink second floor. I planned to watch Chad-Two very carefully. I didn't want to make any mistakes. It would be a disaster if he found out I wasn't the real Chad-One!

Chad-Two went to the first big touch pad on the floor and pulled on a pair of boots, then he stamped on the orange touch pad six times.

I waited for something to whoosh or glow. Nothing happened.

He walked over to the first green touch pad on the left wall and thumbed it. A long oval door opened, revealing another tiny room only a little bigger than a coffin. It was identical to the one I had seen before.

The next thing Chad-Two did surprised me. He grabbed the bars on either side of the little room and swung his feet up. They stuck to the ceiling!

He hung there upside-down like a bat, his arms crossed over his chest, and his hair hung straight down. He stared at me. "Go on," he snapped. "Get in your own sleep chamber, will you?"

I crossed over to the big touch pad on the floor and pulled on the boots. They fit, but kind of grabbed my feet and ankles tight, and they felt prickly inside.

I stamped on the big orange touch pad six times, the way Chad-Two had, then went to the second green badge on the wall near his.

My thumbprint opened the closet I had guessed was Chad's room. Now I knew why there were bars on the wall.

Trying to copy Chad-Two's movements, I grabbed the bars and swung up. It took me three tries to get my feet to touch the ceiling. I hoped that didn't make Chad-Two suspicious.

I nervously let go of the bars. I figured I would fall on my head any minute. But the boots felt as if they were welded to the ceiling.

I started to feel dizzy. I wondered if I would ever be able to sleep in a position like this.

But I didn't want to fall asleep. I needed to stay awake so I could try to escape.

"What's the matter with you, anyway?" Chad-Two grumbled.

"I feel sick," I said. That was no lie!

"You act sick, but it's not any illness I've seen before!"

"Maybe I caught something at school."

"Not a chance. Not after all those vaccinations we had when we first got these bodies!"

When they first got these bodies? Oh, man! What do they *really* look like? Maybe they have six eyes and two heads and eight long arms! I shuddered at the thought of them in their true form.

"If you caught anything at school, it was a bad attitude! We should never have let you do this week! Except I couldn't have taken that math test."

So both Chads *did* go to school? And nobody noticed the difference? Wow. I still couldn't figure out why there were two of them. But it's not like I could ask Chad-Two!

"And your observations are better," Chad-Two continued. "But now I know why. You *like* those horrible, slimy humans! And to tell you the truth, it's beginning to give me the creeps!"

I was giving *him* the creeps?

"You have to stop hanging around with humans." Chad-Two went on lecturing. "One of them might find out the truth! And you know what will happen to you if you let one of the humans get too close. We won't have any choice." Chad-Two's voice lowered ominously. "You know what we'll have to do with you—*mind tailoring.*"

10

Mind tailoring? Oh, man! What was that? It sure didn't sound like anything good!

And mind-tailoring was something they did to *each other* for just getting close to a human.

"You remember Zoink from back home?" Chad-Two asked. "Well, after he explored the Quarex galaxy, they mind tailored him—and now he has no memories. No brain at all. He just sits in his pod with that blank look on his face. You don't want to end up like Zoink, do you, Chad-One?"

I gulped. "No. I don't."

"Good," Chad-Two said. "Then remember that story the next time you feel like hanging out with those slimy humans."

I couldn't believe it. If the aliens did things like this to each other, they were sure to do horrible things to me if they discovered what I really was.

My heart started pounding in my ears.

I had to get out of this house!

But I didn't even know how to get off the ceiling!

I had a terrible thought. What if they already knew I was human? They lured me into hanging upside-down. I'm trapped. Now they could do anything they wanted to me!

"I'm watching you," Chad-Two warned. "You'd better clean up your act soon! Shut your door and go to sleep."

Even if I could get down off the ceiling, I couldn't sneak out now. Chad Two was still awake. If he caught me trying to sneak out, I'd be mind tailored for sure. I had to pretend I was going to sleep.

But first I had to figure out how to get my door shut. I stared at the three touch pads near my hand. One of them was green, like the other door controls I'd used before. On a hunch, I touched it.

Bingo. The door to the closet whooshed shut and disappeared.

I was in total darkness, hanging upside down from the ceiling like a trapped fly.

In a house full of aliens!

Great. Just what I had in mind for the weekend.

The darkness wasn't quite total. The three touch pads glowed.

My Chad act was probably still working. Since I followed Chad-Two's orders, maybe now he'd leave me alone.

I couldn't imagine falling asleep with so much on my mind, and I wanted to stay awake and figure out what to do next. But a weird fizzing started in my head, and I conked out.

My eyes popped open. *Why is it still dark?* I reached for my alarm clock to see what time it was.

I noticed three floating bubbles of color off to my right. *What are those things?* I wondered.

Then I realized I was hanging upside-down from the ceiling. That *really* didn't seem right!

In a heart-sickening rush, it all came back to me. I wasn't Will. I was in Chad's body.

Only there were two Chads.

I was hanging upside down in a house full of aliens with sitcom damage and scary food!

And they were threatening me with mind tailoring! They said they'd take away my memories! That I'd have no brain at all!

I had only been awake for two minutes, and already I was shaking and sweating from fear! I had to do something, quick!

I touched the oval pink pad on the wall. Instantly my feet let go of the ceiling and I crashed to the floor.

Well, I had figured out how to get down off the ceiling!

The room was so small I didn't fit on the floor. I ended up on my back with my legs stretched up the wall.

For a minute I felt just like my clumsy old Will self.

I must have fallen onto a touch pad, because when I landed a pale blue light came on.

I looked around and discovered some other touch pads. Maybe one of them opened a window! Maybe I could sneak out that way!

I scrambled around and stood up. These weren't the touch pads that glowed in the dark. I was just reaching to touch a dark purple pad and see what it did when a hollow thunking sound came from the door.

"What's with you?" Chad-Two yelled from the other side of the door. "It's time for breakfast! Why aren't you up?" He knocked again.

I pressed the green touch pad and the door opened. I stepped out into the pink windowless round area.

Chad-Two was already out of his boots, and he was wearing different clothes.

I wondered where he had gotten them, but I couldn't search around now. Chad would know where his own closet was! Chad-Two stood in the pink room, watching my every move. *Better to keep on these clothes and worry about changing later.*

I slipped off my sleep boots and put my hightops back on. Then I followed Chad-Two downstairs.

The dining room table was already set. I guess breakfast wasn't one of the Chads' chores.

I peered into the bowl at my place. It was filled with dried-up nuggets shaped like starfish. They floated in blue milk, and smelled salty and rotten.

Mom and Dad were already seated at the table. Dad was reading the newspaper upside-down. Aliens made mistakes, too, I guess. Mom wore another frilly pink knee-length dress with a puffy skirt, an apron, and that dopey smile.

I glanced down at the bowl. At least these starfish things weren't looking back at me!

I was starving by this time, so when I took my place at the table, I shoved a big spoonful into my mouth.

Mistake!

It was much worse than it looked. Like biting into totally salty, greasy, rotten cat food treats with crunchy bones in them!

And what was worse—the cereal stabbed like needles in my mouth!

I couldn't spew them all over the table. This could be Chad's favorite dish.

I drank something yellow and milky that was in the glass at my place. It tasted like hot glue! I thought it would help the cereal go down, but it just coated my tongue and made my throat close up.

I looked at Mom. Smiling. Dad. Behind his upside-down newspaper. Chad-Two. Wolfing down that poisonous cereal. Happy campers.

I couldn't take it. I leaped up and ran!

I bolted from the house, not even closing the front door behind me. I didn't want them to catch up with me!

I had to get home. I had to get Chad to switch back *right now!* I couldn't eat that food. I couldn't stay in a house full of aliens. I couldn't wait around for them to tailor my mind!

I was so hungry I could hardly think. I needed some food!

I darted into the Stop 'n Shop.

I bought Twinkies and a Coke. Real food! Then I crossed the street to the park by the high school and collapsed onto a bench.

I tore open the Twinkies package and crammed a whole one into my mouth. I love the way they squish!

A second later I was gagging! It tasted like chalk. Dry chalk! It sucked all the spit out of my mouth and made me cough!

I spat it out.

My mouth was so dry from the chalky Twinkies, I chugged half the Coke.

The Coke tasted like gasoline!

My stomach hurt. I started sweating. I felt dizzy and sick.

I had to get home—fast!

I shook a little when I got up from the bench. My legs kind of wobbled as I tried to make it to my house. *Will's* house.

I had to stop and rest a lot. I was feeling sicker and sicker. My stomach hurt, my muscles ached, and I was sweating so much my shirt was wet through.

I tried to run. I tried to walk. Then I couldn't do anything but sit down. Right on the curb.

"What have you done?" somebody yelled.

I looked up. Chad-Two!

"That's it!" he bellowed. "You're coming home with me!"

I felt so sick, my head was spinning. But I still knew exactly what Chad-Two had planned.

He was going to mind-tailor me!

Chad-Two yelled at me all the way home. He was really mad. For one thing, he practically had to carry me. I was sweating and freezing and then sweating again. I couldn't stand up by myself. Way too rubber-kneed!

He told me I was an idiot to eat Earth food.

"No wonder you're sick!" Chad-Two shouted. "Everything on this planet is poisonous to us, even in these bodies! How could you forget?"

I hung on to his shoulders and tried to get my feet to walk. It didn't work very well.

I wondered if I would die from eating Twinkies!

Chad-Two dragged me up the porch and into the

front room of the aliens' house. He dropped me onto the couch.

"Don't move," he ordered before going into the next room.

He came back a minute later, carrying a bowl.

"Eat some of these skwoos," he instructed, plopping a handful of live bugs into my shaking hand. They looked like giant cockroaches, only they had more legs.

I didn't much care what I did now, I felt so terrible! I couldn't feel any sicker than I already did!

I shoved the squirming bugs into my mouth and chewed.

I couldn't believe it! They tasted like beef jerky. One of my favorite foods in the world. It was horrible the way their legs moved in my mouth, but they tasted so good, I ate them all.

A couple of minutes later I felt a little better.

"You are such a spidunk!" Chad-Two said. "Maybe this poisonous food is what's messing up your mind. Take this box of skwoos with you, and take this pinter, too."

He gave me two small boxes, a pink one and a brown one. Each had a little black touch pad on it.

"Put them in your pocket," he said. "If you eat any more local food by mistake, take two skwoos right away, and then a pinch of pinter. Can you remember that?"

66

I nodded and put the boxes in my pocket.

He glared at me. "Earth food! What were you thinking? This place—these *people*—have warped your mind. We're not here to make friends. Have you forgotten that?"

"No," I mumbled.

"Well, make sure you *don't* forget!" he snapped.

Chad-Two led me to the sleep chamber. I flipped upside-down and closed my eyes. That strange, fizzling sensation came over me.

As soon as I'm feeling better, I thought, *I'm going to find a way out. Just as soon as I'm better.*

My eyes shot open. Chad-Two stood in front of me—and he was upside-down. He looked right at me and said something in another language. It wasn't like any other language I'd ever heard.

I stared at him. What was I supposed to do now?

"Whoops! I forgot." Chad-Two smacked his forehead. "We're supposed to speak in Earth languages only. Good job, Chad-One! You're obviously returning to normal. Now, get out of bed and let's go test the shink."

I had no idea what a shink was, but I tried to act cool about it. "Why do we have to test it *today?*" I asked. "It's Saturday!"

"Shut up, you groober! You know we have to do it today. Now, hurry up or I'll test it on *you.* Then

67

you'll know how your human friends feel when we use it on them!"

The shink was what they used on humans? What kind of machine was it? What could it do to me? I didn't want to find out. But I had to follow Chad-Two to the yard or he'd get suspicious.

I flipped out of bed and put on my regular shoes. I caught up with Chad-Two as he strolled across the backyard. "First we need to collect a test specimen," Chad-Two said.

He led me past the mushroom shed. And into a tangle of trees behind it.

"Catch anything you see," Chad-Two told me.

Catch anything? How?

"There!" he urged, pointing up into a tree.

A crow sat on a low branch, glaring down at us. How was I supposed to catch a crow?

I snuck closer, then jumped as high as I could, grabbing for the bird.

It flew away, cawing.

"You dummy! What are you doing? Where's your merister?" He pulled a little metal tube from his pocket.

What was a merister? "I left it in my other pants," I said.

"You spidunk!" He tapped the tube on a little black spot, and it got bigger. Whoa! It looked like a ray gun from those space-alien movies.

"Turn over that log," he ordered.

I crossed to the log. I pushed it and it rolled over.

A big black rat the size of a small cat raced out from under the log! I jumped back.

Chad-Two aimed his merister at it, and a web shot out of the barrel. It caught the rat and yanked it back to Chad-Two. "This should do nicely," he declared, holding up the net. I could see the rat struggling inside.

He tapped the merister a few times, and it folded up into a little metal lump.

Chad-Two led the way back to the silver puffball shed. Once we were inside, he set the net with the rat in it in the middle of a big yellow circle on the floor.

He picked up a little yellow box with black patches on it.

One of the sides of the box was fuzzy. Chad-Two turned the fuzzy side toward the rat, then he pressed the big black patches—two taps on the big square patch, three on the smaller round patch, then another two on the big square patch.

The rat shrieked! It was a horrible, ear-piercing sound!

When I saw what was happening, I wanted to scream, too.

I watched as the terrified rat began to shrink.
Shrink!

From rat-size to mouse-size to marble-size to pea-size!

Chad-Two chuckled to himself. It was an evil, awful sound. Then he turned to me and said, "That's what I'll do to any slimy human that finds out about us!"

12

I swallowed hard. That's what Chad-Two would do to humans like me.

I stared at the tiny rat. Chad-Two picked it up. It was frozen as stiff as a statue and about the size of a BB pellet.

For a second I couldn't even move, I was so scared. This was much worse than mind-tailoring!

I would have to be extremely careful. I could never let him know I was a human!

I caught my breath. "P-p-perfect," I stammered.

He handed me the tiny rat.

It was as hard as a rock! I held it up to look at it. It was like a teeny-tiny statue of a rat.

Oh, man! This could be me!

Chad-Two took the rat back and tossed it over his shoulder. Then he glared down at his human hands. "There's only one worthwhile thing on this whole planet," he said.

"What's that?" I asked.

"Slinkies! I've never seen them anywhere else," Chad-Two continued. "They fascinate me, the way they move, the circles, the spirals, constantly shifting. The way they compress and expand, and move down inclines by themselves. They're so beautiful! In fact, I want to go look at Slinkies right now!"

I followed him into the house and up to the pink room upstairs. Then we wiggled through a long tunnel into a workroom full of books. It was full of sunlight that streamed in through three oval-shaped windows.

"You forgot to write down your impressions of the school day yesterday," Chad-Two said. He pointed toward the notebooks. I grabbed one of them.

I picked a pen up off the table and pretended to write.

While I wrote, Chad-Two pressed a green touch pad on the wall and a drawer flipped open. He took out two big metal Slinkies.

He touched something else on the wall and four things like steps slid out, each one lower and larger than the last.

He started the Slinkies going down the stairs.

He sat on the floor and watched the Slinkies going end over end until they wound up on the floor.

He was so fascinated, he wasn't watching me anymore.

Maybe I could sneak out of the house while he was distracted!

I put the pen down and stood up as quietly as I could.

I made it all the way to the door.

When it whooshed open, Chad-Two looked up. His eyes widened. "Where are you going? Are you done already?"

"Just thought I'd get a snack," I said. "You want anything?"

"No eating between meals, Chad-One. You are so polluted from spending time with those humans!" IIis face looked cold and mean. He pointed at the desk.

I thought of the rat after he used the shink on it. I shuddered!

I sat down and picked up the pen again.

After dinner Chad-Two and I went back upstairs. Chad-Two quickly shut the door to his chamber and went to sleep.

My heart started to beat faster. This was my chance. No Chad-Two spying on me! Maybe now I could get away!

I peered down the stairs.

Mom and Dad were still in the living room just below me.

They appeared to be watching TV.

At least, that's what you would think if you saw them through the front window.

But the last I saw, they had been playing with little metal machines in their laps, making them transform, then using the machines for things I didn't understand.

I can't get past Mom and Dad. So how do I get out?

I glanced at the boots lined up by the touch pad. *Hmmmmm.*

Would they only stick to the sleep-chamber ceiling?

I rushed over and put the boots on. I stamped the touch pad. Then I lifted a foot and stamped it on the curving pink wall. But the boot didn't stick to it. Maybe the pink wall was too slippery or was coated with special nonstick wallpaper.

I snuck back into the workroom. The minute I stepped over the threshold, my boots stuck to the floor as if they had Super Glue on the bottoms.

I couldn't get them to let go!

Frantically I jiggled the boots sideways. Three jiggles, and they popped loose!

I grabbed my sneakers from my sleep chamber,

then carried the boots and sneakers over to the window.

Sitting on the windowsill, I tied the sneakers together by the laces and looped them around my neck. I put on the boots.

This had to work!

I swung my booted feet outside and stamped the boots to the outside of the house.

They stuck!

I let go of the windowsill. The boots held me up!

I could feel gravity trying to pull me to the ground two stories below. But the boots didn't let me go!

Now came the tricky part. I jiggled one foot three times, and the boot came loose!

I stamped it farther down the side of the house, and it stuck again. I jiggled the other one loose, and stamped it lower on the side of the house.

I was walking down a wall! Spider-Man had days like this! Only he could go lots faster because he didn't have to jiggle between each step.

I was sweating by the time I reached the ground, but I sure felt happy. I was almost out of there!

I jiggled the boots loose of the wall and stepped onto the grass. I sat on the lawn and took them off. I pulled the tennis shoes from around my neck and untied them.

Then I froze.

Something stepped out of the shadows.

Not some*thing*. Some*one*.

"Chad-One, what are you doing out of bed?" Mom demanded.

For once, she wasn't smiling.

13

"**A**aaaaahhhhh!" I screamed and dropped my tennis shoes.

She had caught me! I was done for! She would guess I was trying to escape!

They would shrink me down to the size of an acorn, and my body would be hard as a rock!

Or maybe they would just tailor my mind. . . .

I screamed again.

"What's the matter with you?" Mom scolded. "Stop making all that noise! You'll wake the neighbors!"

I shut up.

"Chad-One? Chad-One, I am waiting for an answer."

What was the question?

I was so scared I couldn't think straight!

Oh, yeah. What was the matter with me?

"I—I had a nightmare," I stammered. Then I panicked. Oh, no! What if aliens didn't have nightmares? My whole body trembled. I was getting dizzy. My stomach twisted five directions at once.

"What?" Mom was staring at me.

"I had a horrible nightmare!" That was my story. I had to stick to it. *Okay, make this good!* "I dreamed that slimy humans found out about us and they were coming to kill us! I had to get away. Then I woke up and I was walking down the side of the house! It scared me! I managed to get to the ground. Then you startled me. I'm sorry I screamed."

Did it work? Did she believe me?

"It's all right." She patted my shoulder like a good sitcom mom. "Don't worry, Chad-One. Those nasty old humans won't come after us. And if they ever do, we'll just shink them, or evaporate them, or something. No human can ever hurt you."

She bought it! I was so relieved, I almost kissed her.

Almost.

"Come inside. You need some tickeree, Chad-One," Mom said soothingly. "That'll help you sleep."

Luckily she didn't notice the sneakers. If she had seen them she might have realized I had planned ahead on my sleepwalk. I left them on the lawn. I would worry about them later.

We went into the house and into the kitchen, where she heated water and mixed it with these worms with gigantic eyes.

I drank it. It tasted like hot Tang. And it did make me sleepy.

When I finally woke up, it was noon on Sunday. That tickeree stuff had really knocked me out. I breathed a sigh of relief. I made it through another night. Even if I hadn't escaped, at least no one suspected that I was a human!

I wanted to call Chad and make sure we both knew the plan for tonight. I was counting the seconds until switch-time!

I had seen a phone downstairs in the kitchen. I hadn't noticed anything resembling a phone up here, or anywhere else in the house.

I flipped out of my chamber to check on Chad-Two. He was already out of bed. I crept over to the workroom. *Bingo!* There he was, playing with his Slinkies.

I crept down the stairs, hoping not to attract attention.

Mom sat by the front door, playing with some weird machine that spun stuff out into the air like spiderwebs. She smiled at me. "Hi, sleepyhead," she said in her best sitcom tone.

"Hi, Mom," I answered and headed for the kitchen.

Dad was by the back door, studying something with a glowing screen. He glanced up and smiled at me, too.

I approached the phone. It was sitting on a counter near me. Okay, I told myself. Be calm.

I waved to Dad, turned my back to him, and picked up the cordless phone. My body covered my move as I slipped the phone into my shirt. Yes! I thought. I did it!

I bounded up the stairs and ducked into my sleep chamber.

I dialed my home number.

"Kennedy residence," a voice answered.

Just my luck. Pepper.

"Hi, Pepper. It's me."

"Me who?"

"Me. Will."

"Who is this? What kind of game are you trying to play? Will's right in the other room, watching cartoons! You don't even sound like Will!"

Suddenly I really wanted her to know it was me. Maybe if she believed me she would help me. I really wanted someone to help me.

"Listen, Pep. You remember that episode of the Judo-Jabbing Coyotes called 'The Imposter Syndrome,' where the High Muckety sent in a fake Newton that looked just like the real Newton, and he really messed everybody up? Copernicus, Galileo, and Einstein didn't know what hit them!"

"Yeah. So?"

"Don't you think Will has been acting strange since Friday?"

She was silent for a while. "He hasn't tripped over anything or spilled anything," she said slowly, "and he can catch the Frisbee without fumbling it, and he runs real good, and he's way too polite."

"I bet he doesn't call you Buckethead."

"Nope. Not that I miss it!"

"I bet he doesn't know your birthday is May eleventh."

"Who *are* you?"

"I'm *Will*. I know it's hard to believe, Pep. But it's true! I switched bodies with that guy Chad. That was *me* on the front porch yesterday. I can prove it to you. Ask me anything!"

"What's my favorite color?"

"Red."

"How would you know? I never told Will my favorite color!"

"That's what color notebook you buy for school every year. That's what color shirt you always buy, if Mom lets you. What else?"

She was quiet for a long time.

At last she said, "Tell me something only Will could know."

"I drew a mustache on your Cabbage Patch doll with Magic Marker when you were five."

"What?" she yelled. "That was you? You rat! You total rat! I knew you did it! I hate you!"

Then she hung up!

I dialed again.

"Hello?" a voice answered. My voice.

"Chad?" I yelped. "Chad, I don't know if I can wait until tonight. Can't you come over now?"

"No, I can't come over now. Or later."

"What do you mean?" I asked nervously.

I heard his mean laugh cackle over the phone lines.

"Give it up, Will. I'm never giving you your body back. *Never.*"

14

The phone went dead.

I stared at the cordless in my hand.

Never!

He was never going to switch back!

I was stuck with these aliens, and they were sure to find out I was human!

The shink was out in the shed, waiting for me to make one more little goof! And I, Will Kennedy, had a lifelong history of horrible goofs!

No way! I wouldn't let it happen.

I would force Chad back here. That's what I would do. I'd get him back into the shed—somehow.

I went into the workroom and found Chad-Two

still sitting there. A bunch of weird equipment was spread on the floor.

If I was going to get Chad over here, I needed some help.

"Where's my merister?" I asked Chad-Two, remembering his net gun from the day before. It might be helpful in getting Chad to cooperate.

"Check your other pants," Chad-Two responded, pointing to a door. I opened it and saw a closet full of Chad's clothes.

I checked through the pockets of the pants hanging there and found several strange objects.

One of them was a merister, just like the net gun Chad-Two used on the rat the day before. I stashed it in my pocket.

Then I checked out another gunlike object. It had a clear ball the size of a big marble on the end of its barrel and two touch pads, one blue and one pink. I held it up to look at it.

"You found your lifter!" Chad-Two said, noticing the object in my hands. "Good! Let me see if it's still charged." He took it from me.

He tapped a touch pad high on the wall. A drawer the size of a piano opened, making a deep grinding sound as it slid across the floor. It sounded *really* heavy.

Chad-Two pushed the round ball against the drawer and pressed the blue button twice. Then he raised the gun. The big drawer rose up in the air! And Chad wasn't straining at all!

He put the lump back down, tapped the pink button twice, and the ball came loose. "Works fine," he announced.

"Yeah," I said.

He tossed the lifter to me.

I wondered if it would lift cars! Or, say, that big bully Eric Rice in Miss Scott's class.

Or Chad-Two?

I put the lifter in my pocket.

"Chad-One! Chad-Two!" Dad yelled up the stairs.

"Yeah, Dad?" Chad-Two shouted back.

"Time for that test drive!"

"Come on, ooligooch!" Chad-Two said, punching my arm. I followed him down the stairs and through the kitchen. I managed to sneak the phone back onto its base.

Mom and Dad came into the kitchen. Chad-Two and I followed them through a side door I had never seen opened before.

The door led to the garage.

There was nothing else in the whole garage but this huge round metal thing with an opening in it. *The aliens' spaceship!*

Dad ducked and crawled into the opening. Chad-Two shoved me, so I followed Dad into the ship.

Chad-Two and Mom crawled in behind me.

We crawled through a narrow dark tunnel for a while. All I could see were Dad's feet ahead of me, and the slick shiny walls. Little lights ran across the walls like fireworks. The floor was damp and spongy.

Then the tunnel opened out into a round room and we could stand up. There were pools of bubbling liquid on the floor, and spiky bad-smelling plants grew from the walls and the ceiling.

When we got to the other side of the room, Dad ducked and crawled into another dark tunnel.

I felt like toothpaste being squeezed out of a tube by the time we got to the other end!

Finally we ended up in a round room with a big console like the Starship *Enterprise*. It had four sets of touch pads on it.

Mom went to one of the center sets and put her hands on two big gray touch pads.

Dad stood beside her and put his hands on matching gray pads in his set.

Chad-Two went to the set of touch pads on Mom's other side, so I took the only set left. I made sure to touch the same two pads everyone else was touching.

"Ready?" said Mom.

"Yes," we all said.

"Good. Now zum."

The others all started humming. I joined in. Then the ship itself started humming!

It was weird. I could feel the metal humming under my feet!

Lights flickered and flashed. For a second I could see right through the ship into the garage. We were lifting off the ground!

I glanced at Dad, and he was flickering and flashing.

I looked down at my hands. They were flickering, too!

I felt as if everything in me was fizzing and sizzling. Like I was burning up! I looked up at the garage's ceiling when the flashes lit it up. I thought we were going to bump into it.

But more flashes, and then I saw the sky! The ship was going right through the ceiling and taking us all with it!

"Uh-oh," Mom said. "Zum down!"

We hummed softer and softer. The ship dropped back down and settled gently on the ground.

"All systems functioning perfectly!" Mom said. "Pack up everything you want to take. Leave the storage module out back for last. We need that machinery up and running until the last minute. Now, we'll want to switch back to our own bodies as close to departure time as possible. Be ready to leave at two P.M. local time."

"Don't forget anything," Dad added. "We won't be coming back."

15

No! It couldn't be!

They couldn't be leaving! As in *leaving the planet!*

Oh, man! What if I couldn't get Chad to give me my body back before two P.M.? Then the aliens would take me with them into outer space! Away from my friends—away from my family!

I was so scared I couldn't even think. I followed as Chad's family crawled out of the ship and went into the house.

The next thing I knew, I was upstairs with Chad-Two in our workroom. Packing for space travel.

Chad-Two opened drawers and took different machines out of them.

He tapped tiny black touch pads on the edges of

the machines, and they shrank down to the size of quarters.

He took a case out of one of the closets and opened it. It had a whole lot of slots in it, and each thing he shrank fit into one of the slots.

"On the next planet we explore, we get to have six legs!" Chad-Two said. "It's got to be better than this dump! I can't wait until we leave!"

Oh, man! Six legs!

Oh, man! Two P.M.? That was really soon!

Leaving! We were leaving the planet!

My thoughts whirled around my brain.

"What's wrong with you, Chad-One? We won't need those where we're going!" Chad-Two snapped.

I looked down and saw I was trying to stuff a pair of tennis shoes into the big case.

"We'll never have to wear these itchy ugly clothes again, thank Sprog!" Chad-Two shrank the notebooks we kept our observations in.

"Sorry," I choked out, putting the tennis shoes back into the closet. What kind of clothes would I wear on some other planet? Maybe none at all. It would be tough to make a pair of pants with six legs!

Oh, *no way!*

I had to get Chad back to that shed. I had to get my body back! *I had to get out of here!* But how could I distract Chad-Two long enough to make a break for it?

Then it hit me.

"Hey, Chad-Two," I said, trying to sound helpful. "Aren't you going to pack the Slinkies?"

"The Slinkies!" he yelled. "Croggers, I haven't had time to transmorph them with shink technology! The Slinkies! I almost forgot!"

He opened the Slinky drawer and grabbed about six of them.

"Help me carry these out to the storage module," he said.

I grabbed the rest of the Slinkies in the drawer.

We passed Mom and Dad, who were collapsing stuff downstairs. Chad-Two explained what we were doing.

"Slinkies!" Mom exclaimed. "Yes! We need to take the Slinkies!"

I followed Chad-Two to the door. *Whoosh!* The door opened. I dropped the Slinkies and darted out!

I had never run so fast in my life.

I crossed Fear Street and zoomed through someone's backyard, putting a house, some fence, and a few trees between me and the aliens.

I reached Kent Place in record time. Then I slowed and snuck up to my house, using the bushes for cover. I glanced down at my watch. It was nearly one P.M. Less than an hour to takeoff!

The station wagon wasn't in the driveway. That meant Mom and Dad weren't home.

I found Pepper, Chad, and Dumbbell playing Frisbee in the backyard. Chad and Pepper tossed

90

the Frisbee back and forth, and Dumbbell ran around barking.

I watched them, trying to figure out what to do. How would I get Chad to make the switch? Or even go back to the change chambers? Time was wasting away.

Then Pepper told Chad she was going inside to get some lemonade.

I crept over to the house and slipped inside. I startled Pepper in the kitchen. She screamed.

"Shh!" I hissed.

"Who are you," she demanded. "What are you doing in my house?"

"Keep your voice down," I implored her. "It's me, Will!"

"Prove it!"

"Your real name is Penelope."

"Ewww!"

"You know it's me, Pep. You know it!"

She shook her head, glaring at me.

"Don't you?" I wanted to shake her!

She stuck out her lower lip. Then she said, "I will *never* forgive you for wrecking my doll!"

"I'm sorry! I'm sorry! I'll never do it again!"

"That's for sure. Since you don't live here anymore!"

"Please, Pep! This body, the whole family, they're aliens from outer space! And they're blasting off in less than an hour! If I don't get my body back right now, they'll leave and take me with them. I'll never see Earth again!"

She snorted. "This is *waaay* too much to swallow!"

"It's true! If you can just help me get the alien pretending to be me back to their house, I can prove it to you. I can show you the body-switching equipment and the spaceship and everything!"

"How am I supposed to get him to go anywhere?"

Good question!

I shoved my hands in my pockets. Maybe some of the junk I was carrying around would give me an idea. I started pulling things out. The merister. The lifter. The boxes of pinter and skwoos Chad-Two had given me.

A light went on in my brain. An idea! Earth food had nearly killed me. Maybe alien food would make Chad sick!

Skwoos wouldn't work. They were big and still alive, and Chad would know not to swallow one. But the pinter . . . Chad-Two had said it was powdered.

I tapped the brown box up to full-size.

Pepper gasped as it grew in my hands.

The box was filled with multicolored powder that looked like ground-up butterfly wings.

"If I put a pinch of this in some lemonade and Chad drinks it, I bet it'll make him sick," I told Pepper. "Then maybe I can get him on a bike and wheel him back to his house."

"Will it kill him?" she asked, peering out the window. Chad was throwing the Frisbee up and catching it as it came down.

"I hope not!" I told her. I didn't want to kill Chad. I didn't want to kill my own body. I didn't want to kill anybody! But I had to try something!

I put a pinch of pinter in the bottom of a glass and poured lemonade over it. I stirred it really well.

I handed Pepper the glass. "Please help me, Pep. *Please!*"

She stared at me for a long minute.

"This is for real, isn't it?" she asked.

"Yeah. It's for real," I told her.

She bit her lip, then went outside, carrying the glass of lemonade.

I hid in the kitchen and watched her walk out and give the glass to Chad. He grabbed the lemonade and drank it all.

Pepper smiled at him.

He told her to go long. He waved the Frisbee at her.

Pepper stared at him, then ran across the yard. He threw the Frisbee in a perfect arc.

A beautiful pass.

Chad was fine. The pinter didn't affect him.

My plan wasn't going to work! I was doomed!

16

They went back to playing Frisbee.

I went back to thinking that my life was over.

I stood staring out the kitchen window more miserable than I've ever been. I'd never get my body back now!

My days on Earth were over.

Pepper tossed the Frisbee and Chad jumped up and caught it in the air—but he tripped when he landed. He fell to the grass.

That wasn't like Chad. Even in my body.

I clutched the sink below the window. I held my breath.

"I don't feel so good," Chad said as he pushed

himself up. He pressed the backs of his hands to his cheeks. His face was red.

Could it be? *Yes!* Chad was getting sick. My plan was working. I still had a chance!

"Come on, Will. I'll get you inside and call a doctor," Pepper said. She pulled his arm around her shoulders and led him toward the driveway where our bikes were.

I slammed out of the kitchen door and stood in front of them.

Chad was wiping sweat off his forehead, but he looked up and saw me. "You! Oh, no. What have you done?"

"Come on, it's just a pinch of pinter!"

"Pinter? You want to kill me?"

"No! I want my body back! Now get on this bike!"

Chad groaned and held his stomach. He collapsed on the cement. His face was red and he was sweating.

"He's dying!" Pepper yelled. "Do something!"

I felt in my pockets and found the lifter.

I headed for Chad, when a shadow fell across the driveway.

I glanced toward the street.

Chad-Two stood there.

And he didn't look happy.

17

"What are you doing?" Chad-Two demanded.

"Who is *this?*" Pepper screeched. "How many of you space guys are there? What do you want?"

Chad opened his eyes, groaned, and slumped again.

"What's the matter with you, Chad-One?" Chad-Two yelled at me. "You've been acting so weird, I planted a tracer on you! What are you doing with these slimy humans? How could you tell them about us?"

"I'm not Chad-One," I confessed. Shink or no shink, I had to tell him. *"He's* Chad-One. He stole my body, and I want it back!"

"I did not steal it!" Chad croaked. "You gave it to me!"

"Chad-One! How could you?" Chad-Two shouted.

"I want to stay here," Chad said.

"You want to what?" Chad-Two was so shocked he squeaked. "You would destroy everything we've worked on for two years local time just so you can stay on this stupid planet?" Chad-Two fumed. "You idiot! You fleeflaw! You groober!"

"Will you help us switch back?" I asked.

Chad-Two's face was purple. For a minute his mouth just opened and closed and no words came out.

Then he blinked a couple of times. His eyes narrowed. He looked really mean. "Oh, yeah. I'll switch you back. And then it's mind-tailoring for you, Chad-One!"

"Fine," I said. I was afraid of Chad-Two. But one thing at a time. First I would get my body back, *then* figure out what to do next. "Pepper, you stay here."

"Oh, no," Chad-Two said. "The larva comes with us!"

"Larva?" Pepper shrieked.

He glared at her and she shut up.

Chad groaned again.

"What's wrong with him?"

"I gave him a pinch of pinter," I explained.

"Pinter? In an Earth body? He needs some sklix right away!"

"*After* we switch," I said.

"Okay," he agreed. "How did you plan to get him back to the storage module?"

"On my bike," I said. I pulled the lifter out of my pocket and tapped it up to size. "Will this work on him?"

"Good thinking," he said. Then he remembered who he was talking to and glared at me.

We lifted Chad to his feet. He leaned on me and I raised his shirt. Chad-Two put the clear ball against Chad's back. And lifted him with no problem.

We left the driveway, me on Chad's right, Chad-Two on his left, Pepper walking beside me.

I sneaked a peek at my watch. Quarter to two!

When we reached the house, we rushed over to the silver puffball mushroom shed out back. I opened it with the touch pad.

"Wow!" Pepper said, staring at the door opening. When we stepped over the threshold, she said wow about fifteen times—every time she looked in a different direction.

Chad-Two went over to the touch-pad console and pushed the pad that opened the change chamber doors.

The familiar, sour smell wafted out.

I took Chad over to one of the big, purple telephone booth change chambers and settled him inside, then tapped the lifter so it let go of him.

I tapped the lifter small. I shoved the lifter and the merister into Chad's pockets—my own jeans pockets—then went and climbed into the other chamber.

"Ready?" asked Chad-Two.

"Ready," I answered.

A second later the doors whooshed shut and I was in the dark again.

It was all just like before.

I felt as if I were jerking sideways on a carnival ride.

But when I opened my eyes again, boy, did I feel different!

I felt hot and then cold. My stomach ached. My throat hurt. I could feel sweat pouring off me and soaking into my shirt.

My mouth felt weird. I ran my tongue on the backs of my teeth. Braces!

They were mine! Will's!

Oh, man! I never thought I would be so glad to go back to being Will the Spill!

The door whooshed open.

Pepper ran over to me. "Will? Are you okay? Are you—*you?*"

"Your birthday is May eleventh," I gasped. My throat hurt as the words came out. "Your favorite color is red. It worked, Pep. Thanks for believing in me." Then I moaned. My muscles were burning!

Pinter! The pinter I gave Chad while he was in my body was still having an effect. It was making me sick!

I glanced around for Chad-Two. He was opening a cabinet in the wall.

Chad-One stormed out of the other change chamber. He looked furious. "I hate you, Will Kennedy!"

Chad-Two came over with a small blue box. He tapped it up, then slid the lid sideways.

Inside was a gray-green bug with a million legs. It started oozing up over the side of the box.

"Take this sklix," Chad-Two said.

I grabbed the bug and ate it. It tasted sour and crunchy, and it fluttered in my mouth. I didn't care.

"Eww!" Pepper yelped. "You ate a *bug?!*"

I started feeling better right away! Oh, man! I was back in my body again, and everything was all right! I was so happy I felt as if I could fly!

I got to my feet. I wiped sweat off my forehead with the back of my hand. Everything about being in my own body felt a little skewed and sideways, but I didn't care. I could adjust! I took some deep breaths.

Then I grabbed Pepper's hand and headed for the door.

I thumbed the green touch pad.

Nothing happened!

Of course. I didn't have Chad-One's fingerprints anymore! Chad-One had said the locks were keyed to specific people!

I pointed at the touch pad. "Can we borrow your fingers? Just for a minute?" I smiled.

"Sorry. Not possible," Chad-Two said. He strode across the room and stood directly in front of me.

"Wh-wh-why not?" I stammered.

"I can't let you two leave," Chad-Two informed us. "You know too much!"

18

"What do you mean? We don't know anything!" I said. "I don't know what planet you're from or what you're doing here!"

Chad-Two shook his head. "You know we were here, and that's enough."

"I don't know what your real bodies look like! I don't know where you're going! We won't tell anybody! I promise!"

"Who would believe us, anyway?" Pepper added.

"Sorry. We have a policy about this," Chad-Two said.

Chad-One came over and stood next to him. Chad-One had a nasty grin. He looked over at the shink.

They were going to shink us like the rat?

No! I couldn't let that happen.

My heart pounded in my ears. My palms felt sweaty.

I shoved my hands in my pockets.

The merister and the lifter were still there! Right where I put them before Chad and I switched back!

I pulled out the merister and tapped the touch pad to make it bigger. It grew until it was just like the ray gun Chad-Two had used to net the rat!

I didn't know if it would work on anything as big as a person, but it was better than nothing!

I turned toward the two Chads and tapped the pad that fired the merister.

Web shot out!

But I had forgotten I was Will! I aimed for the Chads, but I stumbled over the leg of a piece of equipment as I headed for them!

The web shot out, all right. But it didn't come anywhere near the two Chads! Instead, it covered the touch-pad console that ran the changing chambers!

Chad-One snickered. "Nice shot."

Chad-Two walked right up to me and grabbed the merister out of my hand. "Come on, Will. The shink doesn't hurt."

"What's a shink?" Pepper demanded.

"They shinked me a couple of body switches ago when I was having discipline problems," Chad explained. "Every time I caused trouble, they'd shink me. You don't really notice anything when you're in the small state. They put the setting on reversible, so I had one of those black touch pads they could tap bigger or smaller. I'll do that for you, too. Maybe I can grow you later and let you loose on some other planet."

"What's *a shink?*" Pepper screamed.

"You'll find out soon enough," Chad-Two said, pushing me and Pepper toward the yellow circle on the floor.

Just then the shed door whooshed open, and Mom and Dad came in. "Oh, good, you're both here," Mom said. "It's time for the body switch."

Then she noticed me and Pepper. "Who are these humans? What are they doing here? This is going to throw off our schedule!"

"I was just going to shink them," Chad-Two said. "Chad-One has been misbehaving. He stole this one's body." He pointed at me. "No wonder he's been acting so strange the last couple of days—he had someone else's brain!"

Pepper grabbed my sleeve and pulled on it. "Who are those people with sitcom damage?" she whispered to me.

"Grown-up aliens."

"What's a shink?" she whispered.

"It's a machine that shrinks you and turns you into a pebble," I whispered back.

"Nobody shrinks me!" she yelled.

104

"It doesn't hurt," Chad-Two said again. He shoved my shoulder to get me moving toward the yellow circle.

I tripped over that blue box on the floor again and fell across the edge of the yellow circle.

I reached out for anything to break my fall and grabbed the shink from Chad-Two's hands.

I hugged it to my belly and curled around it as I fell.

I'm not sure exactly how it happened. Only it was way better than falling into a tray full of spaghetti!

I had the shink in my arms, and Mom and Dad and Chads One and Two were racing toward me.

They all looked horrified!

I felt as if everything were moving in slow motion.

I lifted the shink. I turned the fuzzy side toward them.

What if I couldn't remember the right way to touch the pads?

They were closing in on me! Mom had her arms out to grab me, and for the first time I noticed how long and red her fingernails were!

I tapped the square black pad twice. I tapped the round black pad three times. I tapped the square black pad twice again!

For a second they kept coming. Then they all shrieked! Just like the rat. They shrank, twisting and squirming, until they were tiny statues on the floor!

19

It was a good thing I had that lifter in my pocket. Otherwise there was no way Pepper and I would have been able to cart all that stuff home, even though we shrank it all down—the spaceship, the shed, the body-switching machines, and all those other gadgets I didn't understand.

I even double-shrank stuff the aliens had already packed into those big hard-sided cases.

The machine was on the reversible setting when I blasted everything. So all the stuff ended up having those little black touch pads on it. I can tap it back up to life size any time I want to.

I keep everything on the top shelf in my closet.

I found an excellent place in my basement to hide

the shink so no one would ever find it. Especially Pepper.

Sometimes late at night when everyone else is asleep, I take out one of the machines and tap it up just to look at it. Just so I can convince myself that everything I went through was real—and not some weird, horrible nightmare!

The aliens didn't shrink down as much as everything else did. They are about three and a half inches high, and you can tell by looking at them that they're people.

Pepper keeps them on the top shelf with all her best dolls.

I'm thinking of starting a cartoon series about this superhero who can make things bigger and smaller and defeats body-switching aliens. And gets revenge on everyone who ever called him a dork.

I still trip over things. And I'm still klutzy. But Pepper doesn't tease me as much as she used to. She has major respect for me now.

Because she got caught in the shink blast, too.

And now—any time I want—I can tap that little black pad on the back of her neck. I can make her really small and really quiet for as long as I like.

I guess you could say things are really looking up for Will the Spill.

Are you ready for another walk
down Fear Street?
Turn the page for a terrifying
sneak preview.

R•L•STINE'S
GHOSTS OF FEAR STREET® #15

FRIGHT CHRISTMAS

Coming mid-November 1996

I grabbed the doorknob and turned it. The door remained locked.

I jiggled the knob.

Tugged on the door again.

It didn't budge.

It was bolted shut—from the outside.

Which meant I was stuck in a closet in Dalby's Department Store! On Christmas Eve!

A small wave of panic rose up inside me.

I stared around the closet.

Relax, Kenny, I told myself. *If you bang on the door, somebody will hear you and let you out.*

I listened.

I heard only the low hum of the electrical control panels in the closet.

"Hey, could someone open this door?" I shouted. "I'm stuck in here."

No one answered me.

"Hey, I'm stuck in here!" I yelled, pounding my fist on the door. "Somebody open up!"

No one came to the door.

With all the people out there, why didn't anyone hear me?

"I'm a kid trapped in this closet!" I yelled as loud as I could. "Help me! Somebody! Get me out of here!"

I banged on the door with my hands. I kicked it hard with my feet.

There! Somebody had to hear that!

Silence.

An uneasy feeling crept into the pit of my stomach. I stood back from the door and took a deep breath.

Then I took a running leap at it, throwing my shoulder against it, hard.

Nothing.

I banged on the door until my knuckles hurt.

Still nothing.

Where is everyone?

I glanced at my glow-in-the-dark watch. 8:15!

Dalby's closes at 8:00.

Did everyone go home?

How could that be?

How could everyone have gone home and left me in here? My mom must have told someone I was missing. Why weren't they looking for me?

My hands began to sweat. I had to get out of this place. But how?

I wiped my sweaty palms on my pants and checked my watch again. 8:20.

It wasn't that late. There had to be someone in the store. A manager. A security guard locking up. One of the department-store Santa's stupid elves. Someone.

Oh, I get it! They *know* I'm in here, I realized. They're trying to teach me a lesson or something dumb like that.

"Come on, you guys!" I yelled. "Please. Let me out of here! Now!"

No reply.

I grabbed the doorknob and pulled with all my strength.

"Help!" I screamed. "Help!"

I twisted the knob. Then I pulled again, as hard as I could.

"Let me out of here!" I shouted.

No one answered my calls. I backed away from the door, wondering what to do next.

That's when I heard the sizzling sounds.

I gazed around the room. I couldn't tell what was making that noise.

Then, suddenly, the hum in the room grew louder.

And the floor began to vibrate.

My legs shook hard.

The humming grew louder. Louder. It filled the room now, shrill and strong. It seemed to come at me from every direction, all at once.

The floor quaked under my feet.

I started to lose my balance.

Started to slam into the control panel—when the door slowly swung open.

I grabbed on to the control panel and caught my balance.

I stared at the door.

It swung open some more. A pale red light glowed through the opening.

I staggered toward the door on shaky legs.

"What took you so long?" I demanded as I stepped outside. "Something crazy was going on in that room!"

Huh?

No one stood outside the door.

The toy department sat in silence. Except for the dull red glow from the exit signs, it was totally dark.

As my eyes adjusted to the dim light, I glanced around. In the shadowy light, I could make out the outline of Santa's Village.

In the glow of the red light, Santa Street looked eerie—like a miniature Fear Street. The deserted end of Fear Street. The part with the abandoned mansions. The mansions that people say are haunted.

I live on Fear Street. I have to admit it—the mansions do look kind of creepy. But haunted—come on! How could anyone really believe in ghosts.

I took a step forward.

"Hey!" I shouted. "Anybody here?"

My voice echoed back to me.

I took a few more steps. My sneakers squeaked on the marble floor.

I stood perfectly still and listened. All I heard was my own heart beating. Really loud.

Then I heard something else.

I held my breath. What was it?

It sounded like . . . bells.

Sleigh bells. Louder now. Coming closer—from Santa's Village.

I took a few steps through the village gate.

"Hey, is someone there?" I yelled.

Footsteps. Slow and heavy.

I squinted in the darkness. I saw something move—down by Santa's sleigh.

I could make out a shadow now—the shadow of a man. A man sitting in Santa's sleigh.

He stood up and stepped out of the sleigh.

Even in the shadows I could tell he was big. And

tall. He walked slowly down Santa Street—right toward me.

"Who's there?" I shouted. "Who is it?" My voice squeaked a little.

The man didn't answer.

He came closer.

I heard his heavy shoes scrape the floor.

And with every step he took, I heard the faint sound of jingling bells.

Barely breathing, I stood there and watched him. Now I could make out his fur-trimmed red coat and red pants.

Joe! The department store Santa.

Joe—still wearing his big white beard. Didn't he ever take that thing off?

"Hey, did you unlock that door for me?" I called out to him.

He shrugged. "Maybe I did. Maybe I didn't."

"Give me a break, Joe." I rolled my eyes at him. "It sure took you long enough," I complained. "I yelled my head off in there. Didn't you hear me?"

"I'm a busy guy tonight," Joe replied. "It's Christmas Eve, after all—the big night."

"Yeah, yeah. Whatever. So you're still mad at me for pulling your beard off," I said sarcastically. "You wanted to teach me a lesson, right?"

Joe walked right up to me and stared down into my eyes. He shook his head slowly from side to side. I noticed a funny little smile under his beard.

"You've been naughty all year, Kenny," Joe said grimly.

"Naughty?" I mimicked his voice. Then I chuckled.

Joe wagged his finger at me, frowning.

"Come on, Joe. Lighten up," I teased. "You don't have to drag out this Santa act for me. Christmas shopping season is over."

I reached up. I grabbed hold of his beard—and gave it a good yank.

It didn't budge.

I pulled on it again—harder this time.

It didn't come off.

No, I thought. *It couldn't be.*

Could it?

About R. L. Stine

R. L. Stine, the creator of *Ghosts of Fear Street*, has written almost 100 scary novels for kids. The *Ghosts of Fear Street* series, like the *Fear Street* series, takes place in Shadyside and centers on the scary events that happen to people on Fear Street.

When he isn't writing, R. L. Stine likes to play pinball on his very own pinball machine, and explore New York City with his wife, Jane, and son, Matt.

Dream

Interpretation
The Secret

David F. Melbourne
and
Dr Keith Hearne

BLANDFORD

A BLANDFORD BOOK

First published in the UK 1997 by Blandford

A Cassell Imprint

Cassell Plc, Wellington House,
125 Strand, London WC2R 0BB

Reprinted 1998

Distributed in the United States by Sterling Publishing Co., Inc.,
387 Park Avenue South, New York, NY 10016–8810

A Cataloguing-in-Publication Data entry for this title is available
from the British Library

ISBN 0-7137-2670-9

Design and electronic page make-up by Chris Warner

Printed and bound in Great Britain by
Creative Print and Design Wales, Ebbw Vale

Contents

To Elizabeth, who is courageously coping with progressive illness.

Acknowledgements

We would like to thank Chris Melbourne for her love and support through years of interrupted sleep; Joan Newby, for checking the manuscript and giving excellent suggestions, and everybody who, over the years, has sent in dreams for analysis. This book would not have been possible without them.

Preface
by
David Melbourne

SOME YEARS ago, during my service with the London Fire Brigade, I underwent my second Near Death Experience, or NDE, which was to have a profound and lasting effect on my life. Every year since then I have had two or three Out of Body Experiences. This powerful phenomenon engendered in me the desire to discover my spiritual side and to try to understand the workings of the subconscious.

My first brush with death came at the age of three, when I was drowning in a swimming-pool. I was hovering out of my body, when my mother came to the rescue. This memory has remained fresh in my mind. Although not enough time had elapsed for me to see a bright light or a tunnel (common features of an NDE), my consciousness was definitely existing outside my physical body. The fact that I was drowning classifies this as the first stage of an NDE.

The second close shave was different: this time I didn't part company from my body. I was on a large burning roof of a furrier's in Whitechapel, London, with Anthony Hall (usually known as Nobby), a dear friend and fellow fire-fighter. We were directing a jet of water into the heart of the inferno which was raging below. The heat was intense and the situation was becoming untenable. Suddenly, our supply of water was cut off, effectively leaving us exposed.

There was no mistaking the seriousness of the situation as we both tried to shield each other from the intense heat. During those moments, before the water was restored, facilitating our escape from danger, I realized that we might perish there. It was then that my life flashed in front of my eyes.

Conscious, and vaguely aware of the surroundings, I went into a trance-like state. It was as if I was being my own judge and jury. As well as poignant memories, I witnessed inconsequential incidents that I had long since forgotten. Later, I learned that only a few seconds had elapsed. However, during the experience it was as if time stood still as I pondered each scene at my leisure. Soon after our escape, the roof collapsed and went crashing into the heart of the fire. There is no doubt in my mind that we had been near death.

Although Nobby and I rarely discussed it, that frightening night has lived with me ever since, so much so that I began a quest which, to a large extent, was eventually to take over my life.

Part of this search for knowledge involved trying to understand the purpose of dreams and their meaning – if any. As you will discover in later chapters, I accept the possibility that some of our dreams might be a way for the brain to act as a sort of clearing house, processing information gathered during the previous day. However, I realized that without a doubt, some dreams bear messages.

I was delighted to discover that I seemed to have a gift for interpreting the meaning of dreams. During the early years, my work was confined mainly to the dreams of my wife and myself; sometimes I would interpret one for a close friend. I discovered that when I interpreted a dream correctly, the degree of accuracy was uncannily high. However, when I got it wrong, I did so in spectacular fashion.

This strange inconsistency nagged at me for years. My failures, although few, were unacceptable. I had to discover where I was going wrong. Like other dream interpreters, I had studied Freud, Jung, the Gestalt theory and the like, and had developed a technique which allowed for each theory and also for my own interpretation.

I found that by developing and using my own theories and methods I increased my accuracy rate. However, I still encountered the odd dream which baffled me. It was then that I decided to delve deeper into the reasons behind dreams. This further investigation was to lead to the discovery of a new and entirely different understanding of dream analysis, using a flow-chart approach.

At about the time of the fire, while I was witnessing my life flash before me, a young scientist at Hull University called Keith Hearne was working for his doctorate. His subject was 'The Lucid Dream'. Dr Hearne, the co-author of this book, is now a leading authority on dreams.

His discoveries and writings, at a new and exciting cutting edge of science, were to take me in a different direction and enable me to solve the riddle of my occasional outrageously inaccurate dream interpretation. His work led me to conclude that not only are there different types of dream, but that each type comes in several varieties. It is simplistic to believe that dreams serve only one purpose.

It is clear that we owe the great dream researchers, Freud and Jung, a debt of gratitude. However, it would seem that they allowed their disputes to side-track them – they couldn't both be right. Unfortunately, in certain quarters the argument between Jungians and Freudians continues to this day.

What the modern analyst hasn't allowed for is the fact that neither Freud nor Jung could possibly have been aware of the intricacies of such phenomena as lucid dreams, false awakenings, sleep paralysis and the hypnagogic state, each of which gives rise to different kinds of dream.

The secret, therefore, of accurate dream interpretation lies in the willingness of the analyst to understand these conditions, maintain an open mind and consider all possibilities and theories. To this end, it is up to each of us to learn as much as possible about past discoveries and current knowledge.

Carrying out an in-depth study of Dr Hearne's work, I discovered that understanding the strange world of dreams can bring tremendous rewards. These come not only from interpreting their meaning, but from putting them to other highly beneficial uses. Therefore, although this book is primarily about dream interpretation, we also intend to cover these other valuable aspects of the subject.

However, there is another important feature: to become an accomplished dream analyst, one must first learn as much as possible about this curious state of brain activity. To become proficient in the field of interpretation, the analyst has to be able to recognize and identify different types of dream. The realization of this fact led me to the reason for my previous errors: not all dreams bear messages.

Dreams come in an amazing variety and unless the analyst can classify them, there will always be a degree of failure in their interpretation. For example, as we will see later in this book, the light-switch effect and the scene-shift effect occur in dreams. If these curious anomalies are not recognized, any attempt at interpretation will be useless.

One important type of dream is the spiritual dream. Regardless of the analyst's religious views, it is imperative that this sort of dream be recognized. It is unimportant whether such dreams are labelled 'spiritual' or 'deep dreams of the subconscious'; they do exist and can sometimes occur quite frequently. Whatever their cause, there is no doubt that they relate to the dreamer's spirituality or conscience. An understanding of this category of dream is vital to successful dream interpretation.

I put my theory to the test and achieved an extremely high degree of accuracy. The result of a practical joke finally convinced me that I had solved my problem. Somebody tried to trick me by fabricating a dream. Although I was suspicious that he was making it up as he went along, I reasoned that its content was coming from his creative subconscious. I decided to treat it as if it were a fantasy message-bearing dream. If my theory was correct, it would still translate into an accurate interpretation. It did. My colleague was shocked at the in-depth analysis of himself it revealed. If accurate dream interpretation can be used successfully on a trickster, this could have significant implications for the world of psychiatry. However, a great deal more research is needed before any conclusions can be reached.

As with all forms of diagnosis or analysis, experience enables the dream researcher to follow the right direction and achieve good results. An analyst must keep meticulous records and file each dream with its interpretation. Over the years, with increasing experience, an instinct for the task develops. Because all dreams are different – although there are common themes, such as falling – it is self-defeating to try to establish universal meanings for dream symbols. Therefore, it is a mistake to give credence to dream dictionaries. Rather, each dream should be assessed individually. Then, and only then, will the analyst begin to accumulate valuable experience and develop an aptitude for the work.

By following my methods, it should be possible – with hard work – to 'hit the bull's-eye' every time. Of course, this success will depend on an ability to distinguish a message-bearing dream from other varieties.

Although I was certain that I had discovered an almost infallible method of analysing dreams, having accurately interpreted literally hundreds of them, I needed to put it to one last test. What better subject for a dream interpretation than Dr Hearne?

As I currently produced the 'Dream Theme' column for *Horoscope* magazine, I had the perfect excuse for approaching Dr Hearne. I explained that I intended to write articles about his work on lucid dreaming and false awakenings, and his invention of the dream machine. I then cautiously suggested that I might interpret one of his dreams for the magazine. When he read my subsequent interpretation, Dr Hearne admitted that he was impressed and sufficiently intrigued to wish to understand my methods. Ultimately, our association led to the writing of this book.

In recent years, in the course of my own research, I have noticed a tremendous increase in the number of letters I receive from people who suffer from nightmares. I believe that I can explain the reason for this. I have also cured people of nightmares by means of interpretive analysis and other techniques without ever having met them. For many years, Dr Hearne has specialized in ways of eradicating nightmares. Our methods will be described in this book.

Our two goals in writing this book are to explain the amazing world of dreams so that the reader can work out their meanings and benefit from their considerable potential, and, more importantly, to establish dream interpretation as a science which can be learned, albeit with hard work and patience. Nothing worthwhile in life ever comes easily.

Preface
by
Dr Keith Hearne

T HE TWO main intellectual influences in my life, psychology and musical composition, developed when I was young. It was a musical household: my sisters played the piano and I started to compose pieces of music when I was about ten. We had no television then, so I read voraciously. I was in my early teens when I encountered Freud's great work, *The Interpretation of Dreams*.

My sister Tina was training to be a teacher and she brought it home as part of the required reading for her psychology course. I was absolutely enthralled by the book. It was heavy going and I was constantly having to refer to a dictionary, but the ideas were undoubtedly persuasive. Freud put forward his theories logically and systematically, with full reference to published sources, and provided numerous case studies to illustrate them.

As a teenager discovering the taboo subject of sex, I found Freud's emphasis on the sexual nature of dreams attractive. I now think that his approach is too narrow, but the book struck a chord with me and was partly responsible for my future involvement with dream research and psychology.

At university I realized how little psychologists knew about many areas of psychology. It is a fairly young science and covers a massive field, so there are many opportunities to discover new phenomena and develop new ideas. While an undergraduate at Reading University I discovered a method of externalizing the visual imagery of hypnotic dreams which I termed '*hypno-oneirography*' (see Chapter 3). My researches indicated that there are indeed

consistent effects in visualization processes, including dreaming.
At that time psychology was still largely influenced by
Behaviourism, a rigid approach dating from the 1930s which basically teaches that psychology should concern itself only with things
that can be physically measured. Exploitative and even cruel behav-
iourist experiments on animals were commonplace. What about
the things I was interested in – dreams, imagery, consciousness?
These topics were virtually banned from the psychology journals
for decades.

A closed frame of mind was typical of psychologists in the 1970s.
As a graduate student, I was speaking to one professor about
conducting some research into lucid dreams. He was interested and
later in the conversation asked what other topics interested me. I
replied, 'Parapsychology'. His demeanour changed visibly. 'Well,
we're a very hard-nosed department here,' he exclaimed, huffily.
That struck me as a very odd response. I was thoroughly trained
in experimental psychology, but he clearly had an irrational belief
that anyone studying parapsychology was not a true scientist.

In any other field of science, an anomaly tends to be seized on
by researchers because it probably indicates that the current theory
is flawed in some way, but science studiously ignores the accumu-
lating data in the field of paranormal experience, despite the wealth
of anecdotal evidence and experimental evidence that the world
is not as it seems. If a scientist conducted an experiment and, finding that certain data did not support the hypothesis, omitted them
from the calculations, they would be castigated – justifiably – for
being unscientific. Yet that is precisely what official, orthodox
science does with the data of parapsychology.

Having gained my degree from Reading University, I moved
on to Hull University, intending to do my doctorate research on
the topic of hypnotic dreams, but I soon found that hypnosis was
not the important element: I decided to study individual differences
in visual imagery. We all vary. For example, when I am awake, I have
no visual imagery. If I think of a high-imagery noun like '*aero-
plane*', I don't 'see' anything, yet others immediately form an image
of an aircraft in the greatest clarity. (Ask people to visualize something and see how their reports differ.) Using recently introduced

computers and brainwave-monitoring equipment, I examined the
brain activity of good and poor visualizers, but this raised many
more questions than answers.

During the course of that research, I became skilled at running
a sleep laboratory. I also read Celia Green's seminal book *Lucid
Dreams*. I had never had a lucid dream, i.e. one in which I was aware
that I was dreaming and could control the events, but several
people told me that they often experienced them. I had a hunch
that a dreaming person might be able to signal from within a dream
and devised a method of enabling sleeping, dreaming subjects to
communicate. This, and my invention of the 'dream machine',
will be covered later in this book.

I met with some opposition from colleagues who didn't approve
of the idea of studying lucid dreams, which they likened to research
into parapsychology. Some thought lucid dreams did not exist,
because they had never had one. Undeterred, I went ahead and
quickly turned my work on imagery into an M.Sc. research thesis.
I was then offered a sleep laboratory at Liverpool University, where
I could continue researching lucid dreaming for my doctorate.

During this time I also performed many parapsychology experiments, most of which were published in the *Journal of the Society
for Psychical Research*. For eight years I made a special study of
premonitions, and was put in charge of BBC Television's
Premonitions Bureau, linked to the *Out of This World* programme.
I broadcast on television and radio with Nerys Dee, a wonderful
woman who was a highly respected dream interpreter – we made
a good team. Unfortunately, Nerys, who was dedicated to helping cancer victims, developed a carcinoma herself and died in 1995.

Science has barely scratched the surface of human experience
in general and of dreaming in particular. Jacob Bronowski, in his
television series *The Ascent of Man*, declared that science progresses
when some awkward individual asks an impertinent question like,
'Does the sun really go round the earth?' I am proud to be such
an individual.

Introduction

IN ORDER to achieve a high level of accurate dream interpretation, it is essential that we understand as much about the
curious world of dreams as possible. Therefore, this book will
cover a wide range of sleep- and dream-related phenomena, including hypnagogic imagery, lucid dreams, false awakenings, sleep
paralysis, precognitive and telepathic dreams and creativity. To
attempt to put a general interpretation on some of these curious
phenomena would prove fruitless, so we must learn to identify and
acknowledge them.

The analysis of true message-bearing dreams can be used
constructively for a variety of purposes, to banish nightmares,
enhance creativity and reveal insights into our deeper thoughts and
the workings of our subconscious, for example.

First of all, let us take a look at a few theories, ancient and relatively recent, in order to highlight some aspects of dream
interpretation.

In ancient Chinese culture, dreams were attributed to wander-
ings of the *hun* or spiritual soul. They were categorized as ordinary
dreams, dreams of terror, dreams on thoughts of the day, dreams
of waking and dreams of joy and fear.

There was a realization that life itself could be a kind of dream.
The great sage Chuang-tsu, (*c*. 350 BC), wrote:

*While men are dreaming, they do not perceive it is a dream. Some
will even have a dream in a dream and only when they wake they
know it was a dream. And so, when the Great Awakening comes
upon us, shall we know this life to be a great dream. Fools believe
themselves to be awake now.*

Ancient Indian texts such as the *Atharva Veda*, written between 1500 and 1000 BC also discuss dreams, linking dream content with the temperament of the dreamer. For the ancient Greeks there were 'true' and 'false' dreams and they believed that the macrocosm might be represented in the microcosm. Thus, a dream where the stars shine brightly would represent a body in good health.

Roman beliefs were similar to those of the Greeks. An outstanding contribution to the understanding of dreams was made by Artemidorus of Daldis (*c.* 200 AD) in his lengthy work, *Oneirocritica* (*The Interpretation of Dreams*). Artemidorus declared that there are two basic varieties of dream: those of the future and everyday dreams. He recognized that associations to dream images are individual, differing from one person to another.

Artemidorus taught that certain information must be established at the outset of a dream interpretation: the name and occupation of the dreamer, the conditions under which the dream occurred, and whether the dream events are natural, lawful and customary for the dreamer. Associations and puns were to be noted. Symbolism, including sexual representation, was very well understood by Artemidorus; for example, a mouth might represent a home and the teeth specific people living there.

In the West, before Sigmund Freud appeared on the scene, it was known that long-forgotten objects can appear in dreams and that impressions of recent incidents frequently occur. 'Typical' dreams (of flying, for example) were believed to be caused by physical stimuli. Various theories attempted to explain the rapid forgetting of dreams on waking and the falsification of some dream memories. Thinking in sleep was considered to be pictorial, ideas being transformed into hallucinations by a process called 'dramatization'.

The progression of dreams along associative pathways was well known. Several theorists and researchers believed that dreams can reveal our true nature. It was also generally accepted that dreams happen in a partial waking state, owing to 'fatigued albumen' in the brain. Some believed that the function of dreams is to eliminate or excrete useless thoughts, others that dreams are simply recreational.

FREUD

Sigmund Freud, the founder of psychoanalysis, considered that dreams have meanings and that they are wish-fulfilments. These ideas were not new; what Freud added was the theory that dreams represent disguised wishes.

According to Freud, the personality consists of: the unconscious Id, which seeks the gratification of basic needs, especially sex and aggression; the conscious Ego, which is in contact with the world and is aware of social constraints; and the Superego, which reminds us how we ought to behave.

In sleep, the Ego is not present, and the Id tries to obtain gratification – which is provided vicariously, in the illusory form of dreams – without disturbing the inactivity of the individual.

In order not to shock or unsettle the Ego or Superego, the dream is forced to gratify the wishes of the Id in symbolic form. Therefore, a large discrepancy will exist between any reported dream (its manifest content) and the underlying dream thoughts (the latent content). The transformation required to evade the censorship of the Superego is known as 'dream work'.

The Freudian dream analyst traces the real meaning of a dream by a process of free association, but certain symbols are universal; for example, the penis is represented by a stick or a serpent, the vagina by a pit or cave, pubic hair by woods, and masturbation by sliding and gliding.

Freud was convinced that dream work involves no intellectual processes. He maintained that dreams arise from the repressed instincts of the Id, or from a conscious Ego desire of the preceding day. A trivial event in wakefulness could set off, by association, a basic repressed wish. For Freud, emotions in dreams usually remain the same in both their latent and manifest forms, although an emotion may sometimes be disguised by appearing as its exact opposite in the manifest version, so that a feeling of hate, say, is expressed as love.

He also described the phenomenon of condensation, whereby different wishes are fused in the latent content, forming strange composites. For instance, the physical features of two people might be combined; here, the important point would be whatever they had in common. A repressed wish for two people to be or behave alike might be fused in the same way. In displacement, the most significant elements are projected on to a seemingly insignificant item in the dream (thus, a strong emotion might be associated with something trivial).

Various experiments have been conducted to test Freud's claims, with differing results. One major objection to his ideas was that anxiety dreams cannot satisfactorily be explained as wish-fulfilment. In addition, the observed association between penile erection and the dreaming cycle which is thought to have influenced Freud's theories is now known to have no cause-and-effect connection.

JUNG

Carl Jung was a follower of Freud, but dissociated himself from him because he disagreed with Freud's insistence on the significance of sex as the basic human motivator. Jung established his own school of psychological thought, called analytical psychology.

He envisaged the psyche as a self-regulating process involving a flow of energy between opposite poles of personality and maintained that during our lives we undergo individuation, whereby our opposing aspects are reconciled. For Jung, the unconscious is not full of repressed desires, but is a friend and guide to us.

Jung thought that dreams have a compensatory function which can reveal any one-sidedness in our nature. He would look at a series of dreams and instead of asking his client to free-associate away from a dream (Freud's method), he would keep all associations relevant to it, using a process he termed 'amplification'. Whereas Freud interpreted his subjects' dreams, Jung said that only the dreamer can really interpret their own dream.

For the Jungian analyst, the structure of the dream is that of a Greek classical drama. First, the person, the location and the time are established; then the problem is stated, the plot thickens and a crisis appears. Finally, a solution is presented.

Unlike Freud, Jung believed that dreams are prospective and can actually anticipate and rehearse future events. Experiments with Jungian theory have also produced ambiguous results, but there is probably some truth in both the Freudian and the Jungian approaches.

OTHER MODERN THEORIES

Since Freud and Jung, the trend in dream theories has been to become less dogmatic and narrow. Alfred Adler believed that thinking is similar during sleep and wakefulness, and that unconscious thought processes are not significant. He saw the dream symbol not as a disguise or metaphor but as a simple representation.

Anne Faraday recommends keeping a dream diary and encourages the dreamer (when awake) to hold discussions with their dream characters to find out more about them – a Gestalt technique. She considers that recent events probably trigger off our dreams and that, to begin with, they should be taken literally – they may provide a reminder or a warning – and then metaphorically. For Faraday, feelings are good indicators of the subject matter of a dream, and the individual's own experiences and current circumstances are important: on a different occasion, the same dream could have another meaning for the dreamer.

Theories such as that put forward by Evans and Newman in the early 1960s hold less and less water these days. They proposed that all dreams are merely serving the function of enabling the brain to do some sorting out – similar to taking data 'off-line'. Early research seemed to reveal that if we are deprived of dreams during sleep, as opposed to non-dreaming sleep (slow-wave sleep), our mental faculties are affected. It was said that laboratory experiments showed that people who were dispossessed of their dreams soon displayed symptoms of mental imbalance and, in certain circumstances, even a tendency towards schizophrenia.

If such a theory were true, then dreams would certainly not be contaminated by external stimuli – which some evidently are. It is not unusual for our dreams to incorporate sounds from the real world. For example, a subject could be dreaming of his previous day's exploits while swimming in the sea. However, in response to the sound of lawnmower, (which he hears during the dream), he might find himself (in his dream) mowing grass. Therefore, we must ask why should the brain incorporate such stimuli in this way if it is merely sorting through the previous day's activities? Moreover, it has since been discovered that certain drugs abolish REM sleep with no noticeable consequences, so the idea is left rather high and dry.

Dr Hearne's own theory, based on transpersonal psychology (which involves the concept of the soul), is that, while dreaming is not a process vital to adults, it can reveal unconscious thoughts in symbolic form, sometimes in disguise rather than in overt images. In addition, the dream-producing process operates within in-built limits, as demonstrated by the light-switch and scene-shift effects, for example.

The dream flows along verbal and visual associative pathways and generally deals with current preoccupations, but with greater insight than is available to conscious thought. However, some themes will be suggested by the unconscious, relating to anniversaries of forgotten but significant events in the dreamer's life perhaps, and there can be elements of precognition or even past-life memories in the dream material. Dreams can help the dreamer to gain important insights and may also be utilized to enhance creativity.

The greatest myth about dreams is that they are over 'in a flash'. It is surprising how many people today accept this idea as true. It originated in the nineteenth century, with a Frenchman called Maury, who reported having had a long and involved dream which culminated in his execution by guillotine. At the moment the blade fell, he was woken by part of the bed collapsing on his neck. Maury reasoned that the whole dream must have been constructed in that moment. However, in his sleep-laboratory studies of lucid dreams, in which subjects signalled information from within the dream by making coded eye movements, Dr Hearne found that the subjects' estimates of time between the signals corresponded to the intervals recorded on the polygraphic chart-record. The dream was happening in real time.

~1~
Sleep and Dreaming

THERE are two main types of sleep: slow-wave sleep (SWS) and rapid-eye-movement (REM) sleep. Sleep-walking, night terrors and sleep-talking occur in SWS. People who are woken during a stage of SWS usually have no recollection of dreaming. The dreams and nightmares we are able to remember happen during REM sleep.

Research has shown that SWS and REM sleep states are governed by the ebb and flow of neuro-transmitter substances at the base of the brain. It is fascinating to observe the states alternating. In a sleep laboratory, electrodes are stuck with tape or glue to the subject's body to detect electrical signals accompanying muscular or nervous activity. Eye and jaw movements, for example, are recorded, and sometimes respiration, body temperature, etc. as well. The data formerly appeared on chart paper emerging from the recording instrument (the polygraph), but nowadays it is more likely to be stored in a computer and displayed on a screen.

SLOW-WAVE SLEEP

SWS has been arbitrarily divided into four stages, according to the number of slow brainwaves of a certain amplitude that are present. (Brain activity is measured with an electroencephalogram, or EEG.) At the onset of sleep, Stage 1, the eyes may begin to roll slightly; the waking alpha rhythm (about ten cycles per second) recorded by the EEG disappears. In Stage 2, there are sudden peaks of brainwave activity, known as 'k-complexes', produced in response to external or internal stimuli. Stage 3 is characterized by large, slow waves and, if over half the record consists of such a pattern, Stage 4 is registered.

After a period of Stage 4 sleep, the sequence is reversed, back to Stage 2, perhaps, and then REM sleep suddenly begins. The EEG record during REM sleep is active, showing saw-toothed waves. Muscle tone is at a minimum. This reflects the bodily paralysis which affects the dreamer during this time.

RAPID EYE MOVEMENT SLEEP

REM sleep usually occurs in 90-minute cycles throughout the night, preceded by a period of SWS. As the night progresses, these intervals of REM sleep increase in length until the last two hours of slumber contain a high percentage of dreams. The first half of the night consists mostly of SWS and the second of REM sleep. Therefore, you are most likely to catch yourself dreaming towards the end of a sleep period, between five and eight in the morning for the average person.

REM sleep is relatively easy to identify in others. REM brainwaves are different from those of SWS and bear a closer resemblance to those of the waking state. There may be slight twitches in the face, fingers and toes, the heart may beat faster and the breathing becomes shallow and rapid, in addition to the more obvious 'REM bursts' of activity from the eyes, shifting under the lids. These eye movements seem to be a mixture of both involuntary and scanning actions.

Genital arousal (in both men and women) is another feature of REM sleep. Most men are aware of the connection between erections and dreaming; it may have been this link which led Freud to assume that dreams are sexual in nature. Experiments have shown that if subjects are woken repeatedly from REM sleep, the erection cycle will get out of phase with the REM cycle, so there is not necessarily a cause-and-effect relationship between the two phenomena.

The REM state differs from the waking state in that the body is subject to external paralysis, only the eyes and respiratory system remaining functional. It is said that the inability to move while dreaming is a safety mechanism inherited from our ancestors which prevents us from acting out our dreams. Although there is no doubt that it stops us wandering off during the night, this safety mechanism probably has a more complex purpose.

It is not just humans who become paralysed while dreaming. Anybody who has watched a cat or dog dream of running, their paws twitching, will recognize that they too have this safety mechanism. Imagine the consequences if living creatures were not paralysed while dreaming: at best, very few of us would wake up in our own beds; at worst, there would be complete chaos. Throughout the night, the streets would be a riot of people and animals running, jumping out of windows, fighting, fleeing from unseen monsters, attempting to fly and so forth.

No evidence has yet been found to suggest that human or animal paralysis during REM sleep occurs as a result of evolution and it seems unreasonable to assume that, by a quirky accident of nature, a few of our ancestors developed this ability and were the only ones who survived, their genes eventually being passed on to the rest of humanity.

Nor can evolution explain how REM sleep paralysis managed to bridge the species divide. Evolutionists might argue that it developed before the division of species, but let us consider briefly the sleeping habits of a few other species. The fact that organisms do evolve is demonstrated by peculiarities shared by several species. Humans and other mammals (except the Australian spiny anteater) experience SWS and REM sleep, but there are great variations between species regarding the amount and quality of their sleep, depending on such factors as whether they are predators or preyed upon.

Cats, for example, sleep for as many as 16 hours a day. Their REM sleep appears cyclically, roughly every 30 minutes. Birds show a SWS–REM cycle too, with partial muscle paralysis; they need to retain a degree of muscular control for perching. Rats may sleep for about 13 hours a day but have many sleep periods, each lasting about ten minutes, throughout the 24 hours.

When we look at the sleeping habits of rabbits, the argument that paralysis during REM sleep evolved before the species divided becomes much less convincing. Rabbits, unusually, do not exhibit this paralysis. They sleep for a total of about eight hours, but, as with rats (their fellow rodents), their sleep is broken up into many short periods.

The evolutionary argument is complicated by the strange sleep characteristic of porpoises and dolphins: one half of their brain goes to sleep at a time. Nor do these creatures show any loss of muscle tone in REM sleep. The curious variations between species demonstrate that there is no clear-cut explanation for the REM sleep paralysis phenomenon. It remains a mystery.

Recent ideas about sleep and dreaming have stressed the evolutionary background and have tried to explain either SWS or REM sleep, but no single theory is fully accepted. The general hypothesis is that SWS keeps us still and out of danger during the hours of darkness, when bodily growth and repair can take place. To use the unsatisfactory analogy of a computer, REM sleep is seen by some as a time when memories are updated and filed and redundant information is discarded.

A few decades ago it was thought that being deprived of REM sleep would result in mental disturbance (see page 15). This proved to be untrue. It is now understood that some drugs, such as some anti-depressants, completely abolish REM sleep, without any noticeable harm to the user. The powerful barbiturates which used to be prescribed for insomnia suppressed REM sleep until the user's body adapted and regained a baseline level of this type of sleep. If they stopped taking the drug, such people would experience a massive REM-rebound effect for several weeks, sometimes with vivid nightmares. If you go without sleep, you will, when you eventually rest, have much more non-dreaming SWS than REM sleep, which implies that dreaming is a bit of a luxury for those short of sleep.

The surprising conclusion is that REM sleep does not seem to be necessary to adults. However, it may be very important to the developing foetus. Because the sleep of a new-born baby is about 50 per cent REM, this type of sleep may play a significant part in the baby's development, programming the brain or providing genetically coded imagery, perhaps. Few psychologists now believe that the mind of a new-born child is a blank slate.

Finally, let us briefly consider the wide variations between individuals regarding colour in dreams. In general surveys on dreams, colour is usually referred to in about a third of cases. If, however, subjects in a sleep laboratory are asked to report any colours in their dreams on being woken from REM sleep, nearly three-quarters can recall colours. The content of the dream seems to be more memorable than its colouring.

~2~
Preparing to Dream

THE FIRST STEP to successful dream analysis is being able to enjoy a good night's sleep. The amount of sleep we need varies from person to person. Some may be able to survive quite happily on a few hours' sleep, while others need as much as ten or more. It is up to each individual to decide the ideal amount and then allow enough time for it every night. Developing regular habits will facilitate this.

There are many superstitions and old wives' tales about certain foods causing bad dreams and restless nights. It is largely a matter of common sense and again, each individual will know from experience which foods need to be avoided. As a general rule, steer clear of anything that is likely to keep the stomach busy and lead to a lot of discomfort, from flatulence, for example. If you eat anything last thing at night, ensure that it is easily digestible.

It may be argued – by the determined few – that alcohol is a good sleep inducer. There is little doubt that it does induce sleep, but is this of good quality? In addition to the obvious red-eye, furry-tongue and throbbing-head syndrome it produces, alcohol inhibits dreaming and can cause REM rebound as the brain tries to catch up by cramming as many dreams into the latter stages of sleep as it can. Thus alcohol disrupts the natural rhythm of sleep.

Sleeping-pills, some tranquillizers, diet pills and other drugs can inhibit dreaming and affect different aspects of sleep. Stimulants, including caffeine, are well known for restricting sleep. However, as we will see, there are circumstances when caffeine is thought to assist sleep.

What if you are a poor sleeper? There are different types of insomnia. Some people find it difficult to fall asleep on going to bed (initial insomnia), while others may awaken in the night and then have trouble going back to sleep (sleep-maintenance insomnia).

Some theorists think that insomniacs may be either under- or overstimulated and recommend sufferers to adjust their life-style accordingly to compensate. Thus, insomniacs who are understimulated should take more physical and mental exercise, while those whose minds are racing when they go to bed should adopt a calmer way of living and learn to relax more. There is evidence that drinking hot malted milk drinks aids sleep. The neural stimulant caffeine should of course be avoided by the overstimulated, but the understimulated may find that coffee or tea assists sleep onset.

Interestingly, it is recognized by sleep-disorder specialists that people can be wildly mistaken in their self-estimates of insomnia. It is thought that in about half the reported cases the individual gets enough sleep but has an exaggerated perspective of the amount of wakefulness in the night. The partners of many insomniacs say that the sufferer in fact sleeps well.

Dr Hearne has found that if logical, straightforward left-brain thinking can be switched to more artistic, creative right-brain thinking typical of the mind in sleep, sleep is more readily induced. Gentle fantasizing relaxes and encourages sleep because it involves a thought pattern similar to those associated with sleep. Self-hypnosis can be helpful here.

Before we can successfully undertake self-hypnosis in order to relax and sleep well, certain criteria have to be met. Obviously, it is important to have a comfortable, well-supporting bed. Ensure that the room is at a suitable temperature and any lighting is gentle. To a certain extent, intrusive background noise can be masked with neutral white noise – the humming of an electric heater or fan, a loudly ticking clock or the splashing of a water fountain, for example.

Probably the most widespread single cause of restless nights is stress. This condition often manifests itself as worry, especially when we are settling down for the night and our minds allow negative thoughts free rein.

Nowadays, thankfully, there are safe alternatives to tranquilliz-ers and sleeping-pills. There are numerous books and tapes available on meditation, relaxation and self-hypnosis techniques designed to alleviate stress. Some of the relaxation tapes can be extremely effective and should not be used outside the bedroom or when operating machinery.

Modern research has proved that inhaling fragrances from essential oils can soothe an agitated mind and reduce anxiety. Because the olfactory nerves in the nose are connected to the brain's emotional centres (the limbic system), aromatherapy can aid sleep and even enhance dreams. Many good books about aromatherapy are available.

Some oils can safely be applied to the pillow-slip or added to a relaxing bath. However, although aromatherapy is generally accepted as a safe alternative therapy, certain oils can occasionally be harmful, causing skin rashes, for example. Therefore, make sure that you understand their potentially harmful as well as bene-ficial effects and follow the instructions for their use to the letter.

Most essential oils used to reduce stress, induce sleep and enhance dreams are extracted from herbs. For example, Melissa (Lemon Balm) is probably the best oil for relieving stress and anxi-ety; it can be effective against restlessness, excitability, palpitations and headaches and is often used as a sedative for the nervous system.

Rosemary has been used as a medicine for hundreds of years. The scent of this oil is known to help clear the mind. Traditionally, both Melissa and Rosemary were believed to counteract night-mares and induce more pleasant dreams.

Lavender is an excellent oil to assist relaxation. Other oils that can reduce stress and promote relaxation are: Petitgram, Neroli, Frankincense, Marjoram, Camomile, Clary Sage, Sandalwood, Ylang Ylang, Mimosa and Rosewood.

When buying aromatherapy oils, ensure that they are unadul-terated (100 per cent essential oil), as they are sometimes diluted with perfumes or vegetable oils.

SELF-HYPNOSIS

The counting backwards method can induce sleep in many insomniacs. It is also useful for anyone who wants to fall asleep in a ritualistic, gentle, relaxed manner. The technique involves a systematic body-relaxation routine followed by the visualization of a tranquil situation while counting down from ten to one. Relaxation increases with each descending number.

You can memorize the following script (not necessarily word for word) and, every night, when you go to bed, run through it in your mind. Alternatively, ask your partner to read it to you. Used regularly, this technique can result in better sleep and allow you to access dreams for investigation and analysis.

You can relax either from head to toes or from toes to head. The latter is recommended, because the complex musculature of the head, face, scalp, etc. is more difficult to relax than that of the feet and so is best approached gradually.

If you are likely to have to get up in the middle of the night to go to the toilet, include instructions to allow for this in your script. Tell yourself that you will quickly go back to sleep when you return to bed. The subconscious is very literal, so give your conscious mind clear and unambiguous instructions.

Begin by telling yourself that you are going to enter a state of self-hypnosis for a few minutes. Then settle down comfortably in bed and in your mind slowly go through the general points of the following script:

> *Just allow your eyelids to close . . . and relax your mind by thinking of something pleasant. . . perhaps a tranquil scene. . . that makes you feel good. . . and as you enjoy that experience. . . I want you to systematically begin to relax your whole body. . . starting with your feet and ankles. . . Tense your toes and feet. . . and then feel them relax. . . Imagine a flow of beautiful warm relaxation gradually spreading upwards. . . to your calf muscles. . . Tense them. . . and relax them. . . Allow that wonderful relaxation to flow up further to your thigh muscles. . . Tense those muscles. . . and relax them. . . Now allow the relaxation to flow to your stomach region. . . Become*

*aware of those muscles. . . and relax them. . . Now let that glow of
relaxation spread to your chest muscles. . . Take a few slow, deep
breaths. . . Let each breath relax you even more. . . [Pause] Now let
that beautiful feeling of peace and relaxation flow to the muscles of
your shoulders. . . Feel the tension in those muscles dissolve away. . .
Notice the muscles of your arms. . . and feel the relaxation spread
down to your hands and fingers. . . Sense the muscles in your neck. .
and allow that flowing peacefulness to relax those muscles. . . Feel it
spread to the muscles of your face. . . and forehead. . . up to the top of
your scalp. . . Now the whole of your body is relaxed. . . and each
breath that you make. . . is spreading that warm feeling of
relaxation. . . throughout the whole of your body. . . [Pause] In a
strange way, too. . . the sound of my voice. . . is part of that feeling
of relaxation. . . like floating pleasantly in a mist of drowsiness. . .
feeling tranquil. . . safe . . . and serene. . .*

*In a short time. . . you will count down from ten to one. . . and
enter sleep. . . Before that. . . I want your subconscious,. . . that
special part of you. . . that is aware of many things. . . beyond
consciousness. . . to be ready to do two things during sleep. . . First, to
ensure that you sleep well without unnecessary interruptions. . . and
second, to awaken you automatically at the end of dreams that are
significant and reflect important aspects of your life.*

*Now, in a moment you will [hear me] start to count down. . .
from ten to one. . . and with each descending number. . . you will
sense yourself becoming even more relaxed. . . sinking deeper and
deeper into a pleasant trance-like state of complete mental and
physical relaxation. . . which will gladly lead to a deep, restful,
natural, sleep. . . Ten. . . Nine. . . Deeper and deeper. . . Eight. . .
Deeper. . . Seven . . . Drifting, drifting. . .Six. . . Deeper and
deeper. . . Five . . . Even deeper. . . Four. . . So relaxed now. . .
Three . . . Going deeper. . . Two . . . Drifting. . . One. . . Now
totally relaxed. . . Totally relaxed. . .*

To summarize: developing regular habits, watching what you eat
and drink before retiring, ensuring your own comfort, practising
self-hypnosis and relaxation techniques and using essential oils will
allow you to sleep peacefully, have pleasant dreams and wake

refreshed in the morning. The benefits of these subtle and mild techniques may not be immediate, but a little perseverance should bring worthwhile rewards.

DREAM RECALL

Once you can get a good night's sleep, you can train yourself to remember your dreams. You will need to understand a little of how the conscious mind, the subconscious and dreams are related.

Recall is best immediately after a dream. The brain is very active in REM sleep and the thought processes can function on waking. Waking from SWS, and especially from Stage 4 sleep, can be very different. A person woken from this state is often disorientated and 'sleep-drunk'.

The reason why we rapidly forget our dreams is probably so that we will not confuse dreams with reality. The memories do not seem to be actually erased – hours later something may trigger the recollection of an entire dream – so much as filed away where we cannot access them easily. Those who want to analyse their dreams in search of self-knowledge and self-development will have to overcome this obstacle.

There are ways of accessing your more complete dreams, which are suitable for interpretation. First, your sleep should be interrupted as little as possible so that the amount of dreaming sleep is increased (we do not dream all the time we are asleep) and meaningful dreams can have time to occur. We remember dreams only if we wake up – even briefly – so if we are constantly disturbed in sleep, more fragments of dreams are likely to be recalled, but we may not have 'proper', structured dreams.

However, you can set up your subconscious mind to look out for meaningful dreams and it will then automatically awaken you at the conclusion of such a dream, enabling it to be recalled for the purpose of analysis.

This alerting technique may also be used to detect the anomalies in dreams that signal the onset of lucidity (awareness of dreaming), or the early signs of a nightmare, so that the dreamer can wake up before it becomes severe, or the nightmare can be converted into a lucid dream (this is known as nightmare eradication and is discussed in Chapter 14).

The watchfulness or 'expectation effect' of the subconscious is quite a powerful influence in many psychological situations, including sleep and dreaming. The subconscious is constantly vigilant. It can awaken a mother when her baby starts to cry quietly. Because the mother is virtually anticipating the crying, she is particularly sensitive to that specific sound even though she may be undisturbed by other, much louder, noises. Dr Hearne frequently encountered the expectation phenomenon in the sleep laboratory setting. In one experiment – on memory-storing in sleep – he used to enter the sleep laboratory bedroom at about 3 a.m. to awaken the subject and test his or her memory of previously learned items. Many subjects stated that they had dreamed that Dr Hearne had already come in and talked to them.

Even more interestingly, in an experiment where subjects were receiving mild electric pulses to the wrist while dreaming to make their dreams lucid, several reported on waking that they had felt the pulses and become lucid, although no pulses had actually been administered. The subjects expected them and dreamed them.

In hypnotherapy, such phraseology as: 'As soon as your subconscious becomes aware of. . . you will. . .' is extremely effective. It brings into play the immense powers of the subconscious. When a subject being treated for say, snoring, starts to snore, a little warning signal will automatically be activated in the mind, triggering a previously determined behaviour, in this case, perhaps, turning over in bed to lighten sleep and avert heavy snoring.

Clearly, then, there are aspects of our subconscious that we can utilize for our own benefit. One method of encouraging the co-operation of the subconscious in these states is to induce the hypnagogic state, which is explained in the following Chapter.

Many people report that their recall of dreams and their insight into their own symbolism dramatically increase if they start to keep a dream diary. (A dream questionnaire is given in the Appendix.) As well as writing down a description of the content of your dream, you can record the categories of features present in it. Over time, you can observe how these vary and may be able to link them to different situations in your life.

The following method for remembering and recording dreams is recommended:

- Position an alarm clock near enough to your bed to turn off with your eyes still closed. Set it to go off about an hour before your usual waking-up time.

- Keep a dream diary notepad and a pen by the bed. Record what food and drink you consumed before retiring and any significant event which occurred during the day.

- When you go to bed, program yourself using the power of suggestion. Tell yourself firmly that you will be able to recall a dream on waking.

- When the alarm sounds, keep your eyes closed (dreams have an annoying habit of evaporating the moment we open our eyes). Try not to alter your position, and remember as much of your dream as you can; go over it several times to recall more and more of it. When you are satisfied that you have recollected as much as possible of your dream, write it down in detail, and add the date and time.

- Then try to distract your mind for a few minutes, perhaps with a crossword puzzle.

- Finally, go back to sleep until your usual getting-up time. This will take practice.

If this routine is followed, you will be surprised how soon you develop a capacity for remembering your dreams. This skill is also essential if you want to induce a lucid dream (see page 47).

~3~
The Hypnagogic State

VARIOUS categories of dream are not open to interpretation and it is crucial for all dream analysts to understand those before embarking on interpretation. One of these curious phenomena is the hypnagogic state, which occurs at the onset of sleep.

The hypnagogic state is the transitional interval between consciousness and sleep, the nodding-off period, during which many people witness visions and/or hear voices. They are neither awake nor asleep, but in a strange world somewhere in between. Hypnagogic dreams are fairly common and to a certain extent the visual imagery in this condition can be controlled, potentially yielding great benefits.

First we need to know something about imagery, visual pathways and how the brain structures and develops scenes.

Probably the most important lesson to be learned in psychology is that there are vast individual differences in how people experience the world. For example, if someone asks you to visualize a high-imagery noun such as 'elephant', do you picture an animal? Some people will immediately describe the animal they see, mentioning colours, scenery, moods and all sorts of small details; to them, the image appears very clear and real, like a hallucination. Others 'see' absolutely nothing. Most people fit somewhere between these two extremes.

We assume that everyone experiences precisely what we do. However, the same word can have a totally different meaning for two different people. For example, when Dr Hearne was a child, one of his teachers said, 'Keith, you know when you day-dream and see the pictures clearly. . .' He thought she was mad. She obviously had good visual imagery, whereas he did not. Day-dreaming to Dr Hearne simply means thinking, without the slightest visual content. However, he has good auditory imagery, which he may have developed to compensate for his inability to visualize. Part of understanding ourselves is recognizing that everything is relative. We all perceive the world in our own way. There is no such thing as a 'standard stimulus', i.e. something that we all perceive in the same way. It is as well to be aware of these differences when comparing our own dream experiences with those of others.

Hypnagogic imagery may consist of a sequence of very clear pictures, often of distorted human faces or various shapes or scenes. Some people report being aware of an eye gazing at them. Occasionally, conversations in a foreign language are reported. You may hear your name called, or meaningless sentences spoken. Sometimes these images seem symbolic; for example, if you have a problem – a 'weight on your mind' – you may picture yourself carrying a heavy load on your head.

Another form of imagery, termed 'hypnopompic', is experienced by some people when they wake up. With this phenomenon, dream images linger for some seconds after waking.

There are other interesting 'borderland' phenomena associated with the processes of falling asleep and waking up which the 'oneironaut' or dream traveller should know something about.

Some people experience a falling sensation just before sleep. Others have some sort of sensory shock, like being struck, hearing a sudden noise, seeing a flash of light, or smelling an odour. It may be associated with a mild or violent involuntary jump known as a 'myoclonic jerk'. These sensations appear to be linked to brain changes that occur naturally as sleep begins and are nothing to worry about.

However, any attempt to interpret hypnagogic or hypnopompic visions or borderland phenomena will fail. They do not carry meaningful messages. In addition, because the dreamer is between consciousness and sleep, any hypnagogic dream may be contaminated by conscious thoughts. Quite often, though, these phenomena can contain precognitive images, visions of the future.

Premonitions received through hypnagogic imagery are said to be particularly reliable.

Hypnagogic and hypnopompic visions can sometimes be controlled to a certain extent. For example, just by thinking about Tom and Jerry, David Melbourne can often make these cartoon characters appear. If he concentrates further, he can animate them and make them perform whatever bizarre actions he likes.

Although the two hemispheres of the human brain are connected by the *corpus callosum* (a neural bridge through which both interact, allowing them to work in tandem), in effect, we possess two separate brains. They process information in different ways and each is adept at performing different functions.

The left brain is associated with logic, verbal and analytical functions, and the right brain with non-verbal and creative functions. Just as there are left- and right-handed people, there are left- and right-brain people. A mathematician, for example, will favour the left brain and have good analytical skills, but an artist will rely more on the right brain and have better visual imagery.

Imagine that a helicopter lands in your garden or street and a squad of soldiers disembarks and advances on your home. Can you picture this scene easily and in detail? Extreme left-brain dependants will be completely unable to visualize it. The 'ambidextrous', who use both sides of the brain fairly evenly, will visualize it, although not in detail. Right-brain dependants will find it relatively easy, and extreme right-brain people will be able to conjure up astonishingly realistic images.

The fortunate people in the last category can, merely by using a little imagination, direct the scene at will. They can shrink or enlarge the helicopter, make the soldiers dance with each other or even stage an attack on the garden shed, leaving a trail of destruction in their wake.

It is likely that such right-brain dependants already play around with hypnagogic imagery as they drift off to sleep. Conversely, the extreme left-brain dependant will probably find it hard to grasp the concept of visual imagery and be unaware of the hypnagogic state. They will have absolutely no recall of the transitional period between consciousness and sleep, but will describe the process in terms such as: 'One moment I'm awake, the next, I'm asleep.'

We are extremely susceptible to the power of suggestion during the hypnagogic state (whether we are aware of experiencing it or not) and, with a little imagination, we can put it to good uses, for healing, lowering stress levels, remembering dreams, or inducing lucid dreams and false awakenings. We can even program ourselves to achieve sleep paralysis, in order to experience OOBEs.

Other good uses might include reinforcing a commitment – to give up smoking, follow a sensible eating plan, or stop nail-biting – and overcoming stress-related insomnia through relaxation. For those who are given to premonitions, the hypnagogic state provides a useful opportunity to develop the prophetic gift too. The list is endless.

For most people it will not be an easy task to extend and maintain the hypnagogic state without drifting into the next stage of sleep. This is something that has to be worked at and can take a long time. Nevertheless, if we want to reap the enormous potential rewards, we have to make a determined and prolonged effort.

There are many good books available on the subject of meditation and some techniques recommend attempting to lengthen the period between consciousness and sleep. However, during our research, we have discovered that it is possible to kill two birds with one stone: extend the transitional period by meditation and at the same time lower stress levels and aid healing. This is an excellent way to start.

As we know, aromatherapy affects the limbic system in the brain, thus facilitating beneficial ways of easing stress, and a similar use can be made of colours. Most of us will be familiar with the sick building syndrome, whereby ill-conceived colour schemes in the workplace can result in above-average absenteeism and sickness.

Colour has a profound effect on everyday life. It is no accident that some police forces paint the walls of their holding cells pink. This colour has been discovered to have a calming effect. Some cultures believe that different colours are allied to different organs within the body and that concentrating on the relevant colour has a healing influence. Others hold that meditating on colours can aid our spiritual development.

Therefore, as you drift between the worlds of consciousness and sleep, concentrate on visualizing colours in your mind's eye. If you feel yourself drifting towards sleep, change the colour. Keep repeating this process until you have exhausted the colours you can imagine, then start at the beginning again. You will soon discover that you are able to extend the duration of your meditation. Ultimately, the dedicated enthusiast will be able to maintain the state of hypnagogic imagery almost indefinitely.

Once you become skilled at holding yourself between consciousness and sleep, you are ready to start implanting suggestions, but be careful. Never underestimate your susceptibility to the power of suggestion during the hypnagogic state. Always bear in mind the importance of allowing only positive thoughts. If you are depressed, ensure that negative thoughts do not encroach on your meditation.

It is not surprising that some people complain of sleepless nights owing to worry or depression. Often they deepen their depression by unwittingly dwelling on their troubles during the hypnagogic state and extending its duration. As a result, the next morning the problem seems even worse; they have reinforced their worries by implanting negative thought patterns.

Try to implant positive thinking while you increase the duration of the hypnagogic state. It seems strange that depression or worry can extend this state for hours, yet, when we are relaxed, we drift off to sleep quite readily. If we could employ the same level of concentration on positive thoughts as we do on our worries, we might benefit enormously.

The following colours are said to be beneficial in healing:

RED affects the base of the spine and acts as a tonic. It also counteracts blood disorders, impaired vitality, defective circulation, depression, fear and worry.

ORANGE rules the solar plexus and is believed to generate general good health. It is also a tonic, aids energy-building, and is effective against depression and bronchial and chest conditions.

YELLOW is allied to the spleen and is said to be an acid neutralizer. It also heals diseases of the skin.

GREEN influences the heart and is said to combat blood diseases. It also relates to nerves of the head and nerves generally, kills germs, cleanses and helps remove abnormal tissue growth.

BLUE affects the throat and is believed to cure fevers, insomnia, headaches, rheumatism, inflammation and worry.

AMETHYST allied to the pineal gland and forehead, is considered to be effective against diseases of the ear, nose and throat, and also against obsessions, nervous disorders and insomnia.

PURPLE is linked to the pituitary gland and the top of the head and is said to alleviate stiff joints, rheumatism, epilepsy, neurosis, neuralgia, and mental, nervous and cerebral diseases.

For those who experience problems in creating imagery, the following method will assist in bringing a colour to mind. First, gaze for a while at a coloured object that has a distinct shape, then close your eyes, retaining the image as clearly as you can. With practice, you will be able to recall these memories.

Colours can be used for self-healing. For example, it has been found that certain types of wart can be eradicated through hypnotic suggestion. Looking at the list of colours, we find that green is said to break down abnormal tissue growth. If you want to get rid of a wart, and are experienced in identifying and maintaining the hypnagogic state, try bringing the colour green to mind. Visualize it bathing and shrinking the wart. At the same time, implant the suggestion that the wart will be eradicated.

Colours are also helpful for our general physical, mental and spiritual well-being. As far as physical well-being is concerned, green should be used for restfulness, orange for vitality, and vermilion and scarlet for inspiration. For mental well-being, indigo enhances restfulness and royal blue, vitality. Violet is good for inspiration. As to spiritual health, midnight blue assists restfulness, gold enhances vitality, and amethyst fosters inspiration.

There is hope for extreme left-brain dependants who cannot create visual images, no matter how hard they try. Just as a right-handed person can learn to use the left hand efficiently, so a left-brain dependant can learn to bring the right brain to bear.

SAMPLE A

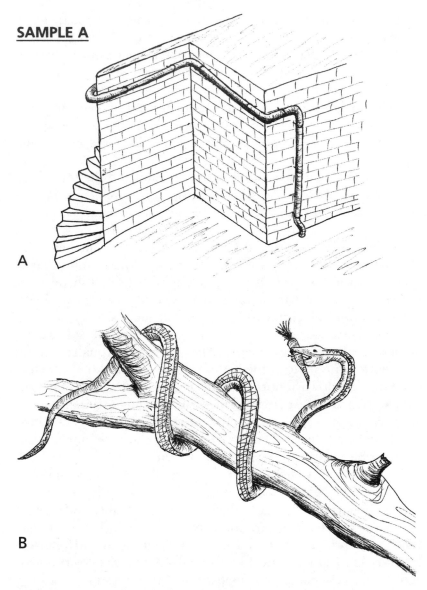

Figure 1 These two sets of 'freeze-frame' pictures were traced from images seen during hypnotic dreams. The before (A) and after (B) pictures of each dreamer include common visual elements, illustrating the scene-shift effect discovered by Dr Keith Hearne.

SAMPLE B

A

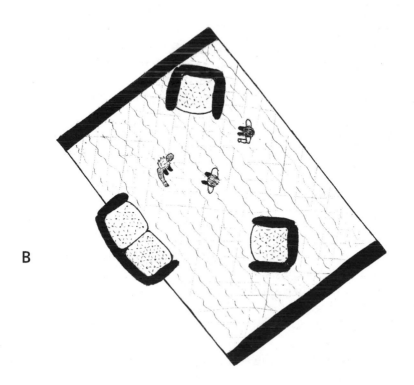

B

Although these people may not be able to identify the hypnagogic state, the best time for them to implant positive thoughts is when they are drowsy, almost asleep.

With regular practice, they should eventually develop the capacity to engage the right side of their brain and achieve a degree of hypnagogic imagery.

THE SCENE-SHIFT EFFECT

Dr Hearne made an important breakthrough when he discovered the 'scene-shift effect' while attempting to externalize the internal imagery of hypnotic dreams. He had developed a successful technique which he called 'hypno-oneirography', (dream-tracing).

In a dimly lit room, his hypnotized subject was instructed to have a hypnotic dream and to stop the dream imagery abruptly and hold the scene when Dr Hearne tapped his pen on the table. The subject was then told to open his or her eyes and project the freeze-framed picture on to a large drawing-board. The subject was handed a pen and asked to trace (not draw) the now two-dimensional scene and describe colours, textures, and so on. Dr Hearne noted down the colours of different objects in the traced dream-scene.

After the whole picture was traced – an operation that could take 15 minutes – the subject was told to reanimate the dream and let it run on to another point. The whole procedure was then repeated for the new scene. Eventually, after a couple of hours or so, Dr Hearne had a set of cartoon-like tracings representing the hypnotic dream. For the first time, the structure of a person's dream was revealed to the outside world.

Sometimes Dr Hearne moved the subject's dream on from scene to scene and a very consistent phenomenon associated with those scene-shifts soon became apparent. He concluded that dream imagery progresses by a sort of 'law of least effort', in that the pictorial elements from one scene are recycled to form the next. The scene is a new one, but it uses a similar number of items, the same colours, and the same common theme as the last. (There is a musical analogy for this phenomenon in key-changing, where common pivot notes are used to smooth the transition.)

Examples from the hypnotic dreams of two different subjects are shown on pages 36 and 37. Subject 1's dream picture, (A), traced before the scene-shift, shows a teacher and two pupils. There are three items of wooden furniture (desks) and a blackboard, and the background colour is blue. The subject's next scene, (B), shows an overhead view of a room. Again, there are three people and three items of furniture. The rectangle of the blackboard frame has been become a large rug and the black of the board has been incorporated into the furniture trim. The rug is the same blue as the background colour of previous scene.

The first picture from Subject 2's dream shows a green snake with a carrot in its mouth coiled around a tree trunk. The next scene, (B), depicts a cellar with a curved green pipe emerging from a wall. The colour of the tree trunk matches that of the wall in the subsequent scene.

The scene-shift effect has also been observed in ordinary nocturnal dreams and there is no reason to suppose that a different imaging process operates in sleep. The implications of this discovery are that the dream-producing process has inherent limitations and progresses by means of linked visual images (it is already known that dreams also follow verbal associative pathways). Dream interpreters must be aware of these basic facts of dream structure and development.

~4~

Lucid Dreams

TRY to imagine being able to heal yourself, stop recurring nightmares, fly, enjoy a romantic experience, or indeed do anything you desire, while in complete control of the situation. These are just some of the things that can happen through the astounding phenomenon of the lucid dream.

The term 'lucid dream' was introduced by Dr Frederik van Eeden in a talk he gave to the Society for Psychical Research in London in 1913. He was a fairly frequent lucid dreamer and recorded some 350 cases in his dream diary. This example illustrates the clarity of thought and observation in his dreams:

I dreamt that I stood at a table before a window. On the table were different objects. I was perfectly well aware that I was dreaming and considered what sorts of experiments I could make. I began by trying to break glass, by beating it with a stone. I put a small tablet of glass on two stones and struck it with another stone. Yet it would not break. Then I took a fine claret glass from the table and struck it with my fist, with all my might, at the same time reflecting how dangerous it would be to do this in waking life; yet the glass remained whole. But when I looked at it again after some time, it was broken. It broke all right, but a little too late, like an actor who misses his cue. This gave me a very curious impression of being in a fake world, cleverly imitated, but with small failures . . . Then I saw a decanter with claret and tasted it, and noted with perfect clearness of mind: 'Well, we can also have voluntary impressions of taste in the dream world; this has quite the taste of wine.'

(van Eeden, F. (1913), *A study of dreams.*)

Another early investigator was the Marquis Hervey de St Denys, a French oriental scholar who produced a book about his own dream experiences in 1867. St Denys experimented extensively with lucid dreams, which he termed 'dreams in which I am conscious of my true situation'. He noticed that dreams represent underlying thoughts, that they progress by associations, and that external or internal stimuli can influence them.

The lucid dream is so real in every respect that it is indistinguishable from full waking consciousness. People who have experienced one are usually left asking, 'Was I dreaming or was it real?' The lucid dream appears to be another level of reality, and they may even wonder whether the waking state is an elaborate illusion.

Any attempt, therefore, to put an interpretation on one of these experiences would be a complete waste of time. Such an extraordinary occurrence has too many variables and, like hypnagogic imagery, is influenced by the conscious mind. This does not mean that some varieties of lucid dream do not carry a message. However, an analyst would have to be extremely skilful to recognize it. It is not advisable to try to interpret a lucid dream unless one is absolutely sure that it is a message-bearing vision.

Some writers have compared lucid dreaming to hallucinations, or sophisticated virtual-reality systems, but this grossly understates the power and complexity of the phenomenon. However, it is hard to find words adequately to describe the process; no technology has yet been devised that approaches the experience of a lucid dream.

A lucid dream can have a dramatic and lasting effect on the subject's outlook on life and it is not surprising that some of the lucky five to ten per cent of the population who have naturally occurring lucid dreams become more spiritual.

Although people have been experiencing lucid dreams for countless years, relatively little was known about them until approximately 20 years ago, when Dr Hearne pioneered a method of communicating to the dream world.

A few writers had published their accounts in books long out of print, but then Dr Hearne came across Celia Green's seminal book, *Lucid Dreams*. This is a collation of reports of lucid dreaming and includes an analysis which found several consistencies between the different experiences.

Dr Hearne had access to a sleep laboratory and was in a good position to study lucid dreams scientifically. It seemed logical that if a person was really conscious in a dream, it should be possible to signal to the outside world in some way. The problem was that the body's musculature is paralysed during REM sleep.

Perhaps the lucid dreamer could communicate through eye-movements? The eye muscles are not inhibited in dreaming sleep. Working on this hunch, Dr Hearne wired up a subject in the sleep laboratory who had reported having lucid dreams about once or twice a week.

The subject was instructed that, on becoming aware of being in a dream, he should make eight regular eye-movements from left to right. These would be picked up by electrodes positioned above and below the outer part of each eye. Other electrodes on the top of his scalp and below his chin monitored, respectively, brainwaves and muscle activity. The measurements from the electrodes enabled Dr Hearne to establish which sleep state the subject was in at any time, as well as monitoring any deliberate eye-movements.

On the morning of 12 April 1975, after Dr Hearne had watched the polygraph recorder all night, the subject (unmistakably in REM sleep), suddenly signalled eight clear left–right eye-movements. It was astonishing. The subject was asleep and unconscious, yet in the dream world he perceived himself to be fully awake and conscious. On waking he described how in his dream, he had been walking around the university and suddenly became aware of dreaming, so he signalled immediately.

Dr Hearne had also taped a micro-switch into the palm of the subject's hand and, interestingly, although he dreamed of pressing it, his general bodily paralysis prevented any action actually occurring. The deliberate movements of his eyes were the only method of signalling.

In a little over half the cases of lucid dreaming studied by Dr Hearne, the subjects realized they were having a lucid dream when they identified an anomaly within it. Further investigation revealed that unfamiliar outdoor locations were the usual setting for lucidity.

This was the case when Dr Hearne had his first lucid dream, some 18 months after he began his research into the subject. An incongruity in a dream alerted him to the fact that he was dreaming, and then he found himself on a unfamiliar beach. This is his description of the experience:

> *The dream was very bright and vivid. I was walking along the beach, which seemed to be Mediterranean perhaps. I looked down at the sand and saw some gold and silver coins. As I knelt down and started to dig them out, they expanded to become as big as plates. My immediate thought was, 'This can't be real. This is a dream!' With that, I stood up and with total clarity looked around at the scenery. It was so astonishingly real. My vision was perfect – I could see individual grains of sand. Children were playing nearby and everything was so relaxed. I could feel the warmth of the sun on me, yet I knew that everything I saw, heard and felt was completely artificial.*
>
> *After a short while, I decided to conduct an experiment and so attempted to conjure up a dream companion whom I 'willed' to appear behind a stack of deck-chairs that was present. I walked over to the stack, looked down at the incredibly detailed sand, and as I raised my eyes I saw a young woman walking towards me. She was short, with black hair, markedly green eyes and had a very pretty face. She approached directly and said, 'Hello, my name's Jane.' We became quite close in the dream. Believe it or not, I actually met that same woman in waking life two weeks later and we were together for two years. Her name was Jane and she was identical to the dream woman.*

Twenty years after Dr Hearne's work on lucid dreaming began some 30 universities throughout the world are examining the phenomenon in dream laboratories. Research is being carried out into the links between lucid dreaming and the lowering of stress levels, the improvement of general well-being, the eradication of nightmares, and the possibility of manipulating a lucid dream to produce precognition. New and exciting data could come to light at any time.

THE BENEFITS OF LUCID DREAMING

There seems to exist a dimension of wisdom and magic within the realm of the lucid dream. With enlightenment and practice, lucid dreamers can learn to take control of these dreams, and put them to constructive use, bringing enormous benefits back to this reality from the inner universe.

According to the Time–Life Book, *Dreams and Dreaming*, some years ago the professional golfer Jack Nicklaus was going through a bad patch, experiencing difficulty with his swing. He credited his return to championship form to a lucid dream in which he changed his grip slightly. He told a reporter:

> *I've been having trouble collapsing my right arm taking the club head away from the ball, but I was doing it perfectly in my sleep. So when I came to the course yesterday morning, I tried it in the way I did in my dream and it worked. I shot a 68 yesterday and a 65 today and believe me, it's a lot more fun this way. I feel kind of foolish admitting it, but it really happened in a dream. All I had to do was change my grip just a little.*

Nicklaus's story is just one example of the tremendous potential of the lucid dream.

Although science has made great strides this century, little is yet known about the brain's deeper functions. Hypnosis, for example, still poses many unanswered questions. How are patients under hypnosis able to will away warts, or cure themselves of psoriasis?

In one astounding, widely reported case, a man hypnotized himself and underwent a vasectomy without an anaesthetic. The surgeon who performed the operation remarked that he was amazed not only that the patient suffered no pain, but the amount of bleeding was negligible compared to a conventional vasectomy procedure.

There is also evidence to suggest that visual imagery can help in the treatment of cancer. Some patients visualize the malignancy, then zap it with imaginary laser beams.

Lucid dreaming has been used to lower stress levels and generate feelings of well-being. Because lucid dreaming stimulates the same centres of the brain as hypnosis, in theory it is possible to put it to similar uses, including the creation of visual imagery. Lucid dreams allow one to conjure up people, so one might be able to summon up a doctor or great spiritual healer, or at least ask for advice or spiritual healing.

Nightmare sufferers can turn their plight to their advantage. The weird or frightening nature of their dream can alert them to its anomalous content so that they realize they are dreaming and can then initiate lucidity. Once lucid, they can neutralize their bad dream. From the tips of their fingers, they can fire pulses or light at the object of their fear to vaporize it or, better still, they can shrink it in size and dress it in comical clothing. You are much less likely to be frightened of a nightmare spider if it is wearing high-heeled shoes and carrying a parasol.

The secret of manipulating dream scenery and events, as if by magic, in a lucid dream is to understand the fact that what you think, you will then dream. Conscious thoughts within the dream act as instructions to the dream-producing process. It makes sense not to have negative thoughts in dreams such as: 'I hope that monster isn't going to eat me.' Instead, while still in the dream, you could, for example, put your hands over your eyes and will yourself to a more pleasant place – a tropical island, perhaps. You will probably find yourself there soon afterwards.

Skilled lucid dreamers use thought control to pre-program their dreams. For example, they can dream of meeting a specific person by deciding to find a door in the dream and willing that person to appear behind it when it is opened.

Accomplished lucid dreamers have reported conjuring up deceased relatives and having conversations with them as if they were still alive. As lucidity appears real in every respect – indistinguishable from full waking consciousness – this could prove to be an efficient way of helping the bereaved to overcome their despair.

However, although these encounters appear so real, it must be remembered that the experience is a dream. We will probably never know if the spirits of loved ones are able to manifest themselves in dreams, or whether these happenings are the product of the dreaming mind.

THE LIGHT-SWITCH PHENONEMON

Many lucid dreamers are reported to have stated: 'I tried to switch on a light in my dream, but it didn't work.' Intrigued, Dr Hearne wrote to eight different lucid dreamers and asked them to switch on a light in a dream and report what happened. The dreamers lived in different parts of the country and had no contact with each other, so they could not confer. When they tried to switch on a light in the dream scenery they all recorded that for some reason the light did not come on; it was as if the bulb had blown.

This is interesting from a theoretical viewpoint because it shows that the dream is not totally free. The dream-producing part of the mind has to work within natural, inherent limitations, such as the inability (probably physiological in origin) suddenly to increase the light level in a dream. It tries to cope, but its failure reveals that, essentially, the dream is fooling the dreamer. It is putting on a show, a performance.

The light-switch phenomenon (there are several other such effects in dreams) offers a salutary lesson to dream interpreters. Until now, not one school of dream analysis has ever suggested that dreams might have such limitations.

A man confessing to a psychoanalyst a frequent inability to switch on a light in dreams might be told that it indicates a problem of impotence. A Jungian enthusiast might see the dream as a message telling the dreamer that he is 'not seeing the light'. Both would be quite wrong, because they have not understood the structure of the dream-producing process.

INDUCING A LUCID DREAM

Here we shall consider those methods which have been studied and proved successful by psychologists and dream analysts. Some readers will be lucky enough to have a lucid dream simply because they have read this chapter. Dr Hearne has often noticed that days or weeks after he gave a talk on lucid dreams, people who had attended the lecture would come up to him and say, 'I've had my first lucid dream.'

It seems that once the concept of lucidity is understood, the state is more easily recognized. Therefore, if you want to begin lucid dreaming, keep a dream diary, read up on the subject and talk about lucid dreams to others so that the topic remains on your mind. Some people practice spotting inconsistencies when they are awake. For example, they occasionally ask themselves, 'Am I dreaming?' and then perform the light-switch test.

A friend of Dr Hearne's, a psychologist called Robin Furman, thought he had woken one night to go to the lavatory. The bathroom light did not come on. It suddenly occurred to him that this might be the light-switch effect, so he tested the state further by jumping down a few stairs. He found himself floating down, which confirmed that he was not awake.

Another method entails hypnotic suggestion. To hypnotize yourself, use the self-hypnosis script on pages 25, adding the following to induce lucidity:

Tonight . . . when you are asleep and dreaming . . . something in the dream . . . will make you begin to realize . . . that you are dreaming. . . It may be perhaps . . . that someone's face . . . will look different from how you know that person to be . . . or possibly . . . their clothes. . . They may be wearing something . . . that you know they would never wear . . .Or perhaps a familiar room . . . may have something different about it. . . At that moment of recognition . . . of a fault in the dream picture . . . you will become excited . . . and say to yourself . . . 'This is a dream . . . I am aware that I am dreaming. . . It is a lucid dream'. . . And you will remember . . . that you can control the dream's activities . . . to your advantage. . .In the lucid dream . . . you can travel

*anywhere you want. . . You can fly . . . or cover your eyes and will
yourself to a new location. . . You can meet anyone you want in the
dream . . . for instance, by opening a door . . . and willing them to be
there. . .You can do anything you want. . .*

A third method is to use induction tapes, like the one prepared by
Dr Hearne which contain suggestions designed to encourage lucid
dreaming. Simply play the cassette before you go to sleep.

Using a dream machine may be appropriate for some people.
Dr Hearne's dream machine (a result of his Ph.D. research) detects
dreaming sleep by monitoring respiration rate, which can double
in rapidity during REM sleep. It then gives the user a series of pulses
which act as a cue for the dream to become lucid without waking
the dreamer.

Another technique devised by Dr Hearne, the FAST (False
Awakening with State Testing) method, requires the assistance of
another person. It is described in the next chapter.

~5~

False Awakenings

HAVE YOU ever woken in the night, looked at a digital (electric) clock, and been unable to read the time, because the clock appears blurred or doesn't make sense? Did you ever reach out to turn on the light, or another electrical appliance only to discover that it doesn't function properly, or can't be switched on (see page 46)? Do you have vague memories of getting up in the middle of the night, trying to open the door, finding that it won't open and going back to bed? If someone told you that you were probably dreaming, would you believe them?

A false awakening is a convincing illusion of having woken when, in fact, you are still in dreaming sleep and the images you see – although seemingly real – are artificial.

There is the same degree of conscious awareness in the phenomenon as in a lucid dream. All the dreamer's critical faculties are working and they can think very clearly. However, what is lacking is the awareness of being in a dream, because the dream is recreating scenery familiar to the dreamer, their bedroom, say. The similarity of the vision to the real scene can be quite amazing, until some inconsistency gives the secret away.

False awakenings sometimes follow lucid dreams, or they can occur separately. Intending lucid dreamers need to be aware of this fascinating phenomenon, illustrated here by a case from our files:

I seemed to wake up from an interesting, vivid lucid dream. My mind was perfectly alert and I looked around the bedroom. It was morning and the room was fairly light. I got up and walked around for a while. Then I went to the window and looked out. Incredibly,

*the road outside was not the road it should have been! The surprise
woke me and I found myself snuggled in bed.*

Some people report experiencing multiple false awakenings, which
can leave them rather puzzled:

*Several times I have known that I was dreaming when it was time
to get up for work. I have tried to wake myself up, but only
succeeded in dreaming that I have woken. This could happen four or
five times in a row before I actually woke up properly. I'll know it's
still a dream usually because the carpet or bed-sheets are a different
colour, or that something else in the room – say, furniture – is not
correct.*

It is not unheard of for some unfortunate souls apparently to wake
up in the morning, wash, eat breakfast, get ready to leave for work,
and then wake to find themselves still in bed. Then they get up
again, wash, eat breakfast and leave for work. Caught in the rush-
hour traffic, and while thumping the steering wheel, impatiently,
they wake up again to find themselves still in bed. This can go on
almost ad infinitum.

The false awakening is more common, however, when dreamers perceive themselves as waking up at home in their own beds;
then they usually turn over and, in their dream minds, go back to
sleep. This can be accompanied by an atmosphere of eager expectation, stress or even apprehension, and these feelings can remain
with the subject for some time after waking.

Celia Green, in her analysis of lucid dreaming, identifies two
varieties of false awakening. In Type 1, the person seems to have
woken from a dream and reflects on things normally. In Type 2,
the individual seems to have woken, but there is a somewhat
oppressive atmosphere:

*I thought I was awake. It was still night and my room very dark.
Although it seemed to me that I was awake, I felt curiously
disinclined to move. The atmosphere seemed charged, to be in a
'strained' condition. I had a sense of invisible, intangible powers at*

work, which caused this feeling of aerial stress. I became expectant.
Certainly, something was about to happen.

(Fox, O., *Astral Projection*.)

So how can we recognize false awakenings when they happen to us? As described earlier, electrical appliances will not function properly – if at all – during a false awakening. Dr Hearne identified this and other anomalies and devised a test whereby the dreamer can assess their validity:

TEN TESTS FOR STATE-ASSESSMENT

1. Switch on an electric light in the dream scenery. If it does not work, or there is a malfunction of any kind, or light switches cannot be found where they should exist, suspect strongly that you are dreaming. The same applies for any other electrical appliance.

2. Attempt to float in mid-air, or fly. Any success is proof of dreaming.

3. Jump off an object, such as a chair. If you descend slowly, you know you are dreaming.

4. Look carefully at your surroundings. Is anything there which should not be present? Is anything missing?

5. Look at your body, e.g. hands, arms, feet, and your clothes. Is it your body? Are they your usual clothes?

6. Look out of a window. Is the environment accurate? Is it the right season? Is the light-level correct for the time?

7. Attempt to alter a detail in the scenery, or make something happen by will-power.

8. Attempt to push your hand through solid-looking objects.

9. Pinch your skin. Are the texture and sensation as they should be?

10. Look in a mirror. Is there anything different about your face?

If you are living with a partner, it is advisable to warn them of your intentions. It would be most disconcerting for a husband or wife to wake in the middle of the night and find their spouse switching electrical gadgets on and off, jumping off chairs and so on. Assistance is invaluable in endeavours of this kind. You could arrange for your partner to prod or talk to you while you are experiencing REM sleep shortly before waking in the morning. Anticipating an interruption to one's slumber can trigger a false awakening.

False awakenings not only precede, but often follow a lucid dream. If this occurs, there is nothing to prevent you running the tests and becoming lucid again. Some dream enthusiasts have experienced lucidity as many as four times in a single night.

When the dreamer becomes lucid for the first time, this may last for only a few seconds before they drift back into REM sleep. This can, of course, be very disappointing, but it has been discovered that the duration of lucidity can be extended by practice. The more adept you become at inducing and controlling lucidity, the greater will be your chances of experiencing and lengthening the phenomenon.

If lucidity seems to be slipping away, concentrating your gaze on the back of your (dream) hands may extend the duration of the experience. It is not known precisely why this should happen, but it seems reasonable to assume that the act of focusing one's thoughts may be responsible.

Having observed the powerful effect of expectation in his sleep lab research, Dr Hearne devised a method of inducing lucidity, based on recognizing false awakenings, which you may like to try. This is the FAST (False Awakening with State Testing) technique and it sets up an expectation in the subject which should result in a false awakening.

You will need an assistant. Every half hour or so after 6 a.m. (when there is more REM sleep), your assistant should enter the bedroom, say a few words, potter around and then leave. Whenever this happens, you must go through some of the state tests listed above, no matter how convinced you are that you are awake.

Occasionally, you will, because of the expectation effect, dream that your helper has come into the bedroom. At that point the testing procedure will reveal that you have only dreamed it. You should then get up, explore the dream environment or relocate by covering your eyes and willing yourself to be somewhere else. For the purposes of dream interpretation, it is important that the analyst understands that people frequently experience false awakenings without realizing it. Here are two typical examples of the kind of letter an analyst might receive:

I have a vague memory of getting up and going to the toilet in the middle of the night. However, I noticed that the light switches weren't working properly. Yet when I got up this morning, they all worked perfectly. Now I'm not sure if it was a dream or not. What does it mean?

I remember getting up during the night, only to discover that the street scenery outside my bedroom window was strangely different. I'm sure I wasn't dreaming, so can you tell me what happened?

Reports that the bedroom furniture was somehow different, or that the curtains were not quite their usual colour are clues that the individual has undergone a false awakening. (If the above descriptions sound familiar, it is likely that you have experienced a false awakening. It is probable that we all have them from time to time.)

In contrast to a lucid dream, where the surroundings are likely to be strange and typically dream-like, the false awakening usually occurs in a familiar environment which seems real (not necessarily the bedroom).

Night-shift workers can be vulnerable to false awakenings, especially if they go to work in a tired condition. They may nod off during a shift, but dream convincingly that they are at work, performing their duties as usual. If they then drift into natural REM sleep, the chances are that they will be unable to distinguish between true and false awakenings.

Why should we take the trouble to find out whether we are dreaming or not? Apart from the advantage of being able to tell reality from fantasy, identifying a false awakening when it occurs provides us with a potent method of initiating a lucid dream. This can enhance our potential to heal and to eradicate nightmares, for example, as well as offering us the opportunity to fulfil exhilarating fantasies, like being able to fly or enjoying a secret romantic encounter.

~6~
Sleep Paralysis

CHARLES DICKENS may well have been inspired by the phenomenon known as 'sleep paralysis' to write one of his best known works. *A Christmas Carol* accurately describes what happens to many people who undergo this sometimes frightening experience.

Imagine a cold December night during the middle of the last century. A miserly old man, whom Dickens appropriately christens Scrooge, puts hot coals into a pan and warms his bed. Shivering, and wearing a long gown, bedsocks and nightcap, he snuggles beneath the covers.

Several hours later, unable to move, he wakes with a start. Sensing a presence close by, he nervously scans the room. When he tries to cry for help, no words leave his trembling lips. Inexplicably unable to move a muscle, Scrooge struggles in a futile attempt to escape the approaching spectre. The harder he tries, the more exhausted he becomes. This experience is identical to that of sleep paralysis.

In some cases of sleep paralysis include hallucinations of intruders or spectres, like Scrooge's ghost of his dead partner, in the bedroom:

> *I heard footsteps on the stairs. The bedroom door started to open and was creaking. I was lying with my eyes open and I could see the door open but could not move because I was totally paralysed. When I woke up, the door was tightly shut.*

Every time you are in REM sleep – for a total of two hours each sleep night – your body is almost totally paralysed. As mentioned in Chapter 1, the purpose of this strange effect is thought to be to prevent the acting out of dreams. The paralysis is a perfectly normal phenomenon.

Sometimes, however, people wake up while their body is still in REM paralysis. They may feel that they are trapped or tightly bound, or even believe they have died, and their natural response is to try to struggle. Both authors have experienced sleep paralysis and know how disconcerting it can be, as these examples show:

> *I thought I'd died. I tried to signal to my husband to wake me up. I tried to nudge him but I couldn't move. All I wanted to do was to wake up. I tried to make a noise. I thought I did but he said he didn't hear anything. I am totally paralysed and fully aware of the fact. I know that it will take something outside of myself to awaken me : a touch, a noise.*

However, the phenomenon does not always occur in this way. Some people will remember waking, being unable to move, and simply going back to sleep.

The condition is also known as 'night nurses' paralysis'. Like a false awakening, it is likely to happen to people working on the night shift. They are supposed to be alert and vigilant and if they fall asleep they may dream that a supervisor appears and, to their, horror, they cannot wake up.

Sleep paralysis is an elaborate illusion, but the person who experiences it is definitely not fully conscious. It happens during REM sleep, but on the edge of consciousness. Sometimes the dreamer will move from an awareness of paralysis back into a conventional dream, but often they wake up soon afterwards.

Both sleep paralysis and false awakenings occur while in the dream state, in familiar surroundings (usually the bedroom) and in both cases the experience is so convincing that the dreamers is certain that he or she is wide awake. Both can happen to shift workers anxious about being caught napping.

There is a difference between the phenomena, however. In a false awakening, the dreamer is able to move – even get out of bed and walk around in the dream – but in sleep paralysis the dreamer is almost conscious, fully aware of being in a paralysed state, yet still dreaming. How does one deal with this sometimes frightening experience? The answer is surprisingly simple. Just think to yourself, 'I know that this is sleep paralysis, which is linked to REM sleep.' Then, having labelled the phenomenon, simply relax and do not fight it. You will lapse into an ordinary dream and the paralysis will disappear. There is no reason at all to worry about it.

In 1996, a case was reported of a woman whose hair turned white overnight after a terrifying experience of sleep paralysis. She found herself paralysed and hallucinated that the Devil was licking her neck. If she had understood the phenomenon, the awful consequences would have been avoided.

To the dream-state explorer sleep paralysis is a very interesting condition. Because it is a REM-sleep state, potentially it could be exploited by experimentation. For example, it might be possible to induce an OOBE during sleep paralysis by rolling out of the body or forcing one's consciousness out through the top of the head, then re-entering in the same manner.

Sleep paralysis is also experienced by people with the condition known as narcolepsy. On going to sleep, instead of going through the various stages of SWS, they immediately enter REM sleep. Sufferers may report, for instance, suddenly feeling very weak during the day, flopping down and starting to see images, unable to move. They are in fact in REM sleep.

Sleep paralysis is not usually recognized as a dream state, so the dream analyst is unlikely to be asked to provide an interpretation for such an experience. However, we have received letters from worried people who describe sleep paralysis and ask for information about what is happening to them. Those who have had the experience for the first time often tell us they thought they were dying.

There is, therefore, a need for the analyst to understand the phenomenon. It can be most rewarding to receive a letter of thanks for putting a worried correspondent's mind at rest. In addition, if the client understands that it was all a dream and that there were no ghastly spectres coming to haunt him, this might stabilize what could otherwise have become a disturbed mind.

~7~
OOBE and Dreams

T HE STRANGE dreaming condition known as sleep
paralysis can be used to initiate astral projection, or an
Out Of Body Experience (OOBE). Is this phenomenon
just an elaborate dream, or can we really separate our consciousness
from our physical body?

Although it cannot be stated categorically, the answer would
appear to be yes. We can leave the body as an empty shell and
travel on the astral plane. Incredible as it may seem, there is a
growing mountain of evidence to support this. In the West, it is a
recent development, yet according to surveys, about a quarter of
adults say they have experienced an OOBE.

There have been reported descriptions of OOBEs for countless
centuries and some cultures accept their validity without question. The ancient Egyptians believed that a mind part of us, the
ka, could project, and a similar idea was accepted in early Greek and
Roman civilizations. In Tibet, it was said that we each have a spiritual replica of our body (the *bardo* body), which contains our
consciousness and leaves the physical body at death, but can also
make temporary excursions from it in life.

Psychic Voyages is one of the publications that cite cases where
people have had OOBEs under laboratory conditions. Although
some astounding results have been achieved, in general the scientific establishment prefers to ignore such findings, arguing that
other factors may have been involved – perhaps some form of
telepathy (this in itself is a curious admission).

In a sleep laboratory, Dr Hearne wired up with electrodes three
people who said they could astrally project at will. In each case the
subjects were in Stage 1 sleep (at the very onset of sleep) when

they reported their unusual experiences, such as perceiving extremely vivid images of floating through the ceiling and travelling rapidly to another location. Technically, they were experiencing hypnagogic imagery. It is impossible to prove that consciousness, or the soul, has become separated from the body with existing technology.

OOBEs are widely reported by people who, having been declared clinically dead, are resuscitated. Typically they report floating above the scene, watching the medical team working on their body. These anecdotal reports suggest that current criteria for clinical death are wrong and the near-death state should be investigated further.

Dr Hearne devised an experiment that might usefully be carried out in a hospital.

As part of the resuscitation procedure, tape-recordings of random words and phrases would be played to the patient via earphones. A television screen, facing upwards, above the bed and completely out of sight of the medical team, would display a randomly selected pattern or picture. A video camera would automatically monitor the room and a doctor would give a running commentary on the procedure so that the period of clinical death could subsequently be identified using the video recording.

Some time after resuscitation, when the patient had recovered, he or she would tick off any recalled words and phrases from a list which would also include words and phrases that were not on the recording. If the patient were able to remember any part of the tape being played during the time when they were judged to be clinically dead, the accepted criteria for death would be shown to be erroneous. Any recollection by the patient of material being broadcast on the television screen would provide evidence for the dislocation of their consciousness to a point above the scene.

Many people have written to us mistakenly claiming to have had an OOBE. It is not merely a case of being dishonest; they are simply confusing the phenomenon with sleep paralysis. To the individuals concerned, the experience seemed real in every respect and they were convinced that they had actually been out of their bodies.

Sometimes subjects provide a perfect description of sleep paralysis, except that they appear to be floating towards a dark tunnel where some sort of frightening experience awaits. Nevertheless, the fact that they are unable to move a muscle strongly suggests they are experiencing sleep paralysis. No paralysis is experienced during a genuine OOBE.

Why should anyone think they are floating towards a tunnel during sleep paralysis? Nowadays, there are frequent reports of OOBEs and also of the tunnel effect characteristic of the Near Death Experience (NDE). Having heard about such things, it is perfectly understandable that some people have realistic dreams about them.

Genuine OOBEs can of course be initiated during sleep paralysis, so it seems likely that the subject is only one step away from the real thing. Maybe their unconscious mind is testing them to assess whether or not they could handle an OOBE.

Most people who write to us about such experiences describe them as frightening, but anyone who has a real OOBE soon loses any fear. They feel they have embarked on the most exhilarating journey the mind can comprehend.

David Melbourne maintains that a genuine OOBE is unmistakable and without parallel; no other dream experience, apart from an NDE, comes remotely close to it. The astral traveller is neither constrained by the parameters of a dream, nor affected by paralysis; it is a fantastic and totally unique happening.

Dreams during sleep paralysis can be very convincing, so how can they be distinguished from a true OOBE? It is unsatisfactory to say that you will recognize an OOBE when you have one. The absence of paralysis will be one indication, but the best answer is to obtain corroborative proof. It will not occur to the subject of an ordinary dream to look for evidence, but this is often foremost in the mind of an astral traveller.

What sort of evidence should you look for? Something you could not have known about when awake. This may not be accepted as scientific proof, but it will leave no doubt in your own mind, which is what matters.

The following is an account of David's own first OOBE, for which he obtained corroborative evidence (this experience occurred soon after his second NDE):

> *I suddenly awoke from sleep and was immediately aware that my entire being was in a state of high resonant vibration. For a moment, there was a loud sound, as if sparrows were squabbling in springtime. First, I became conscious of having an erection. Then, to my utter amazement, I began to levitate up through the bedclothes. Next, as if falling out of bed, I flipped over and headed – horizontally – towards the floor. It happened so fast that I put my hands out to protect my face.*
>
> *To my horror, they went through the floor, and as they did, I could feel the texture of the carpet, the wooden floorboards and the space in between, then I felt the plasterboard which formed the ceiling above the living-room. Next, I floated up until I could see my body reclined in bed next to my wife.*
>
> *It was at this point that I thought that I was dead, and began to panic. Then a strange calm came over me and I started to enjoy it. I floated back down again until my face went through the floor and I was seeing into the living-room. It was as if I was being shown something deliberately, to prove that the occurrence was real and not a hallucination. My gaze focused directly on a small scrap of torn paper. It was covered in dust and was sitting on a bookshelf. At first, it didn't make sense and I felt the urge to get closer. The moment I had the thought, I drifted nearer to it.*
>
> *It was then that I recognized it. Written in faded red ink was the name 'Ronnie', above a telephone number. It was the number of a friend with whom I had lost touch. Some three years earlier I had met a mutual acquaintance, who had given me his number on the scrap of paper. I had since mislaid it, yet there it was before my eyes.*
>
> *As soon as I acknowledged what I had seen, I felt myself being drawn back towards my body. But I was enjoying the experience so much that I didn't want to go. I floated back through the floor and into the bedroom again. No matter how hard I fought against it, I couldn't resist merging with my body.*
>
> *Then, with a jolt, I regained full, conventional consciousness. The first thing I did was waken my wife and tell her all about it. I even*

told her Ronnie's telephone number. Full of excitement, I persuaded
her to come downstairs with me, there and then. At first, she wasn't
too pleased at being disturbed, but when she realized how thrilled I
was, she agreed to leave the warm bed and accompany me.
   Standing on a chair, I reached up and groped around the book-
shelf. When I showed her the dust-covered scrap of paper with the
same number, she was amazed, yet I had known that it would be
there. Although this doesn't constitute scientific proof, that incredi-
ble experience was more than adequate proof to me!

It might be argued that David's subconscious could have remembered where he had left the scrap of paper and somehow
manufactured this extraordinary experience. Yet he cannot begin
to imagine how it came to be on the top shelf of the bookcase in
the first place. Perhaps it became caught between the pages of a
book and fell out when the book was put on the shelf, especially
as the bookshelf was directly above the telephone, directories, pens
and pieces of paper.
   There appear to be several different types of OOBE. Usually
they occur spontaneously and subjects often report, as David
Melbourne did, having a deep buzzing sensation throughout the
body at the start of the episode. In his account, the presence of an
erection in sleep suggests that he was in or on the periphery of
REM sleep, which is associated with dreaming. That doesn't inval-
idate the experience. It suggests that if astral projection occurs, REM
sleep is conducive to separation. The ancient Chinese thought
that the soul (*hun*) could travel anywhere during sleep.
   The letters we receive from people who have dreamed of having
an OOBE usually ask for an explanation of the meaning of the
experience. It would be foolish to try to suggest an interpretation
for either a dream of an OOBE or the real thing. An analyst must
not be afraid to inform a client that a specific dream appears to be
unsuitable for interpretation. In these cases we usually explain the
reasons why and include a stamped envelope for their response.
   In our experience, most members of the public are interested
to learn and accept our explanation. However, there are those who
insist that they have undergone an OOBE, despite reporting that

they were paralysed. Because these dreams can be very convincing, it is usually not worth arguing the point.

Analysts who make the mistake of trying to interpret these extraordinary phenomena are, at best, risking making fools of themselves; at worst, their efforts could prove damaging to the client. Imagine that somebody has dreamt of having an OOBE, during which evil entities or monsters were encountered (this does happen), and seeks your advice as to its meaning. It would be totally irresponsible to allow them to believe they have experienced a genuine OOBE. This might suggest that all manner of horrors lie in wait for them should a true OOBE occur, and lead to terrifying nightmares. It would be better to reassure them that their dream was the product of their imagination, brought about by self-hypnotic suggestion.

Finally, although modern astral travellers have reported having a ghostly 'subtle body', some of our clients have described perceiving themselves as points of light. Interestingly, some of Dr Hearne's many past-life regression subjects have also described themselves as being points of light. It would seem that those points of light represent the very beginning of individuality: the universal 'big bang' was not an explosion of matter, but the fragmentation of a super-consciousness.

~8~
Creative Dreaming

WE COULD ALL learn to utilize the dream for creative purposes. Dream construction is a dynamic, building, wandering process that naturally connects pictures, thoughts, sounds, ideas, etc. that would not normally be linked. With the additional element of conscious awareness – as in a lucid dream – the products of the unconscious may be critically studied and evaluated as they develop.

The ability to control a lucid dream enables the dreamer to engineer situations where creativity may be encouraged. For instance, an artist could dream of going to a gallery to look at new works of art. Dr Hearne has done this himself. Some of the pictures he observed were spectacular, but he is not an artist and on waking could not reproduce them satisfactorily.

Clearly, in order to transfer dream creations into waking life we need well-developed, appropriate skills, but each of us is a potential Mozart or Michelangelo, with a wonderfully creative mind.

There have been many instances of inspiration coming in a dream. Kékulé, for example, hit upon the idea of the shape of the benzene molecule in a dream. He was troubled by the problem that the chemistry of benzene did not fit the supposed linear shape of its molecule. When he fell asleep, still thinking of the molecular shape, he dreamt of a snake with its tail in its mouth. Kékulé woke up instantly, realizing that this was a symbol of the molecular ring structure of benzene. He told a scientific audience, 'Gentlemen, we must learn to dream.'

At the beginning of this century, Otto Loewi won a Nobel prize from an experiment that his unconscious suggested in a vivid dream. Using frog hearts, he was able to demonstrate that conduction in nerves was in fact chemically transmitted.

The Lock-Stitch sewing machine became reality when a dream of warriors advancing with their spears going up and down gave the inventor Elias Howe the idea for the design of a mechanized sewing needle.

The inspiration for Robert Louis Stevenson's novels, *Treasure Island*, *Kidnapped* and *Dr Jekyll and Mr Hyde*, came to him in dreams, and like several well-known composers, Dr Hearne sometimes hears music in his dreams and writes it down on waking.

The unfinished poem 'Kubla Khan' was written by Samuel Taylor Coleridge after he had read a passage in *Purchas his Pilgrimage* relating to the Khan Kubla and the palace he commanded to be built and fallen asleep in a chair. On wakening, he was conscious of having composed in his sleep two or three hundred lines on this theme and started to write them down, only to be interrupted by a visitor. When he went back to it, the rest of the poem had vanished from his memory.

What is the source of dream creativity? The nineteenth-century student of dreams St Denys offers a cautionary tale: a musician friend of his wrote down a piece of music from a dream and discovered years later that it was an old established melody, although he had no recollection of hearing or seeing it before. However, St Denys also pointed out that he himself saw bizarre images in his dreams that could not have been based on actual memories. He believed, as we do, that novelty in dreams results from the associations between the elements of the different scenes as they develop and flow into one another.

The subconscious, therefore, working at a level beyond our comprehension, is the source of great creativity and efficient solutions to problems. David Melbourne is currently responsible for producing all of *Horoscope* magazine's short fiction, stories relating to astrology, tarot, dreams, palmistry and so on. If he runs out of ideas for story lines, David meditates during the hypnagogic state, asking his subconscious to supply him with a creative dream containing material for the next short story. Nine times out of ten, when he wakes in the morning, he has had a dream that fits the bill perfectly.

Other, more obscure kinds of creative dream may not be so obviously useful. However, they often relate to a dilemma the dreamer is facing in waking life. If the dream is studied carefully, it usually furnishes a solution, though the answer may be presented in a convoluted or bizarre manner. Dreams of this type are difficult to dissect and attempts at interpretation may give incoherent, incomprehensible results. The analyst has to pay close attention to the way in which the dream is described. The details of the presentation are every bit as important as the content of the dream itself. For example, the subject may say, 'The dream reminded me of something I've been going over and over in my mind for the past few days' or 'My car has a wheel which wobbles just like the one in my dream.'

When this happens, more information has to be sought. Dream interpretation is a process involving painstaking investigative work. The analyst must try to identify, from the contents of the dream, any clues relating to the waking dilemma, and decide whether or not these point to a solution. Often, a connection is made and the answer found.

No one would turn up at a doctor's surgery expecting to receive an instant diagnosis and cure for their illness without answering appropriate questions and undergoing a medical check. The same applies to dream interpretation. All available information should be collected in order to provide the correct solution.

It is possible for creative dreams to be confused with another type of dream, which is thought to be produced when the brain, acting as a filing clerk or clearing house, sorts through all the stimuli that have bombarded the conscious mind during the day, storing items of relevance and discarding what is unimportant. Under normal circumstances, these dreams are not remembered, but if you are disturbed during sleep you may stumble across them. It is pointless trying to analyse them.

~9~
Symbols

DREAM INTERPRETATION is extremely complex, fraught with pitfalls, and symbolism is probably the most common cause of inaccuracy. We have only to consider the bitter disagreements between Jung and Freud, both of whom insisted they were right, to understand how easy it is to come to the wrong conclusions.

Symbols can have recurring themes, but it is a mistake to assume that any symbol has a fixed, universal meaning. An excellent book on the subject is *The Secret Language of Symbols*, by David Fontana, which guides the reader through the history and mythology of symbolism.

Dream dictionaries offer the general public the most readily available method of interpreting a dream and are therefore quite popular, although most people are also aware of their limitations, especially when they provide contradictory interpretations for aspects of the same dream. They can be useful for suggesting possible symbolism, but each individual has his or her own language of symbols.

To attribute any single one meaning to a specific symbol is futile and irresponsible. The mere fact that dream dictionaries rarely agree on the meaning of certain symbols testifies to the superficiality of their interpretations and such misleading material should not be taken seriously.

Some dream dictionary symbols are based on verbal puns from other languages, so they have absolutely no relevance to dream interpretation in another country. The various schools of interpretation also explain symbols in widely differing ways. For a Freudian, a rocket might have sexual significance; for a Jungian, it might be a sign of great progress by the dreamer; for another analyst, it could be a pun, symbolizing admonition.

Thoughts are represented in picture form in dreams but, simplistic, fixed methods of analysis can lead to wildly inaccurate interpretations.

The analyst has to delve deep when defining the meaning of a symbol. If, for instance, a musical record, cattle, a rainbow, grass, a forest, a tiger, a house or any other symbolic image appears in a dream, what does it mean?

At least one dream dictionary implies that buying a record in a dream means there will be a death in the family. Because records are a fairly recent invention, no symbolic meaning can logically be attributed to ancient superstition or religious beliefs, so this incongruous interpretation seems irresponsible at the very least.

A lot depends on the context in which a symbol appears in the dream. Other factors are also involved; for example, the dreamer's life situation, temperament, problems, ambitions and so forth.

It is ludicrous to assume, without firm evidence of intelligent research, that if a child who is a budding musical prodigy dreams of purchasing a record, a death is imminent in the family. A deaf person, or somebody who works in the music industry, could equally well have this dream. The same meaning simply cannot apply to everyone who has such a dream, because it takes into account neither their personality nor their circumstances.

'I dreamed about a bull. What does this mean?' A simple enough question on the surface, but, for the purpose of dream analysis, one which cannot be answered without a great deal more information. Bulls are sometimes said to symbolize power and authority. However, this would be a superficial interpretation of the dream.

It would be necessary to find out, for example, whether the bull appeared threatening, friendly or uninterested, where the dreamer was in relationship to the animal, and what happened in the dream. What was the dream environment? Was the dreamer a Westerner, or from India or elsewhere? Does the subject work on a farm? These and many other questions have to be addressed before any interpretation is attempted.

Let us return to the dream image of the musical record. A disc is always round, flat and usually black; it has a hole in the middle; there is an undulating groove which spirals in towards the centre, stopping short of a label with printed information. Generally, a record is associated with instrumental music, songs, or both. It can convey messages of love, war, tragedy, happiness – anything at all. Records have to revolve and a needle or stylus follows the contours of the groove to produce sound. They are usually purchased in a paper sleeve, which is in turn inside a cover. On the cover there are graphics and written information.

Many more pertinent features could be listed. All these details are considered by the dedicated dream analyst, who continues searching until the true meaning becomes evident. If the analyst is already privy to information about the dreamer, it will only be a matter of time before the unmistakably correct interpretation is discovered.

This process often takes hours of dedicated study and is invariably a labour of love. To analyse the simplest dream usually takes at least an hour. Occasionally, to ensure accuracy, David Melbourne has found himself toiling away for days in an attempt to unravel a complicated dream.

One should never trust an interpretation given on the spot; dream analysis simply cannot be an instant process. First, the dream must be written down and studied in its entirety in order to grasp its general atmosphere or 'feel'. Then each symbol should be singled out and a flow chart drawn up. As we have seen, even something as ordinary as a musical record will produce an almost infinite number of linked themes (see Figure 2).

Each flow chart should be compared with the rest and a common theme sought. The next step is to see whether the connecting theme is appropriate to the dreamer's disposition and fits in with the rest of the dream. If it does not, the process has to begin again. Eventually, the real meaning will leap off the page. With luck it may be recognizable straight away, but more often than not hard work and patience will be required to complete the interpretation.

A flow chart for a musical record is shown in Figure 2 to illustrate a small proportion of the many linking associations such an object could have. In this context, a clear link with death is being sought. Dreams, by their very nature, can convey their message in ambiguous and convoluted ways; nevertheless, in this instance, no obvious association with death can be found.

The chart includes an ambivalent link with births, deaths and marriage. Straight away, investigation has moved away from musical records to records of events. The link is extremely weak, in that it also suggests birth, the opposite of death. As for marriage, with a stretch of the imagination, it could perhaps be argued that marriage represents the death of single life.

The second, slightly more credible, link with death comes via connections with music, songs, parties, alcohol, driving and accidents. This hardly leaps off the page as the only clear-cut interpretation for a dream about purchasing a musical record. At best, such a conclusion would be questionable; at worst, dangerous and totally misleading. For example, the client who has dreamed about buying a record may be suffering from depression because their beloved partner is ill. Imagine the likely effect of being told that their dream symbolizes impending death.

To emphasize the point about not taking dream dictionaries too seriously, it would be useful to consider briefly the other symbols mentioned earlier, beginning with cattle. Most of us are familiar with the story in Genesis of Pharaoh's dream about the seven thin cows which ate the seven fat cows, and Joseph's interpretation: seven years of plenty followed by seven years of famine. Supposing the dreamer had been an ordinary person and not a Pharaoh? More to the point, what if the dreamer's religion regarded cattle as sacred? All such details are relevant and must be taken into account.

A rainbow might signify wealth – to somebody who knows the myth about the crock of gold at the end of the rainbow. Rainbows are generally thought to signify either good health or money in the West. For a person with an African background, the rainbow could have an entirely different meaning. Some cultures hold that it represents energy which flows back and forth between heaven and earth. To a Hindu, it might suggest the highest state of meditation that can be attained. Jews and Christians, remembering the story of Noah, might equate it with a solemn promise.

Some dream dictionaries connect grass with wealth, others with

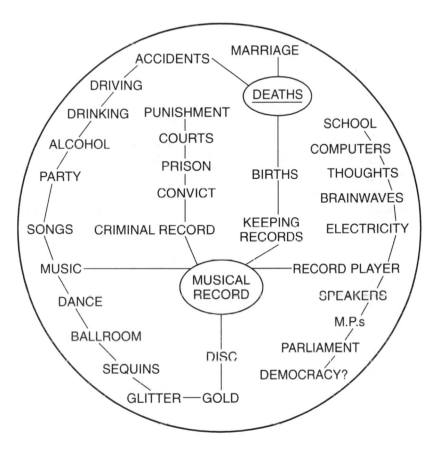

Figure 2 Flow charts are used to list possible associations suggested by images, characters, phrases, etc. that occur in dreams in order to find a common theme. One dream dictionary states that dreaming about buying a record indicates an imminent death. The above example demonstrates that such a narrow interpretation would be artificial and unconvincing.

poverty, health or enemies. Again, we have to take account of other factors. What was the dreamer doing in relationship to the grass (if anything)? Was the grass green and luxuriant, or parched and yellow? Were there any trees in the area? Was the grass on a hill, on a plain, or in a valley?

For example, if the grass was growing on a hill, it might signify the dreamer's spiritual development, the ascent from earth to a higher understanding. However, a grass-covered hill or mountain could represent masculinity. Conversely, a valley rich with grass might suggest the feminine side of one's nature. There are far too many connotations to make an exact interpretation without weighing up all the evidence and considering the dream in its entirety.

Similarly, there are numerous possible interpretations for the image of a forest, including good news, bad times, wealth and happiness. To somebody who is self-confident, a forest could indicate inner strength and longevity. On the other hand, a person of a nervous disposition might see it as a dark, sinister place, hiding fearful perils. The analyst must find out, for example, which trees predominated in the forest. Were they mighty oaks? Silver birches? Did they appear stunted or flourishing? Were they being battered by the wind or still and unruffled? Were they in leaf or bare? Did the dreamer feel comfortable about the forest, or experience a feeling of foreboding?

In dream dictionaries, a tiger can represent almost anything: passion, love, enemies, illness, wealth, bad news or danger. One dictionary suggests that cats in general may mean occult protection. If the dreamer comes from India or China, there may be other interpretations. The Chinese regard the tiger, not the lion, as the king of beasts and associate it with vitality and raw strength, whereas in some parts of India tigers are considered sacred, with the power to afford a village protection.

A house is sometimes believed to denote financial security or stability, but it is also said to symbolize worry (heavy mortgage repayments, perhaps). A wide range of alternative meanings can be found in dream dictionaries. However, since ancient times the house has frequently been regarded as a symbol of the dreamer. In this context, the roof and attic space represent the mind and higher spiritual functions. A bedroom often indicates affairs of the heart. As always, the disposition of the dreamer must be taken into account when an interpretation is made. A house may mean just that – a house.

Finally, let us take a brief look at colours. A dream dictionary might tell us, with some accuracy, that the colour red represents a warning. Should it therefore be assumed that a dream about a red budgerigar represents a warning? Perhaps the next time the dreamer puts a hand in the cage, will the budgie will turn savage? Green might plausibly indicate nature or the natural order of things. If a man dreams of wearing a pair of green trousers, does this symbolize a deep desire to return to nature?

When dealing with dream symbols, therefore, it is wise to refrain from taking dream dictionaries too seriously. Use them rather as a form of entertainment or as a source of inspiration in your search for accurate interpretations.

The scene-shift effect also casts serious doubts on the notion of universal symbols. For example, you might dream of a bull and find that the scene suddenly changes, so that the bull is replaced by a cat. Bearing in mind the brain's capacity for advancing scenes by the law of least effort, it is possible that the scene-shift effect is at work here. You must then decide which symbol the dream is trying to communicate, the bull or the cat. This process might continue until the last creature in the dream – a snake, say – is the definitive symbol. Or is it?

Important factors that must be taken into account in dream interpretation are the verbal and visual pathways of association, including the pun, or play on words.

It has long been known that dreams can follow verbal pathways; thus a cat can become a mat and so on. For instance, Dr Hearne had a dream in which he was on a train that pulled into a station called Akpinar. In fact, this was the name of a psychologist whose papers he had been reading the day before. Then the scene changed and he was in a park, a typical municipal park with flower-beds and areas of grass. On waking, he quickly realized that 'in a park' is an anagram of 'Akpinar'. (He loves crossword puzzles.)

Puns are well known for appearing in dreams. Anne Faraday noted several forms:

Verbal (e.g. gilt – guilt)

Reversal (e.g. feeling full – fulfilled)

Visual (e.g. baseball game – base game)

Colloquial metaphor (e.g. shooting me down)

Literal (e.g. bare chest – getting something off one's chest)

David Melbourne interpreted a dream for Dr Hearne in which he was in a coach with a person whom he described in his dream account as 'a lady-in-waiting'. Once it was realized that this meant not a courtier but a lover yet to come into Dr Hearne's life, the dream analysis clicked into place.

Using the flow-chart method (see above and Chapter 11), a sensible constellation of associations for each dream symbol can be written down and, eventually, a common theme will suddenly present itself. With this approach, dream interpretation becomes a fascinating and valid exercise. The technique is straightforward and workable. Anyone can do it.

However, to make an accurate analysis of a dream symbol, you will need to be a conscientious detective, possessed of the patience of Job and the determination of a bulldog. Each dream should be filed and meticulous records kept and, in time, you should develop a sixth sense when it comes to recognizing linking themes.

~10~
Developing Self-Knowledge

'OWAD some pow'r the giftie gie us to see oursels as others see us.' When Robert Burns wrote these words he was acknowledging one of the cardinal human weaknesses: blindness to one's own true character. It is this lack of self-knowledge which often hinders interpretation of one's own dreams.

For accurate dream interpretation, it is crucial to know some facts about the dreamer before embarking on an analysis, such as their age, nationality, gender, marital status, and whether they are basically extravert or introvert.

Knowing nothing about the subject will result in a sketchy, general interpretation which may or may not be accurate. Applying an interpretation of one person's dream to that of another will produce a disjointed result. This tends to happen when self-analysis is attempted, because our self-perception is often distorted. Neither are we able to view and interpret our dreams with the necessary detachment. We are too close, too involved, to remain impartial. In consequence, we may force our interpretation to fit.

It can be most embarrassing and quite a shock, to hear or see a recording of ourselves that we didn't know existed. 'That's not me, is it?' is a common response to such a revelation. Then the ego usually comes to the rescue with a natural defence: denial of the truth.

It is perfectly natural not to want to see ourselves as others see us. For some, a 'warts and all' exposure can be harmful; for others, beneficial. Denial may therefore be helpful, but acknowledging that there are aspects of our appearance or character which we do not particularly like is a more mature and healthier reaction, even though this awareness may be pushed to the back of our minds. The bizarre nature of dreams may be the result of a defence mechanism that attempts to hide from the conscious mind (by various methods of disguise) potentially uncomfortable or shocking information deriving from the unconscious. However, it may simply be that dreams are mainly the product of the right brain, where visual/symbolic representation is the natural language. Another possibility is that both these processes are involved. Whatever the reason, dream imagery can be decoded and, theoretically, we should be able to access information that not available in conscious awareness.

We all possess elaborate psychological defence systems that protect us from things that are too disturbing. Rape victims, for example, often say that they dissociated during their attack so that, in a sense, their conscious mind was not present. Also, someone who does not want to acknowledge that their partner is being unfaithful, for example, will fool themselves by disbelieving their own senses and completely fail to read the signs of impending trouble obvious to everyone else.

Similarly, scientists can be so attached to a particular theory that they foolishly overestimate findings that support it and play down any negative evidence, and those who suffer from anorexia perceive themselves as overweight, when it is obvious to the world that they are pitifully emaciated. There are, indeed, 'none so blind as those that will not see'.

Therefore, the dream interpreter has to be aware that most people either do not know themselves very well, or do not fully accept themselves as they are. In addition, they may consciously be denying disturbing events or other factors in their lives.

For centuries it was accepted that certain individuals had a flair for interpreting dreams. In the West, however, there is now an increasingly popular, though mistaken, belief that the best person to interpret a dream successfully is the dreamer.

This might well be the case if we were able to analyse our dream material – and ourselves – with objectivity. Where we come up against the first hurdle. To view anything dispassionately and analytically, we have to step back and adopt a neutral stance. When we interpret dreams, we must be able to see ourselves as others see us.

The accomplished dream interpreter relies heavily on the ability to recognize certain facets of other people's characters. It is not necessary for the analyst to know their clients inside out; all he or she needs is sufficient information to make a brief mental sketch of the personality and background of the individual concerned. Naturally, the more knowledge that can be gleaned about the dreamer, the better.

Nowadays there are many tapes on the market which claim to induce lucid dreaming for the purpose of dream interpretation. A word of warning: the likelihood is that these tapes will induce lucid dreams only in people predisposed to experience lucidity because they are hearing about it for the first time. Such people are just as likely to achieve lucidity simply by reading about it.

Inducing a lucid dream can be difficult; once achieved, hard work is required to extend the duration of lucidity, and it takes sustained and determined effort to learn to manipulate and skilfully direct a dream. Then, and only then, is it possible to conjure up a guru to explain the meaning of our dreams, providing that the dream state can be prolonged sufficiently to allow us to grasp what may be a complicated interpretation.

Other tapes claim to be able to program our subconscious so that when we wake up we will understand the meaning of our dreams. However, we have to be dispassionate and honest, and recognize the less attractive side of our nature, before we can understand any interpretation that our subconscious may be trying to communicate. Therefore these tapes are likely to prove disappointing.

Any reader who is considering purchasing such tapes should not be surprised if they do not work as expected. This is not to say that they will not work, for a small minority. For most of us, however, the road to successful dream interpretation is paved with obstacles which have to be overcome. Nevertheless, the determined dream enthusiast will succeed, one way or another.

To summarize: much can be done to develop the art of interpreting our own dreams. First, we must be willing to discover and accept the less appealing aspects of our character. Unless these are taken into account, any attempt at interpretation will inevitably be distorted.

The next step is to learn how to remain detached from the dream material and view it impersonally, to take it apart, look for linking themes, identify them and then reconstruct the dream. A successful outcome relies on resisting the urge to make certain features of a dream fit. If one fragment of the interpretation doesn't slot in with the rest, the temptation to ignore it must be withstood and the whole process of analysis begun all over again.

How can these hurdles be overcome? We must begin by learning about ourselves, peeling back the layer of self-deception, of ego. There are various techniques which can be employed in the task of self-discovery. Perhaps one of the most efficient and certainly one of the speediest ways is to use guided imagery.

This should not be confused with the sort of imagery used for healing, whereby a growth is pictured in the mind and then zapped with imaginary laser beams, for example. The imagery needed here involves careful observation. A series of mental exercises are performed which entail visualizing certain images and events, allowing them to run their course, then observing and reporting on the outcome.

Helen Graham, a psychologist and lecturer at the University of Keele in Staffordshire, is an acclaimed authority on guided imagery and its uses. Having run several courses on the subject in recent years, she has discovered techniques whereby we can learn to identify our fears, anxieties, likes, dislikes, ambitions, potential and physical, spiritual and mental awareness. Many of her students claim to be able to see themselves as complete persons for the first time in their lives. Some of Helen Graham's methods are described in her book *A Picture of Health*, which recommends techniques like the following:

- Relax, paying as little attention to distractions as possible. When you are ready, visualize yourself in a place where you feel comfortable. Next, imagine that a famous sculptor has created a statue of you which will soon be displayed in public, and that you enter the room where, completely covered by a dust-sheet, the statue is housed.

• Before you pull the dust-sheet away, examine your feelings at the prospect of the statue being exhibited in public. When you feel ready, remove the cover and study the statue meticulously. Note its size, what sort of material it is made of, and its texture. Absorb as much detail as possible and note your feelings at the time. Then try to pick out one feature about it that you find sticks in your mind.

• On finishing this exercise, write down as much of the experience as you are able to remember, even the slightest detail, no matter how inconsequential it might seem. Study the notes and begin an analysis.

Many people are surprised by the results of this exercise. Some imagine that the statue is larger than life, while others see themselves as small and hunched. Some picture themselves sculpted in cold stone, whereas others envision the texture of richly grained wood, warm and inviting.

Some feel proud and full of confidence at the prospect of having their statue displayed in public. Others are embarrassed and even afraid at the thought of being exposed to public scrutiny.

The outstanding feature recalled by one person may be a nose larger than normal, suggesting that they are rather inquisitive. Another person might see the shape of a large heart beneath the statue's skin.

The above example is just a quick outline of one of Helen Graham's mental exercises, but it illustrates the huge potential of guided imagery as an aid to self-discovery.

Some people, however, will be unable to produce visual imagery; they are likely to be predominantly left-brain users. If you find it difficult to visualize anything, let alone a detailed image of a three-dimensional statue, try sketching a statue covered by a sheet. Then draw the statue as it is revealed, stage by stage; finally, draw the complete figure. Next, make notes about what you think the statue is made of, your feelings about it, and so forth. This exercise should produce helpful results.

Once you have recognized and accepted yourself as you are, you will be better equipped to view your dream material dispassionately. Begin by dividing the dream into sections: symbols, action, scenery, dialogue, emotion, etc. Then break down each section into small segments and start looking for linking themes (the full method is described in Chapter 11).

For example, suppose there is a horse in your dream. The horse is standing outside a door acting strangely. A voice says, 'That's not a real racehorse!' and you feel suspicious.

This may just be a small fragment of a lengthy dream but you already have many facts to study. If you consult a dream dictionary to find out what a horse symbolizes, you will be bewildered by a plethora of horsy meanings, many of them spurious, probably ranging from wealth, marriage and good news to happiness, misery and misfortune.

So you must play the role of detective and become your own analyst. The horse is acting strangely – why? Then a voice announces that it's not a real racehorse. Perhaps these two factors indicate that the horse is not what it appears to be. It is outside an entrance and you feel suspicious. All these facts, put together, might suggest a Trojan horse. Therefore, the horse may represent some sort of deception.

Assuming that this analysis fits in with the rest of the dream and interpretation as a whole, you can feel reasonably comfortable about it. But if other factors in the dream suggest facets of your own character, your darker side, the horse may be a representation of your 'other self'.

Unless you can see yourself as others see you, you will never make this connection; you may even, unconsciously, deny this aspect of your character and construct an inaccurate interpretation to protect yourself from the truth. However, if you have acknowledged your other side, and are able to view the dream with detachment, the symbol of the horse may alert you to the fact that you are behaving unjustly or deceitfully towards somebody else.

On the other hand, your objective, careful dream analysis may guide you to an interpretation promising love, happiness and wealth.

~11~
Interpreting Message-bearing Dreams

IT IS IMPORTANT to be able to tell message-bearing dreams from the other varieties, which (as we have seen) are unsuitable for analysis. There are different types of message-bearing dreams: normal, precognitive, inspirational and spiritual, for example. They are usually easy to distinguish. For example, they tend to be vivid, because they are intended to be remembered on waking. For the same reason, they often present their message using bizarre imagery and/or spectacular events.

We remember few of our more mundane dreams because the content, not indended to convey a message, is simply dull. If sleep is interrupted during this kind of dream, the chances are that the dreamer will recall at least part of it, but not very clearly. It is not worth trying to interpret such dreams.

When a normal message-bearing dream comes to an end, the dreamer will generally wake up and spend some time reflecting on the contents of the dream. Most of the reports we receive describing message-bearing dreams end with the words: 'Then I woke up'. This is no accident: the subconscious has completed its message and wants the conscious mind to think about it.

Because our subconscious wants us to remember these powerful dreams, they may be accompanied by compelling emotions that remain long after waking. We find ourselves going over and over the dream during the day until it fades. It may be that we relive the experience until the emotion has been exhausted and, in so doing, unconsciously get the message or exorcize a fear or anxiety.

Successful interpretation is defined as

So, vivid dreams with strong emotional overtones that linger after waking are invariably message-bearers and should lend themselves to successful interpretation. The more striking the dream, the more important the message, and the easier it will be to analyse. Most precognitive dreams are extremely vivid. On waking, the dreamer usually has a strong feeling of having seen a vision of the future and guesses that the dream was precognitive. Sometimes such dreams occur during Stage 1 sleep, in the nodding-off stage, and contain hypnagogic imagery. Barbara Garwell (a well-known precognitive dreamer) sometimes realizes the predictive nature of her dreams only when the event of which she dreamed is reported on the news, although her precognitive dreams are always very vivid. Others have felt as though they were being shown something in such dreams, like a pupil at school. Dreaming of dates in the future and a feeling of anticipation are further clues that a dream may be precognitive.

Spiritual dreams can be difficult to identify. They range from seemingly normal message-bearing dreams to unmistakable visions of spiritual beings. However, research reveals that there is one recurring theme which can alert the analyst to the possibility of a spiritual dream: the dreamer may describe being in a foreign country – nearly always there is some confusion as to which country they were in – and the people in the dream may be speaking in a foreign language.

Creative dreams can resemble inspirational dreams, which are thought to act on a deep, subconscious level and may therefore not be readily recalled upon waking. Instead, elusive fragments may be remembered the following day. These dreams can help the dreamer reach a decision about something that has been troubling them; having solved the problem, they may then recall the dream.

General, or normal, message-bearing dreams are the most common. On analysis, they tend to reveal a logical structure, so that the interpretation has a beginning, a middle and an end, which may represent the past, present and future. Remarkably, they often follow a plot, with the main story reaching a dramatic climax. They generally lead the analyst to a clear and cohesive interpretation, even though the dream itself may have been disjointed and confusing.

Not all message-bearing dreams will yield a well-structured interpretation, however. Some are intended merely to reassure or comfort, others to warn the dreamer. The imagery of warning dreams is sometimes intended to recreate circumstances that should remind the dreamer of a difficult time in the past, or to draw their attention to a problem of which they are unaware in waking life. These types of dream are less frequent than general message-bearing dreams. It may not be possible to translate them into a structured meaning, but a sensible and comprehensible interpretation should be achieveable nonetheless.

There is not enough room here to cover all the other types of dreams you may experience, such as healing dreams and collective-consciousness dreams, but the wide variety of dreams underlines the fact that it is essential to learn as much as possible about the world of dreams before starting to interpret them. It would be pointless for an analyst to try to analyse a healing dream, for example, unless they fully understood this type of dream.

DREAM INTERPRETATION

Once you can confidently identify a message-bearing dream and are aware of the pitfalls of symbolism, you can begin to interpret your own or other people's dreams.

First you will need a steady supply of dreams to work on. It is an advantage to have friends or relatives who are willing to help. If you live alone, or are afraid of being ridiculed, your own dreams will have to do, although analysing your own material can be harder than working on someone else's. You could set up or join a dream group, so that you can make your early mistakes with like-minded people.

Eight Steps To Dream Interpretation

1. Obtain a psychological profile of your subject and any other potentially useful information by using the Melbourne-Hearne Questionnaire (see Appendix). It is helpful to know, for example, if the dreamer is currently preoccupied about anything; any possible cause of stress; whether a special event is anticipated; the dreamer's thoughts before going to sleep, and their psychological state on waking.

2. Write down the dream description and study it in its entirety to get the general picture (several times, if necessary). Try to persuade your subject to provide a written account, and remember that additional clues are often provided in the way the dream is presented and by remarks in the dreamer's accompanying letter. For example, someone may say that in their dream they were laughing and joking with another person 'although I can't stand them in real life'. Important clues like this should always be taken into consideration.

3. Ascertain what type of dream it is; is it suitable for analysis? Lucid dreams, for example, are not. Look out for concluding phrases like 'Then I woke up', which suggest that the subconscious is trying to make the dreamer take notice of an important message in the dream.

4. Sectionalize the dream into categories: setting, action, dialogue, symbols, emotion and anything else that seems relevant.

5. Draw up flow charts for each category and start looking for a common thread or linking theme. Allowing for all dream-interpretation theories, note down any reasonable associations. Look out for plays on words and always bear in mind the subject's circumstances and background.

6. If one part of the dream doesn't fit in with the rest of your interpretation, look for a different linking theme. Repeat this process as often as necessary.

7. Remember that dreams often reveal a logical structure on analysis. If there is a beginning, middle and end to your interpretation, check whether it represents the past, the present and the future.

8. When all options have been exhausted and only one interpretation satisfactorily fits the dream content, your analysis is complete.

The data gathered by the questionnaire can be used to help find associations to key words and symbols in the dream report. Such associations will depend to a great extent on such factors as the dreamer's work, interests and educational background.

Read all the information given by the dreamer several times. This data must, of course, be treated absolutely confidentially. Never reveal information about your subjects or their dreams to another person without their full permission, and keep all your records in a safe place.

The emotional content of a dream is extremely important. It seems to be the feature most closely linked with the underlying subconscious thought and thus serves as the basis of the interpretation. However, remember that the opposite of a reported emotion may occasionally be identified as the real key to the analysis.

Message-bearing dreams are often very strange, but they are usually trying to put a message across in simple terms, so always begin by looking for the most obvious interpretation.

Read the dream report aloud several times and listen very carefully to every word and group of words for verbal puns. Homophones (words that sound the same but have different meanings) frequently crop up; for example, son/sun; vane/vain. Approximate homophones also appear; for example, wisteria/hysteria; Germans/germs.

Pay attention to the words rather than the superficial story. Consider what other connotations each word and group of words may have. The words 'weigh' and 'heavy weather', for instance, accompanied by a feeling of dissatisfaction on waking, may indicate either a problem with the dreamer's diet or their frustration at having to wait for something.

Look for anagrams, especially when the dreamer likes doing

crosswords, and even for acronyms. For example, the written phrase 'big old motorbike' could represent 'bomb' (perhaps an emotional bombshell).

There may be visual puns, such as a horseman riding on a roof, possibly symbolizing someone 'riding a high horse' (the dreamer may perceive someone else as arrogant, or be feeling guilty about their own arrogant nature).

In dreams we are often represented by other people, by animals or even inanimate objects, which is why Gestalt theory encourages the dreamer to view the dream from the point of view of all the characters and elements in it. For example, if you came across a patch of mud with an old fence-post sticking out of it in a dream, your subconscious might be telling you that you are an old stick-in-the-mud!

Dream characters often represent past, present or even future aspects of the dreamer. Sometimes sub-personalities, fixated at times of significant traumas or happier events earlier in life, appear and have their say in a dream.

Flow charts are essential for identifying people in a dream. For example, if a queen appears in the important symbols category of your analysis, write down any associations that come to mind, such as the names Elizabeth, Mary, Anne, Cleopatra and Antoinette. Consider the dreamer's country of origin, education, occupation, etc. Do any of the names correspond to people significant to the dreamer, or is someone called Philip listed, for instance? The queen could represent the dreamer's wife. Equally well, it may refer to a homosexual or to a mother figure. Make as many connections as possible. Ask yourself what links the dreamer might suggest.

Remember that the dream follows visual associations and that at scene shifts it is common for the pictorial elements (including colours, characters and objects) to be rearranged into the new picture. There will be strong links between the two scenes even though the written account describes two apparently different settings.

Watch out for the phenomenon of opposites in dreams. For example, a funeral might signify a birth or a wedding. The discrepancy is not necessarily the result of a devious attempt at disguise.

Also look out for an overall metaphor in the dream. For instance, if the general theme is one of losing control (in the dream, first a vehicle and then a child is out of control), the dreamer may in waking life be afraid of losing control in a significant area, maybe financially, or emotionally. Often a dream, or all the dreams of one night, can be summed up in a single metaphor.

Keep referring to the information given in the dreamer's questionnaire and always look for a simple explanation first. A dream may merely reflect something that is happening in the dreamer's life. For example, a person who dreams of looking over a house for sale may recently have done that in reality, in which case it may be inappropriate to assume that the house symbolizes the body (although there may still be meaningful connections between two such explanations).

Start every interpretation afresh, trying not to be influenced by, say, your memory of what a similar dream meant to you or someone else. Eventually links will be discovered and suddenly everything will seem to fall into place. Do not impose an interpretation artificially; the right one will suggest itself quite naturally.

Finally, it is important to obtain feedback about the accuracy of each interpretation. Always ask your subjects to give you an honest opinion about your analysis of their dreams.

~12~
Precognitive Dreams

ABOUT four out of ten reported psychic experiences seem to involve some awareness of the future. In descending order of frequency, premonitions – which parapsychologists tend to call 'precognitions' – come in the form of dreams, waking thoughts, waking imagery and sleep-onset (hypnagogic) imagery.

A premonition can be defined as an experience (such as a dream or a waking thought) which appears to anticipate a future event that could not reasonably have been inferred from information available before the event. The fact that most premonitions relate to unpleasant things is reflected in the term itself, which derives from the Latin word *praemonere*, to forewarn. Sometimes the person who has the premonition does not know precisely what will happen but has a feeling that something untoward will occur; it is then known as a foreboding or presentiment.

Both authors have had personal experience of precognition. Here Dr Hearne gives his own account:

I had never considered myself to be at all psychic, but one day something happened that made me wonder whether I might have some psychic ability.

In 1981, I was living in Hull and used to visit a colleague, Robin Furman, perhaps once a fortnight or so. Robin lived in Grimsby and the journey involved crossing the Humber estuary; the suspension bridge was not yet open. It was a journey I was very used to. However, on one occasion, as soon as I took my seat on the ferry, I experienced a strange feeling of concern. I knew with absolute certainty that there would be some untoward event on the ferry trip.

I didn't know exactly what was going to occur, only that something would. The feeling was so urgent that I wanted to tell the captain, but a moment's thought made me realize that he would think I was mad. I could have still got off the boat at that point, but I was intrigued to see what would happen. It was rather cold so I sat below deck.

It was the last ferry of the day and darkness was descending rapidly. After about half an hour we were about 200 metres (220 yards) away from the landing stage on the other side of the estuary, when there was cry of 'Man overboard!' I went up on deck. A man had somehow fallen off the bow of the ship. The captain stopped the engines and people peered into the blackness. There was no sound. The victim's young wife stood, shocked, holding a young baby in her arms. Everything was silent. As the minutes passed, we assumed the man had been swept away and drowned.

Eventually the engines were re-started and the boat circled the area. Suddenly, something was seen in the water. It was the man. He was dragged aboard with boat-hooks and a crew member performed mouth-to-mouth resuscitation on him. He revived, and when the boat docked he was rushed off to hospital. To be honest, I was excited about my presentiment of this alarming event.

Having spent about 14 years as a fire-fighter, David Melbourne occasionally dreams about fires, which seems perfectly natural. Some of these dreams carry messages, while others appear to refresh his memory by bringing back faces of old comrades who have since been forgotten. This indicates that some dreams also serve yet another purpose: recharging the battery of our memory. He also maintains a strong belief in precognition because, from time to time, he experiences the phenomenon himself. In the following account he describes a very vivid dream he had recently:

In my dream, I found myself standing just inside the porch of a wooden house, gazing at a fire which had recently started next to the porch door. The fire was beginning to spread up the wall. Looking round, I saw an old-fashioned 'soda acid' fire extinguisher, the kind where water is forced out when a knob on the extinguisher is struck, causing the soda and acid inside the cylinder to mix and generate carbon dioxide gas.

I struck the knob, only to find that little more than a dribble of water was expelled by the extinguisher. However, being extremely careful, I managed to put out the blaze. Just as the last flame died, the fire brigade turned up with a high-pressure hose reel.

When I awoke, I decided that, because the dream was so extraordinarily vivid, it must be recorded on paper for analysis at a later date. Despite the dream's startling clarity, I did not recognize it as precognitive, although upon waking, my memory of it was accompanied by a feeling of anticipation.

That same afternoon, having seen our local ferry dock, I set off to collect my post. As I was getting into my car, I noticed smoke issuing from my nearest neighbour's roof; the house was built from Canadian pine. My neighbour told me that there was a fire in the cavity of the wall, between the wooden exterior and the plasterboard interior, next to the porch door. He had called the local fire brigade. The sounds of fire crackling away behind the plasterboard were clearly audible.

All the owner had been able to do was rig up a garden hose, which was supplied from a water tank. The absence of pressure resulted in little more than a trickle from the hose. I ran my hands over the wall, checking for heat, in order to ascertain the exact location and extent of the blaze. The fire seemed to be confined between two wooden partitions, which were about 3.2 metres (4 feet) apart.

Knowing that the island's fire crew consisted of part-timers, I realized that there might be some delay before they arrived. They have to drop what they are doing and make their way to the fire station from various scattered locations before they can get under way.

During the brief time I spent assessing the situation, I was aware that the fire was beginning to get hold and was showing signs of spreading into the roof. I had to make a snap decision whether to wait for the fire brigade or to try to contain the blaze with what few resources were available.

With the noise of the fire growing louder every second, I decided to punch a small hole in the plasterboard near the ceiling. This would not let in enough air to speed up the burning, but it would enable me to push the end of the hose through into the cavity and attempt to extinguish the flames.

The resulting hissing noise, as clouds of steam were generated, was music to my ears. After a few moments, I instructed my neighbour to punch another hole about 30 centimetres (12 inches) below the first one. Again, there was an encouraging hissing sound. We repeated the procedure several times, working our way down the length of the plasterboard.

Finally, the crackling ceased and I decided that it would be safe to tear down the plasterboard to facilitate access to the interior surface. As the first section came away, the fire gave one final burst of defiant flame before being extinguished completely. At that point, the fire brigade turned up with a high-pressure hose reel.

Clearly, my dream, which came to mind while I was considering whether or not to tackle the fire myself, had portrayed a vision of the future. Somehow, I knew exactly what would happen and that there would be a satisfactory outcome.

When Dr Hearne met his friend at Grimsby station, after his experience on the ferry, he told him about his presentiment and said that it had made him decide to alter the emphasis of his parapsychological research from the artificial set up of the laboratory to the real world, where such phenomena happen naturally.

He asked Robin if he knew anyone who had had a premonition. Robin instantly described an extraordinary case concerning his niece, Lesley Brennan, who had a precognition (confirmed by witnesses) of the Flixborough chemical plant explosion.

Premonitions happen quite frequently: surveys show that seven out of ten people accept the existence of premonitions and over a quarter of the population report actually experiencing such things. Little research has actually been conducted into premonitions as such. Most scientific effort has gone into laboratory studies involving the statistical analysis of precognition using card- or pattern-guessing.

After he had published articles about his initial research in several national newspapers, hundreds of people wrote Dr Hearne and completed questionnaires regarding their premonitions. The data he received showed that nine out of ten reported premonitions were experienced by females. There was a possibility that a reporting bias was operating, in that men were perhaps unwilling to admit to being psychic, so Dr Hearne asked his subjects whether anyone else in their family had premonitions, but the ability proved to be an overwhelmingly female one. About a quarter said their premonitions were always on a particular theme, such as plane crashes.

Four out of ten subjects said they had had between two and ten premonitions, about a third said between ten and fifty and about a fifth estimated that the total exceeded fifty. Most had experienced their first premonition between ten and fifteen years of age. The latency period between the premonition and the event itself was usually between a day and a few weeks.

The subjects took a personality test, which revealed them to be significantly more emotional, or neurotic, than average. This finding might indicate that their emotionalism helps these people 'tune in' to others' distress.

PREMONITIONS IN HISTORY

If premonitions were just a recent phenomenon we could be dubious about their reality, but they have been reported in all cultures since history began. Cuneiform-script clay tablets from Assyria and Babylonia, for example, testify that dreams including foreknowledge were experienced thousands of years ago.

The ancient Egyptians believed that dreams were messages from the gods and that knowledge about the future could be conveyed through the vehicle of the dream. They had special temples (serapeums) where dreams could be encouraged or 'incubated'. After fasting and various cleansing rituals the incubant would sleep in the temple and await a special dream – often about the future – which would be interpreted by 'the learned men of the magic library'. Several papyrii listing different dream symbols have been discovered.

An ancient Indian book of wisdom, the *Artharva Veda*, dating from about 3,000 years ago, commented on premonitory dreams, stating that the time of night in which the dream occurs gives a clue as to when the foreseen event will happen. Thus, a premonitory dream occurring early in the night will be realized later than one occurring near dawn.

The ancient Greeks were also fascinated by dreams. Aristotle believed that some dreams are self-fulfilling prophecies and that some apparently precognitive dreams of future illness may be 'prodromic', in that the dream reveals symptoms not yet available to the conscious mind.

The Bible, of course, refers to precognitive dreams. There are about fifteen in the Old Testament, most of which helped change the course of history, including Pharaoh's dream (mentioned earlier) of the seven fat and seven thin cattle. Joseph interpreted this dream as a warning of seven years of abundance followed by seven years of famine.

TYPES OF PRECOGNITIVE DREAMS

Most precognitive dreams concern unpleasant things. Many of them are about the unexpected death of an immediate member of the family or someone close to the dreamer. Here is one such case:

> *I had a recurring dream every night for a week. In the dream my mother, who was dead in reality, paid a visit and told me, 'You will not see Doug and Joy again. They will not be here long.' Doug and Joy were my brother and his wife.*
>
> *The dream was very disquieting and I wanted to warn my brother but my husband told me not to be so silly. Two days after the last dream I bought the local paper and on the front page were pictures of my brother and Joy. They had been killed flying to Spain. I had no idea they had gone on holiday.*

Other premonitions concern disasters but where the victims are not directly linked to the dreamer:

I was in the sixth form at school when I had the first of many, many experiences of seeing unpleasant events in advance. There was a boy in my form whom I didn't know well and he had a younger brother also in my school. The younger brother was about 13. One night, I had a dreadful nightmare in which I was crossing the nearby Lough in a sailing boat with the younger boy. The boat capsized. As it sank I extricated myself from the ropes and rigging, but I could see the young boy struggling to free himself. I tried to free him but was unable to do so. I awoke with a terrible sense of doom and fear.

During the day I met a friend, a lecturer at the university who was a colleague of the boy's father, and told her of my nightmare. That evening she phoned to tell me that the same young boy had apparently tried to cross the Lough that day in bad weather (he was apparently a good helmsman) and his boat had capsized. The boy was drowned.

While the events they dream about seem destined to happen, dreamers are apparently unable to take any avoiding action:

After having completed my apprenticeship as an aircraft engineer, I left London to work in the Midlands with a light aircraft maintenance company. One of my duties was to fly as observer on air tests, with our managing director as pilot. Air testing can be dangerous, as the aircraft is taken to its limits in stalls, spins and single-engine climbs.

At first I enjoyed the thrill of flying but I soon became dogged by a recurring dream of sitting in the right-hand seat attempting to pilot the aircraft with my boss next to me, unconscious. The problem was that I could not fly the plane.

After a while the dream began to haunt me every time I got into a plane to carry out an air test, until one day my nerve went and I refused to fly. The next plane taken for an air test crashed, killing both the managing director and the apprentice.

An especially accurate variety of premonition identified from Dr Hearne's data is the media announcement dream, where the premonition comes in the form of a public announcement, such as a television or radio news flash or a newspaper hoarding), that is dreamed or hallucinated in some way. Perhaps one in 50 reported premonitions is of this type, although many may go unnoticed because the precognitive element is not recognized. Some premonitions seem to be of fairly inconsequential events in the dreamer's life. For example:

> *I was 20 years old and had just begun a new job as an assistant librarian in Newcastle. I dreamed that a Dutchman came into the library to ask about some Dutch-language novels. In the dream I went to the file where such requests were kept and could not find this one, but eventually tracked it down to the back room, where another assistant was dealing with it.*
>
> *The next day this event happened. The Dutchman came in about his request for Dutch novels. Instead of searching the file I went straight to my friend in the back room who was in fact working on that request*

A small fraction of premonitions actually anticipate happy events:

> *I had a dream of someone telling me a horse was going to win a race; its name was Bean something. Over breakfast I asked my husband if he had heard of a horse by that name. He said he hadn't, and we joked about it because I have never had a dream about a horse winning and I am hopeless at picking a winner at anything. My husband sent my son to get the daily paper but when he read it he said he couldn't see a horse of that name listed.*
>
> *As I sat down for a coffee at ten-thirty. I grabbed the paper and straight away I saw the horse listed: Bean Boy. I was so excited that I rang my mother, my sister, my brother-in-law and a friend, Harry, who likes a flutter. They each placed a £1 bet on the horse. We put £20 of the mortgage money on it. The horse won (at seven to one). I was thrilled.*

Dr Hearne's research approach has been two-pronged. First, he obtained large numbers of reported premonitions in order to establish categories, frequencies, latency periods and so on, and, second, he investigated a few subjects very closely. Barbara Garwell, who lives in Hull, is someone whose premonitions Dr Hearne has studied over many years. Barbara is a very sweet, sincere, Roman Catholic lady in her sixties who has had premonitions since childhood. She seems to be able to foresee major assassinations before they happen. For example, 21 days before the killing of President Sadat of Egypt, Barbara woke from a vivid and violent dream in which she saw some 'coffee-coloured' men spray a group of dignitaries with machine guns at a stadium. The scene seemed to be in the Middle East. President Sadat was actually killed, with several others, while taking the salute at a military parade in a stadium. Soldiers ran from a vehicle to the saluting base and fired Kalashnikovs. Although Barbara had not not identified the country, the details of her dream were very accurate.

In 1981 Barbara had another assassination dream, this time a more symbolic one, featuring members of the Nazi SS. In the dream, a man got out of a limousine. He had a 'pock-marked' face and Barbara 'knew' he was a former actor. One of the SS soldiers also in the dream drew a pistol and fired several shots at the actor, who fell. Exactly 21 days after the dream, an attempt was made on the life of President Reagan (a former screen actor) when he was climbing into a limousine. John Hinckley, the gunman, had been a member of a neo-Nazi group, the National Socialist Party.

Intelligent analysis of both these dreams could, in retrospect, have revealed what was soon to happen, and to whom.

Many other startling premonitions that Barbara has received are catalogued in Dr Hearne's book, *Visions of the Future* and in her own book, *Dreams that Come True*. Coincidence alone cannot explain them. Sceptics have suggested that she records only those premonitions that come true.

To test this hypothesis, in 1981 Dr Hearne collected every single premonition Barbara had in that year. She entered each on a form and sent it to him. There were 52 in all. Two impartial judges later examined events that happened in the following 28 days and rated each premonition for accuracy. The judges did the same for a another, control, year.

The premonitions for 1981 (the correct year) scored significantly higher than those for the control year, but the most interesting result of the investigation was the consistent 21-day latency period for several of Barbara's major premonitions.

Some people who have premonitory dreams are afraid that in some way they are causing the ensuing disasters. This seems implausible. Often, several people will dream about the same disaster; it is difficult to believe that they are all responsible for the same event. It is more likely that they are each passively receiving information about the impending event.

It seems that the future is formed a few months in advance. Major events become fixed or 'set' and can be detected by certain individuals, but the element of free will enables people to avoid them.

Premonitions, more than any other paranormal phenomena, are clear evidence that our ideas about the nature of the universe and ourselves are completely wrong. Whereas telepathy, say, may be explicable within the limits of current scientific knowledge, precognition is unacceptable to scientists because it requires an acknowledgement that an effect (the premonition) can exist before a cause (the event).

However, several theories formerly rejected as scientifically impossible, such as the fact that the earth orbits the sun, and the existence of other planets, have since been proved to be correct.

The evidence tends to suggest that foreknowledge exists. This calls into question the existence of the physical universe. It also suggests that we live in a mind world, a mentalistic universe, and that life itself is a dream. This is a tremendously exciting idea. It allows for clairvoyance, miracles, synchronicity, coincidence, poltergeists and the whole panoply of the paranormal dismissed by science today.

If an analyst accurately interpreted a precognitive dream foretelling a specific disaster and people were prepared to listen and take evasive action, many lives might be saved. For instance, working with the BBC's *Out Of This World* programme, Dr Hearne identified seven premonitions warning of the 1995 earthquake in Japan which caused many deaths and devastating damage to property.

By their nature, precognitive dreams bear messages and they

usually depict scenes closely resembling events that later happen in real life. They are often accompanied by a feeling that they are precognitive and generally require little analysis. Symbolic precognitive dreams normally translate into clear interpretations, which can be confirmed when the incidents depicted occur.

One of Barbara Garwell's dreams is interpreted in Chapter 18. She regards this dream as an ordinary message-bearing dream, although it clearly contains premonitory elements. In addition, Chapter 21 includes an astounding precognitive dream and its interpretation.

~13~
Telepathic Dreams

TELEPATHY is simultaneous mind-to-mind communication. Information in the form of thoughts, images, feelings and sensations can apparently be transferred instantaneously from one person to another some distance away without any form of physical communication. The information is conceptualized as coming from a sender or agent to the receiver or subject. In precognitive dreams, at the time of dreaming the predicted event has not yet happened, but in dream telepathy information that already exists in only one person's mind is communicated to a dreamer.

Dream telepathy seems to be a widespread phenomenon. Most of us, including sceptics of the paranormal, know someone who has had a telepathic experience. One of the most fascinating and comprehensive collections of corroborated material on the subject was obtained in the last century by Gurney, Myers and Podmore in their *Phantasms of the Living*.

We have such cases in our own files. Unpleasant circumstances affecting the sender can be reflected in a warning dream experienced by the receiver. For example:

> *I've had dreams before that relate to things that will happen or are happening at that moment. One I had recently was a dream in which my sister, who is in Australia, had collapsed on the floor in her home. I was concerned and rang her in the morning. It was amazing. She said she had indeed fallen from a ladder while painting a ceiling and had lain there for quite a while in pain. We worked out that the dream and the accident did in fact correspond in time.*

The following is an interesting variation of dream telepathy because the dreamer manipulated a lucid dream in order to obtain information telepathically:

I was in a vivid dream and some inconsistency made me realize that I was dreaming. Suddenly I had full, insightful awareness of the situation – that I had become lucid and all the dream scenery was in fact fake. I decided to try an experiment. I saw a telephone, so I dialled a doctor friend of mine who was in India. He told me he had been very ill with a fever and gave specific details of the illness. On his return, all the information he gave proved to be correct. He was indeed dangerously ill at the time when I had my dream.

Sometimes receivers seem to be warned of events, such as crimes, that are happening elsewhere and concern them in some way. They may be picking up the ill will in the minds of the miscreants. For instance:

I woke from a dream in which I clearly saw some burglars at my shop. The shop had always been safe, so the thought of a burglary was certainly not on my mind. I couldn't go back to sleep because the dream had been so vivid and unusual. Eventually, I decided to get in the car and go and look. Imagine my surprise when I got there and found that the shop had indeed been robbed.

Telepathic dreams are not necessarily about important events. The following case simply concerns the arrival of some photos. It is classed as telepathic because, although the dreamer had not yet seen the pictures, information about them may have been in someone else's mind at the time:

I was asleep and being shown some photographs by a young man. He was saying, 'This is so and so,' etc. When I woke in the morning, the postman had left a packet for me. Inside were photographs from a recently discovered cousin of mine. The first photo I looked at was unmistakably of the young man in my dream. He was my maternal grandfather's first cousin, and I had no idea until I received his

*photograph that morning what he looked like. I did not know the
photographs were being sent.*

In addition to such anecdotal accounts, some research into telepathy has been carried out in this century by a few brave and open-minded scientists. In the USA, J.B. Rhine pioneered the study of telepathy using card-guessing techniques. These experiments were refined over the years, providing strong statistical evidence in support of the existence of telepathy.

The dream state is reputed to be particularly conducive to telepathic communication and some interesting laboratory experiments have been conducted to test this possibility. Various studies were undertaken by Ullman and Krippner in the 1970s at the Maimonides Laboratory in New York.

In one of the several successful studies they carried out, eight pairs of senders and receivers were used. The receiver slept in a sleep laboratory. When the receiver was dreaming, the sender, who was over 22 kilometres (14 miles) away, was placed in a sensory bombardment chamber. The sender was exposed to strong visual and auditory stimulation in the form of slides and recordings of music and effects corresponding to a randomly chosen theme, such as space flight, from a pool of six themes.

The sleeping receiver was woken at the end of the dream period and asked to report any dreams. Judges later linked the themes to the dream transcripts. The results were highly significant statistically and would have been achieved only once in 250 such experiments by chance alone.

With regard to analysis, telepathic dreams are complex and difficult to classify. A person may dream of an event at the precise time it is happening. Usually the reported incidents are major and involve other people; disasters are not uncommon. In these cases, the dreamer may wake up experiencing strong emotions.

As telepathy requires a sender and a receiver, it seems reasonable to assume that in a heightened state of emotion, during a disaster, for instance, a person might transmit telepathic signals, perhaps of distress. Under these circumstances, the dreamer might act as a television set, receiving the signal and witnessing the sights and sounds of the event. (Bear in mind that the other senses, smell, touch and taste, may also be stimulated.) Some people are very moved when they witness tragic scenes on television, such as those of refugees in war-ravaged countries. Telepathic dreams may have a similar effect, especially as they are often accompanied by powerful emotions. Although the dream may not be remembered, the recipient might awaken feeling shaken and distressed and decide that some positive action about an important issue must be taken.

One of the strangest forms of telepathy occurs when two people share the same dream. Many such cases have been reported and David Melbourne has personal experience of this phenomenon:

Over the years, my wife, Chris, has grown accustomed to some of my more eccentric behaviour, which includes scenting the bedroom with various essential oils to find out which ones produce the most vivid dreams for me. There is also my peculiar breathing when I meditate during hypnagogic imagery, sometimes for hours, switching the bedside lamp on and off several times in the middle of the night, as I establish whether I am experiencing a false awakening or not. In addition, there are occasions when I leap out of bed and rush to my office to check something out with Dr Hearne's findings, or frantically scribble down as much of a dream as I can remember.

She is a very patient lady. She sits up in bed and gazes back at me sleepy-eyed as I relate my dreams to her – one of the penalties of being married to an obsessive dream researcher, I suppose.

Nevertheless, during October, 1981, it was just such an occasion which led us to an astounding discovery. As I ramblingly described one of my dreams, I noticed Chris suddenly became wide awake. 'That's impossible!' she gasped. 'That's exactly what I was dreaming.'

Soon we were excitedly swapping notes, each anticipating what the other was going to say next about the contents of the dream. To say that I was overjoyed at this discovery would be an understatement. Chris, too, seemed enthusiastic. Since then, we have shared the same dreams on several occasions and are still just as amazed each time it happens.

Unfortunately, there is no way of knowing how or why this occurs. Indeed, at the time of writing, we still have not established which of us is transmitting and which receiving.

It is possible that shared telepathic dreams take place far more frequently than researchers realize. Many people do not discuss their dreams. However, if everybody achieved good dream recall, then related most of their dreams to their partner and/or friends, it might turn out that this phenomenon is fairly widespread.

~14~
Nightmares

REM NIGHTMARES

THESE ARE what we typically understand as nightmares. They are vivid, visual dreams where there is a story and a progression of events which builds up to a massively frightening finale. The dreamer wakes up shaking in a state of extreme terror, sweating profusely, with racing heartbeat and extreme mental agitation.

Ninety-six per cent of nightmares are of this type. If the individual is wired up in a sleep laboratory, the gradual increase in stress is monitored over several minutes. The breathing rate begins to soar from, say, ten breaths a minute to thirty or more a minute. The subject does not toss and turn because of the bodily paralysis characteristic of REM sleep, although the sufferer may, in the dream, be running and fighting desperately to avoid the clasps of an alien monster, for example. The dreamer may be screaming hysterically, but again the natural paralysis of the state inhibits vocalizations. A blood-chilling scream may be emitted at the moment of waking as muscule control is re-established.

Here are two examples from Dr Hearne's files. The first is from a woman who has between one and three nightmares a week; 75 per cent are on a recurring theme:

I am in a house. There is a room that I know contains something terrible. The room is always at the top of a flight of stairs, on the right. The stairs are narrow, steep, dark and musty. I have to go past this room, and always find myself having to go in. On one occasion the room tricked me into thinking it was another room and

when I went in it changed into the room I fear. The atmosphere in
the room is always intense and frightening and sometimes stays
with me all day after waking. I always know that I'm dreaming,
but I can't wake myself up. The dream is very vivid and I can
remember the details and colours easily. I have had the dream since
I was about four years old.

This person sometimes has several nightmares in a night:

I always wake up screaming, petrified and very often crying. My
husband can usually hear me building up to a scream and gently
tries to wake me before I reach screaming point. I think I am
usually running away from someone or something, or trying to
catch someone or something. I sometimes call out for my mother or
husband but usually let out blood-curdling screams. I remember
recently dreaming that my husband and I were about to be stabbed.
In my most recent nightmare I woke up screaming when a large
stone fountain sprayed liquid chocolate at me.

As part of his research into nightmares, Dr Hearne looked at the
frequency of different themes. The eight most common were, in
descending order:

- Witnessing horror or violence
- Experiencing attack or danger
- Flight from someone or something
- A sinister presence
- Being late and frustrated in travel
- Suffocation
- Seeing nightmare creatures
- Feeling paralysed

Contrary to what might be expected, the most frequent category
of nightmare is where one is observing nasty things happening to
others.

The sense of being tied down or unable to move – sleep paralysis or night nurse's paralysis – was described in Chapter 6. The way to deal with it is not to fight, but simply to relax. The experience will then drift into an ordinary dream and the paralysis will disappear quite spontaneously on waking.

As mentioned earlier, REM nightmares can also be produced as the result of withdrawal from certain drugs. REM-rebound tends to produce intense nightmares. The DTs (delirium tremens) of alcoholics are caused by a similar process.

SWS Nightmares

About four in a hundred nightmare experiences are 'night terrors' occurring in SWS. They are different from nightmare dreams in that, whereas the emotional distress in REM nightmares escalates over several minutes, night terrors kick in instantly, with no prior warning, in SWS.

This condition may sometimes be observed in children. The child may wake up screaming and run about in a state of distress. In the morning, though, the child usually has no memory of the episode. Taking the child to a doctor only causes confusion and worry.

Dr Hearne monitored one case of night terrors in the sleep laboratory at Liverpool University. The subject was a 19-year-old female student. Dr Hearne was in the control room and an hour after she had fallen asleep noted from the polygraphic recorder that she was in deep (Stage 4) SWS. All her physiological measures were normal. An intercom amplifier from the bedroom was switched on to monitor sleep-talking and teeth-grinding.

Suddenly, there was a very loud scream, amplified several times by the intercom system. All the lines on the polygraph chart were flat. Dr Hearne dashed into the bedroom and discovered that the subject had leaped out of bed, in so doing somehow pulling off all the electrodes from her body. She was very frightened but could give no coherent account of any nightmare.

After five minutes or so she was calmer. Dr Hearne reattached the electrodes and resumed the experiment. In the morning the girl had no memory whatsoever of the incident.

In SWS people have muscular control and can therefore act out their bad dreams. These may have some visual content, but generally the situation is not typically dream-like.

Some night terror sufferers imagine they are back in a situation that was traumatic for them at the time, such as a war event. A man might be found kneeling on his bed, petrified, saying that there are mines all around. In his dream, he was reliving a wartime experience.

Some people imagine that their sleeping partner is someone who wishes to hurt or destroy them and react violently. In one case, the husband and wife could no longer sleep together because the man frequently attacked his wife thinking she was an enemy. The treatment involved hypnotherapy, which can be very effective with sleep problems. The husband was instructed, under hypnosis, that as soon as he felt rage building up in him, he would instantly recognize it as a cue to relax. This worked immediately.

CAUSES AND CURES

What sort of people have nightmares? Intrigued by this question, Dr Hearne administered Cattell and Eber's personality test to 39 nightmare sufferers. The test produced a personality profile for the average nightmare sufferer, who was discovered to be emotional, apprehensive, tense, undisciplined and self-sufficient. A little over half of the subjects tested thought that their nightmares had begun as the result of a trauma.

We are all different physically and psychologically. The same trauma – a rape, say – will cause nightmares in one woman but not in another. Our basic sensitivity to events dictates how we respond to them. Nightmare sufferers appear to be more vulnerable to psychological damage than other people.

Most REM sleep is present in the second half of the night. This is also when most dreams, including lucid dreams, occur. Yet most nightmares reportedly happen in the first half of the night. This is strongly anomalous and suggests that psychological factors do not cause nightmares. Surely the rich variety of dream images in REM sleep would randomly touch upon frightening themes if psychological factors were responsible.

On the other hand, stress may cause nightmares early in the night and the resulting reduction in tension may ensure that no further bad dreams are experienced that night. However, if tension-reduction, i.e. the venting of pent-up emotion, were the principle behind REM nightmares, they would be very emotional at first and then decline in intensity. Quite the opposite is reported by sufferers and shown by polygraphic studies.

This is a possible explanation: nightmare sufferers tend to be nervous people and, in sleep, their nervousness persists for a few hours (and may actually increase for a while), but gradually their arousal thresholds rise and they become less anticipatory. It is known that sudden noises, such as electrical equipment or heating systems switching on, can trigger SWS nightmares (wearing ear plugs can therefore alleviate them) and it may be that external or internal stimuli can trigger a general alarm signal which may escalate into a full-blown nightmare. The nightmare may be a conditioned response, a learned habit.

Studies have shown that the therapeutic technique of behaviour modification can deal with nightmares. Using 'unlearning', for instance, the subject replays the nightmare in a therapy session, but associates it with feelings of relaxation. Dr Hearne believes that it is not necessary to look for any deep psychological causes for nightmares. It is the person's basic nature rather than their memories that is significant.

Some nervous people often dream of being attacked by intruders. In these cases, simply putting a lock on the bedroom door considerably alleviates their fear and reduces their nightmares.

How can REM nightmares be stopped? One method developed by Dr Hearne is based on converting nightmares into lucid dreams, in which the dreamer becomes aware that they are dreaming and can then alter the dream scenery.

The technique came about as a result of a letter he received after he had been talking about lucid dreaming on the radio. A woman wrote to him saying that she had had a recurring nightmare every night for years. In the dream she went downstairs and discovered a coffin with her husband in it. A sequence of nasty events then ensued. The woman said that the last time the dream happened, she suddenly remembered – in the dream – that Dr Hearne had said that dream images can be controlled. She simply willed the nightmare to turn into a pleasant lucid dream, and it worked.

In fact, nightmare sufferers have a great advantage over others in the development of dream lucidity. The onset of the nightmare acts as a cue that one is dreaming. Nightmares are nearly always preceded by some recognition (a thought, feeling or both), of what is about to happen. At this point the dreamer should stop thinking, for example, 'Oh my God, here's the nightmare!' and say, 'Great, wonderful – here's the nightmare. That means I'm dreaming, and I can control my dreams.'

If you have nightmares about being chased, try turning to your pursuer, pointing your fingers at them and sending imaginary laser beams at them from your fingers. Your foe will be vanquished and you can then change your dream location. Try the method of covering your eyes in the dream and willing yourself to somewhere like a desert island.

This is informational therapy. It involves no drugs, no expensive therapy sessions. People can stop nightmares by reprogramming themselves, just as sleep-paralysis victims can change their mind-set and, instead of fighting the feeling of being bound, simply relax and accept it.

Helpful Nightmares

Dr Hearne believes that the subconscious mind probably tries to assist, protect and guard us. The function of some nightmares – usually short ones – is to wake the dreamer. This can be for a specific purpose (like catching a train) or to draw their attention to something significant that happened in the dream shortly before it became nightmarish.

When Dr Hearne had to get up early to go and give a lecture, he would sometimes decide to have just a little more sleep before rising. In such situations his subconscious would wake him up with a short, frightening dream if the additional sleep period went on for too long.

For example, he was once having a pleasant little dream when suddenly, and for no apparent reason, he dreamed he saw a man fall off a building, hitting the ground heavily. Dr Hearne was jolted into wakefulness, just in time to rush off to his lecture at the university.

In the experience of David Melbourne, nightmares are usually powerful message-bearers and demand to be interpreted. Surprisingly, they often translate into a pleasant message. However, they can also alert us to some danger in the workplace, warn of unpleasantness ahead, point to the darker side of our character, open up old wounds, etc. Invariably, there is a reason behind the nightmare.

For example, a butcher once reported waking up frightened after dreaming that his fingers had been severed by a bacon slicer. Some weeks later, he noticed that the bacon slicer in his shop sounded different. Remembering the dream, he took particular care to check out the machine and discovered a potentially dangerous fault. This indicates that nightmares can also be precognitive.

In one of David Melbourne's own nightmares, his shadow, sitting next to him in the passenger seat of a car, continually tried to poke out his eyes. The interpretation warned him that in waking life, he hadn't seen that he was driving somebody too hard.

Nightmares often open up old wounds. When a dream relates to a painful experience in the past, there are clear reasons for this. It might be that something untoward occurred some years ago and the subconscious has identified a similar threat looming on the horizon.

CHILDHOOD ABUSE

The most common nightmare of recent times relates to some form of abuse in childhood, physical, mental or sexual. Most abused clients who write to David Melbourne even though they have not positively identified the implication behind their dreams, stress that they desire strict confidentiality. The fact that they tend to labour this point when they first make contact suggests that they suspect their nightmares are caused by childhood abuse.

Another common factor is that most of them have managed to bury their past and get on with their lives in their own way. However, the amount of publicity afforded to abuse nowadays seldom allows such people to forget; television and radio reports and articles in newspapers and magazines concerning child abuse abound. As a result, spectres from the past are continually being resurrected and manifest themselves as nightmares.

It must be stressed that sexual abuse is not necessarily the over-riding factor. Nevertheless, the word 'abuse', currently so frequently used, is assumed by some people (erroneously) to refer mainly to sexual abuse. This idea can lead them to search their past lives for evidence of such abuse and mistakenly conclude they have suffered from it.

The sexual angle apart, it depends to some degree on what each individual regards as abuse. For instance, somebody might have childhood memories of continually going out into the cold to fill the coal-scuttle; looking back, such a task may well constitute abuse to that person. There does appear, however, to be a link between the increased number of letters about dreams with an element of abuse and the amount of media coverage about abuse in childhood.

These dreams can come in many forms. The following examples (of the commonest types) must not be regarded as the only possible interpretations. These dreams include: being in a hospital environment, sometimes filthy, where there is a great deal of blood and disease; witnessing people being operated on without anaesthetic; being forced to perform such surgery; seeing dismembered corpses, in a morgue, for example; being compelled to clean up pieces of flesh; watching people being dismembered; faeces strewn about, sometimes where people might unwittingly come into contact with them; being covered in faeces or sprayed with urine; being locked in confined spaces where there is an overpowering sense of danger, or with venomous snakes, or where one is cursed and spat at by other people.

Other common themes which often crop up in connection

with abuse are pets, toys, playrooms and anything connected with childhood that the client can recall fondly. It is quite common, for example, to dream of a once cherished cat, dog, rabbit or hamster. The dream often follows a pleasant sequence of events, then suddenly the dreamer notices that their beloved pet is beginning to suffer.

It is the way in which the animal suffers that transforms the dream into a nightmare. It may develop a visible cancer, which spreads rapidly across its body until only a small area remains free from contamination. Maggots, boils, open sores or bleeding may feature.

Toys and inanimate objects in nightmares are invariably associated with a pleasurable childhood memory, but become damaged. In a playroom, the wallpaper may fall from the walls, revealing an ugly type of rot spreading underneath. A favourite toy might become broken or twisted or start to rot.

Let us consider the hypothetical case of a person who, as a child, was very fond of a rocking horse. The rocking horse might symbolize the person's innocence as a child. In nightmares, it could sprout thorns over its entire body, thereby destroying this innocence.

Pets rarely seem to die in nightmares, but often hover on the edge of death, which may symbolize the death or loss of innocence, possibly through mental, physical or sexual abuse. The animal's survival often represents the dreamer surviving the abusive experience, albeit feeling tainted, cheated or soiled in some way.

To illustrate the point that we must never believe that a specific type of dream can have only one meaning, let us return to the dream image of the rocking horse. If a jockey, show-jumper, or indeed anybody with something to do with horses, had the a nightmare about a rocking horse, their dream might easily conceal a quite different meaning. Similarly, if a theatre nurse or a mortician has a nightmare about a dead body, for obvious reasons, the dream might have an entirely different meaning, just as somebody suffering from a bowel disorder might dream of faeces.

Most dream symbols do not have a universal meaning, and it must be stressed that if a person dreams of any of the above images, it would be wrong to insist that some sort of abuse is signified. Each dream has to be viewed in great detail and in its entirety, taking into account the dreamer's background, before any interpretation can be attempted.

Much can be done to banish the terror of recurring nightmares. Many sufferers endure nightmares every night without realizing that, by following a few simple procedures, a cure can often be effected. David Melbourne's techniques involve tackling each problem on several fronts, and rely partly on the willingness of the subjects to confront their pain.

Living on the remote Scottish island of Hoy, he rarely has the opportunity to meet his clients personally, and advises them by post. Some people write back with letters of thanks, saying that the frequency of their nightmares has decreased and in some cases they have completely stopped. Writing down a nightmare may somehow exorcise them. In fact, it appears that merely seeking advice and sharing one's fears can bring about a dramatic reduction in the number of one's nightmares.

Although it can be painful to write down the contents of such dreams, it is necessary for two reasons: first, it compels the subject to confront the pain (confrontation is often a good way to begin the healing process); second, as the nightmares reduce in frequency, a common theme or root cause can more readily be identified and isolated in the subject's remaining nightmares.

When dealing with clients who suffer nightmares on a nightly basis – sometimes several times a night – David can almost guarantee to reduce the frequency of the experience immediately. This led him to the realization that people who frequently suffer from bad dreams do so because they are anxious about recurring nightmares. These can be self-perpetuating. In other words, the more you worry about nightmares, the more likely they are to occur.

Therefore, the first step is to advise the client how to get a good night's sleep and to point out that anxiety about recurring nightmares is probably one of the causes for their frequency. Then it is explained how lucid dreaming can be used to neutralize a bad dream. The client should also be told how to implant positive suggestions during the hypnagogic state. It is important that they keep written accounts of their dreams so that an analysis can be carried out.

When clients share a closely guarded secret of childhood abuse with somebody impartial, their nightmares often cease. Sometimes it transpires that they have gone through life feeling cheated, or in some cases, unclean – even partly responsible for the abuse. Once their secret is understood and they are convinced that they were neither sullied by the abuse nor responsible for it, the nightmares generally stop completely.

A similar process occurs with nightmares that are not related to abuse. Once the root cause is identified, shared and discussed, the bad dreams tend to disappear.

When a person suffers from recurring nightmares, it must be established whether or not they are is taking any medication, for depression, nervous complaints or insomnia, for example. As has already been observed, drugs may cause REM-rebound, which can result in frequent nightmares. The subject may then be locked into a vicious circle that is difficult to break. The more nightmares they suffer, the more drugs they take. More drugs often lead to more nightmares.

Under these circumstances, therapy will have only a marginal effect. Unless such subjects consult a doctor, begin to decrease their drug dosage and commit themselves to eventually coming off the drug altogether, their battle against nightmares cannot be won.

Children quite often have recurring nightmares. In these cases, when the children are settling down to sleep (i.e. entering the hypnagogic state), a parent should suggest that if they have a bad dream, they should bring Mummy, Daddy or both into the dream. Once in the dream, their parent(s) will deal with the problem and make it go away, so that it never comes back again. Children usually respond very well to this treatment.

Mrs B's Dream

To illustrate how effective interpretive therapy can be, in the following case a recurring nightmare was analysed, the root cause was isolated and made known to the sufferer and the result was an instant cure. One year later, the client reports that she has not been bothered by bad dreams since.

At the time, Mrs B, from South Yorkshire, reported that this nightmare continually troubled her and always left her feeling very frightened upon waking. In her dream, Mrs B found herself in a large, dark room, in the company of two men. One was smartly dressed, and although she sensed the presence of the other, she was unable to see or identify him.

She was discussing with them something very unpleasant that had been happening outside at night. The man whom she could see got up and announced that he was going home. However, instead of going outside, he walked across the room, descended some steps and opened the door of a cellar. She called out to ask if he was all right. He told her that he was. She then indicated to the unseen man that she suspected that the man in the suit was responsible for the unpleasant occurrences.

Upon entering the secluded cellar, the man had left the door ajar, so that Mrs B could see inside. Peering in, she saw a white sheet covering a single bed on which there was a blue pillowslip. The man then put on a body-suit with a broad leather strap running round the neck; attached to it was a heavy tethering chain. Then he clothed himself in a very large single boot which had an enormous buckle. Finally, overcoming these restrictions, he left through another door and ended up in the open air. At this point, Mrs B would always wake up feeling very scared.

This is the interpretation given to Mrs B, which she acknowledged to be accurate, and which enabled her to identify the root cause, thus putting an end to her nightmares:

> Your dream is very interesting indeed. Although it contained elements which frighten you – often this is the only way our subconscious can draw our attention to a problem – there is no need to be pessimistic. It carries a positive message and is showing you a way to overcome a difficult situation in your life.
>
> Sometimes when we dream of other people, they appear as

and a represention of themselves. However, there is a clue in your dream which suggests this is not the case here. All men have a feminine side to their nature and all women a masculine side. The fact that you could not see one of the people in your dream, yet were aware of his presence, indicates that he is your alter ego. This suggests that the man in the suit represents the masculine side of your nature.

You were in a big dark room (a problem in your life which you are unable readily to identify). You were talking about something disagreeable that had been happening (the problem again). These unpleasant incidents had been happening outside at night (a state of darkness reinforces the idea that you have not fully recognized the problem yet). The scene is set. So far, the dream is telling us that you are troubled by a problem in life with which you have not come to terms.

The man who is smartly dressed is telling us that the masculine side of your character is clever (smart). He says that he is going home (in this instance, home represents security). In other words, he is pointing the way to a situation with which you feel comfortable. Yet he goes down steps into a cellar. This indicates that, although you feel used to a situation, subconsciously, you know it is dragging you down; you will have to take this less savoury route before finally getting home.

You tell the other person that you think it is this man who is doing the unpleasant things (the masculine, smart side is causing your problems). You ask if he is all right (you are concerned as to whether this side of your character knows what it is doing). He answers in the affirmative, indicating that your masculine side is indeed competent.

The door being left ajar, allowing you to see inside, represents the opportunity for you to open your mind and comprehend the problem. It would seem that the bed represents your situation, because the man is not lying on it. There is a white sheet (representing purity or, in this case, honest endeavours) and a blue pillowslip (a pillow is where you lay your head); in this instance, blue represents smart thinking. So the practical side of your nature knows how you can get out of your problem.

However, you feel that if you follow logic (the man you can see), you will be dragging your feet (the huge boot). In this case, the large buckle represents a burden. You also feel that, by taking this route, you will be tied down or tethered to the situation, (the body-suit, leather strap and chain).

The man then gets up, goes out of another door and is outside (away from the problem). By persisting with the situation, your masculine side finds a way out of your dilemma.

Let us summarize the dream. You are in a situation in life where you feel tethered in a rut, or tied down. The temptation is to act now, and possibly in a rash manner, by taking a snap decision, but the dream is telling you that you would do better to listen to your inner voice and be guided by logic, even though you suspect that acting sensibly has led you into this situation in the first place. In other words, follow the path you know to be correct, despite the fact that, initially, you will feel even more entrenched in the rut. With patience and persistence, you will eventually overcome and distance yourself from the problem.

There is nothing in your dream to indicate that your problem is an affair of the heart. Having said that, it could point to a situation where you are looking after somebody else's welfare and feel trapped. The dream suggests that it has something to do with a situation in your life which you consider to be static.

Mrs B replied:

Thank you very much for interpreting my bad dream for me. I understood the interpretation very clearly. You summarized the dream so well, it was easy to identify the problem and put it right. I am no longer troubled by it. Thank you for what you did for me.

~15~
Teri King's Dream Interpreted

THE DREAM ANALYSED in this chapter was provided by Teri King, who is a writer, television personality and lecturer on astrology. The dream is packed full of symbols and would make a marvellous setting for a fantasy novel. The creative power of the unconscious mind, capable of generating any event in any number of settings, may well be limitless. Most of us occasionally experience vivid dreams, but Teri has them most of the time. Such astonishing imagery can be very enjoyable. Unfortunately, however, it can also be disconcerting (as in this case) or even terrifying.

Dreams as vivid as this example bring a message from the unconscious to the conscious mind. Usually, the unconscious achieves this by means of seemingly bizarre dream imagery, although the analysis often produces a reasonably clear message.

The route towards finding the meaning of Teri's dream was very long and far from straightforward. At first, it led in several directions; only after a lot of thorough checking and cross-referencing was the significance revealed. Nevertheless, every message-bearing dream, bizarre or not, can be interpreted. In this instance the interpretation proved to be a particularly enthralling exercise.

TERI KING'S DREAM

I was in a vast dream scene, which was not of this world. It was so huge that it didn't seem to have parameters. Resembling dinosaurs, there were all sorts of prehistoric animals flying about, some of which looked as if they were far too big and heavy to fly. They had scaly skin and were brightly coloured: yellow, green and purple. It felt as if I was flying on one of them, although I didn't actually see it. The animals were fighting each other, and we were flying over a vast canyon filled with a sea of purple, above which was a green sky. I wasn't involved, but viewing everything from a position which was high above it all. It was quite frightening.

THE INTERPRETATION

Knowing that you are an accomplished astrologer helped enormously to untangle what would otherwise have been an extremely complicated dream to analyse. We start with the dream setting: an alien world. Apart from the links with spacemen, rockets, science fiction and the like, there is a more obvious direction for us to follow, namely, space, planets, stars and astrology. This dream has a direct link with your astrological career.

The fact that the dream scenery was so vast – without parameters – reflects the size of the potential market for this hugely popular subject. You seemed to concentrate on a canyon filled with a sea of purple. In this case, the canyon represents a hazard, into which the battling dinosaurs could fall. This is corroborated by the purple sea. The colour purple is a mixture of red and blue, and can have many symbolic meanings. In this case, however, it represents financial failure for anything which might plunge into its depths.

The larger dinosaurs represent the various businesses which encompass astrology, among other things: newspapers, magazines, television and so forth. Although they appeared to be too big and heavy to fly, they were flying (they were staying aloft financially).

Some of the smaller dinosaurs represent your fellow astrologers. The fact that they were fighting one another signifies the very competitive market they are in; the purple sea is always waiting beneath.

The fact that the dinosaurs were different colours is also significant. Although yellow is suggestive of gold, it can also symbolize faithlessness, betrayal and sometimes cowardice – regrettably, traits which are all too easy to find in the world of competitive business. In this instance, a green dinosaur represents growth and a purple one a combination of power (red) and wisdom (blue). Their scaly skin points to resilience and a constant weighing-up of the market.

In this case, the sky represents attainment. However, it is green, and green can indicate many different things. According to David Fontana's book, *The Secret Language of Symbols*, the Celts used to believe that there was a blessed island, hovering above a green sky, where souls went after death. As stated earlier, green can sometimes indicate growth, but it may also signify decay. Jealousy is associated with the colour green, too. Here it symbolizes natural sensations and nature itself.

Your dream is clearly pointing out that you have achieved a high level of success through a natural approach. You have a unique way of communicating the message you want to put across. Therefore, a large part of your success is directly attributable to the individual manner in which you do things and to your natural personality.

The animal you feel you are flying on represents your main business interest (you are unable to see it because you are so closely involved with it). The fact that it is with you, high above the turmoil below, indicates that you are good for each other, regardless of whether or not you think you are ideally suited. Through your natural approach and the company's willingness to go along with it, you have both improved your status and attained a higher level of achievement (rising above the dinosaurs below).

Finally, you found the dream quite frightening. First, this is an indication that your unconscious mind wanted to bring the dream to your attention. Second, your emotional state is pertinent to the entire dream's interpretation.

The dream is telling you that you have climbed to the top of your profession, largely through your unique approach. It is also reminding you that it is a hugely competitive market, not always easy to survive in. However, you are already aware of this and the dream shows that, in consequence, you are not complacent. Your unconscious is not giving you a pat on the back, but alerting you to something else.

It would seem that at the time of the dream, you had certain concerns about your position and particularly about your approach to your work. Perhaps you were having second thoughts about how to tackle a new challenge. This brings us to the main thrust of the analysis. The dream contains the clear message that, in order to remain at the top (dispassionately viewing the dinosaurs below), you must continue with your winning formula. Stick with your natural instincts and unique way of putting your point across. To a significant extent, these have been, and will remain, your key to success. If you start to slip, or compromise your individuality, you will be drawn back into the fray which you have surmounted.

When Teri King read this interpretation of her dream, she commented that it made a lot of sense. She had indeed gone through a time when she had thought of taking a different tack. She emphasized that often her dreams are colourful and frightening. 'So much so, that at one point, I thought I was going off my trolley,' she joked. She added that she was relieved to receive the interpretation, which had helped to put her mind at rest.

You will notice that Teri's description of her dream is about the same length as others in the book. It did, however, contain more symbols than usual. Apart from Teri's flight above the fighting dinosaurs, there was no action. When this happens, the analyst's task is a difficult one. It became obvious from the outset that Teri's dream was going to be a challenge to interpret.

This illustrates the importance it is of knowing a few facts about the person whose dream is to be analysed. For example, suppose Teri had not been a famous astrologer, but an actress. The interpretation might have been totally different. The alien environment might have indicated a set in a science fiction film, for example, and the colour of the sea and sky may have had other connotations. If she had been a vet or an athlete, what would we make of the prehistoric animals? The analyst must have some prior knowledge of the subject and make full use of it.

Although dream messages can show themselves in convoluted ways, you should first look for the obvious. The unconscious is trying to communicate a message to the conscious mind, so ask why should it want to do this in such a complicated fashion. Nine times out of ten, if you look for the obvious interpretation and keep on looking, it will stand out. Only after it appears that the meaning might be hidden should even more complicated detective work be undertaken. The golden rule is: keep things simple.

It takes quite a time to interpret a dream to the point where there is a strong sense of insight and completion about the task. The effort is worthwhile, though, and is far superior to rough and generally unsatisfactory attempts to glean a meaning using dream dictionaries. The procedure requires patience and a genuinely open mind so as not to impose a particular analysis on the material that is presented. It is a problem-solving exercise, using information that needs to be viewed intelligently with much lateral thinking.

In Teri's dream account, the words 'not of this world', are an extremely strong clue, bearing in mind her work and interests, that the theme concerns astrology in some way. Always study, very carefully, the wording of the dream report. Read the account through several times as a first step to understanding how various aspects of the dream were experienced by the dreamer, but also read it almost as a proofreader would and examine individual words and phrases for clues. Remember, the whole basis of the dream may have been a simple phrase which crop up in the account in a straightforward and innocent way.

Explore the dream account for puns and double meanings. Everything described or mentioned by the dreamer is important. Teri took particular notice of the scaly skin of the creatures in her dream; therefore the word 'scales' seems to be significant, and of course it has more than one meaning. This is how the interpretation needs to progress.

People who are doing well in their job often have a consistent dream image of themselves as high-flying planes or rockets zooming into the sky. The high vantage-point of such dreamers would seem to refer to their successful status.

Clearly, too, the unusual colours in Teri's dream were significant features and the possible meanings of the particular colours had to be worked out.

Teri's dream did not have a long plot and complicated developments. Instead, it was an observational type of dream that concerned a situation she was in and caused an emotional response in her.

~16~
Linda O'Byrne's Dream Interpreted

LINDA O'BYRNE, the fiction editor of the highly popular women's magazine, *Bella*, described several short dreams, each involving the same empty house. It was decided to select the salient features from each, knit them together and analyse the result as a single dream.

LINDA O'BYRNE'S DREAM

I am visiting an empty house, one which I have dreamed about many times before. It is large and I have concentrated on different rooms in different dreams.

I am trying to decide whether to buy it or not. There are two very small rooms at the back, with no view, and a larger room at the front which looks out onto a high grassy mound. On the other side of the mound is a river, but I am unable to see it. I know that if I buy a house further down the road, I won't have the mound in front of it and I will be able to see the river. I never go to look at the other house, but just wander between the rooms, wondering what to do. I am not alone, but can't say who is with me. There is a section downstairs which is shut off from the main part of the house and which I keep forgetting about. I am in the kitchen watching my partner breaking down the back wall to make it bigger. I am not particularly worried by this, just watching.

THE INTERPRETATION

We know the house, with its many rooms, is not your real
home and the fact that it continually appears in different
dreams signifies that it is symbolic of your position in life at
the moment the dream occurs. This is corroborated by the
fact that you are not alone but cannot say who is with you (it
is your alter ego). Each room represents a different facet of
your life and the distinct rooms indicate that you have a tidy
mind: you compartmentalize individual aspects of your life.

The fact that you are considering whether or not to buy the
house indicates that you feel torn between maintaining the
status quo and pursuing an alternative. The room you
concentrate on most within the dream reflects the part of
your life you are concerned about at the time.

You have focused on different rooms in different dreams.
In this context, a kitchen symbolizes the home, a bedroom,
affairs of the heart, a living-room, general finances, a dining-
room, all matters relating to yourself (health, personal
finances, fashion, etc), a study denotes work and so on.

The two small rooms at the back without a view represent
two nagging problems about which you are undecided. The
rooms downstairs which are shut off, and which you keep
forgetting about, indicate past problems which you would
rather forget.

In this instance, the grassy mound represents financial
security (grass being the basic food of life), and the river on
the far side is indicative of the encroachment of others (a
possible drain on your resources).

Your partner breaking down the back wall in the kitchen
suggests the revelation of a different outlook concerning
matters of the home. However, it doesn't seem particularly
important (you were not worried, but just watching).

The house down the road represents another way of life
which you have the option of taking. This would entail a
financial risk, in that there is no grassy mound there (nothing
to act as a buffer between you and the river). Nevertheless, it

is tempting (you wander backwards and forwards between all the rooms trying to decide what to do).

When Linda read this interpretation, she commented that it was extremely interesting and accurate, although she is not at all certain about the tidy mind, as she is an extremely untidy person in reality.

It is good practice in dream interpretation to work out first what is fairly straightforward, i.e. state the general message in non-specific terms, and then concentrate on the more difficult aspects within the picture as a whole. Thus, the overall story of this dream reflects the dreamer's thoughts about being in one situation or set of circumstances – as regards employment or the location of her home – compared to another.

Linda's reference to wandering around in the dream is probably a phonetic pun reflecting her 'wondering' about some matter. Here, the house in general could symbolize an actual house (the simplest idea should be examined first), or aspects of Linda.

Linda would like to be in a situation where she can see the river, which will have a specific meaning for her, but, where she is, there is a mound or mount (a verbal pun on the word 'amount'?). The mound probably represents financial commitments or financial security, which is very much a part of the picture for the dreamer. The situation is better 'further down the road', i.e. in the future, where there is no mound.

The emptiness of the house would indicate that a decision has yet to be made, or has been made recently, although Linda's partner is already keen to proceed.

Now let us interpret the same material using dream dictionaries. To begin with, one dictionary claims that if you dream of purchasing a house, you are likely to find yourself in money troubles and will have to sell your own property for a smaller, cheaper one. Others claim that you will enjoy financial security, a fortune, happiness, or that you can expect to be taken to court. Unfortunately, the closest match found to Linda's dream indicates that she should sell her house and buy a cheaper one because of financial problems.

There are a plethora of meanings attributed to rooms. However, the nearest that can be found to fit this dream is 'a room in a home', which apparently means poverty.

Next we have the grassy mound. The interpretations for grass are legion, from deceit, illness and poverty to the downfall of one's enemies, longevity, a joyful love life and good reputation. No mention is made of a grassy mound as such, so we must choose between two interpretations of the image of grass. One says that a woman who dreams of grass can expect a joyful love life. The other states that if a literary person dreams of grass, her reputation will remain intact. For the sake of argument, let us amalgamate the two.

Next, we have the river. There are pages and pages of different meanings attributed to rivers. However, one of the most pleasant indicates happiness within the home.

Then we have the other house down the road. Here, let us use the same interpretation as before: selling the house for a smaller one because of money trouble.

Nothing similar to sectioned-off rooms at the bottom of a house can be found. However, according to one dream dictionary, to dream of an empty cellar means riches. There is no mention of forgotten rooms. Nevertheless, to lose one's memory is a warning of impending dishonour.

Finally, we have the kitchen wall being knocked down. As expected, to come anywhere near Linda's dream description, this image must be treated in two parts. Thus we find someone who dreams of a kitchen can expect a visit from a family member. If they dream of a wall falling down, they can expect losses in business.

Let us reconstruct Linda's dream using dream dictionary meanings and see what we come up with. For a start, she will have money troubles, forcing the sale of a house for a smaller one, which ties in nicely with the poverty attributed to dreaming about rooms.

However, she will have a joyous love life and her reputation will remain firmly intact. This also ties in with the idea of happiness in the home. Therefore, although Linda will have money troubles to the extent that her house will have to be sold, the new, smaller one will be a happy little house and a good love nest.

Unfortunately, there is another house in the dream, so Linda's happy little love nest will have to go in favour of an even smaller one. Somehow this will bring riches, as indicated by the empty cellar, but these riches will somehow result in dishonour (the loss of memory).

No doubt it is the riches that will attract the visit from a family member, and this will somehow result in losses in business.

This represents a genuine attempt to reach a fair interpretation using dream dictionaries. As you can see, the result borders on the ridiculous.

~17~

Cash Peters'
Dream Interpreted

CASH PETERS, author of *The Telltale Alphabet*, supplied this dream. It is a lengthy dream, which at first glance looks as complicated as it was to analyse. It took approximately six hours to decode and further time to write up and check for accuracy.

Cash states that throughout this dream he had a great sense of mission, though without really grasping what the urgency or purpose was. In view of the interpretation, this makes perfect sense.

During the routine gathering of background information, Cash was asked if he regarded himself as an extrovert or introvert. He gave a very interesting answer which helped enormously in the interpretation of his dream. He said that he considered himself to be very much of an introvert at heart, but that all the years he has spent working in the media have helped him to graft on a convincing extrovert exterior. He added that nowadays it is hard to say which side of the fence he is on.

This piece of information proved to be extremely valuable. As the interpretation took shape, a clear picture started to develop which reinforced Cash's statement.

CASH PETERS' DREAM

It began in a street I did not recognize. Deciding to return home, I ascended into the sky and flew close to the roof-tops, as though it was

*a perfectly normal alternative to walking. I propelled myself
forward with a vigorous breast-stroke motion.*
*My 'home' was a couple of blocks away. It seemed to be
American-style and fairly old, with a wooden framework. Stepping
inside the front porch, I found a window slightly ajar owing to a
broken lock. Being small, square and overgrown with leaves outside,
it looked fairly inaccessible to any burglar. Nevertheless, I was
bothered and experimented with it for some time until, from out of
nowhere, I produced a bright metallic, golden-coloured contraption,
rather like a Heath Robinson corkscrew, which fitted precisely into a
hole in the window-lock and fastened the window tight shut.*
*Immediately, a close female friend – the co-author of my latest
book – drove up the driveway in a station-wagon. She is in her
sixties and seemed out of place at the wheel of such an enormous
vehicle. Round about the same time, I became aware that there was
a strange Eastern European man sitting in an armchair in my
front room watching television. He was overweight, with a beard,
and was in his shirt-sleeves. Though previously quite welcome, his
presence now seemed an inconvenience. I found him perturbing and
wanted to be rid of him, but he was firmly ensconced and unwilling
to budge.*
*Next, I was asleep. Suddenly, I woke up in the dark, concerned
that, although my female friend had been given a bed, another
friend – a man – had been neglected and made to improvise. I
pictured him fully clothed and uncomfortable, on the sofa without
sheets or pillows. There was no sign of the Eastern European
gentleman.*

THE INTERPRETATION

The street you did not recognize represents a new idea
(venture?) you have thought about. However, you decide to
return home (stay where you are). The fact that you elect to
fly signifies that, in waking life, you consider that you would
be tied down or somehow trapped or restrained if you were
to pursue this idea. It would require too much of a

commitment, perhaps. Incidentally, flight by means of the breast-stroke is fairly common in dreams.

A house or apartment can be a representation of the dreamer. In this case, your 'home', which seemed American-style and fairly old, with a wooden framework, symbolizes you. Now we see a picture of your subconscious beginning to develop. America is a relatively new country and therefore your house represents new thinking. However, it is fairly old, which indicates that you are blending new ideas with established thinking.

Stepping inside, you find a window slightly ajar owing to a broken lock. You go on to mention a concern about security. In other words, the window represents a small inconsistency in your ideas, vulnerable to invasion from outside (the burglar). Initially, it would appear that you are concerned about having some of your ideas stolen. However, that avenue of thought does not gel with the rest of the interpretation, so we have to follow another path.

Although you feel reasonably secure in your thoughts, some doubt remains. You are concerned that there is a small hole in your theories (an unanswered question, perhaps?).

You go on to say that you were 'bothered' and 'experimented with it' for a while. Then, out of nowhere, you produced a contraption which fitted and secured the window. This indicates that you have plucked some sort of golden answer out of the air which, although you don't fully understand how it works, seems to satisfy and seal the window of vulnerability. The spiral shape of the corkscrew is significant here: no matter what point you track it from, it will eventually lead to the same place.

Now we come to your close female friend, the co-author of your latest book. Here we are given a clue as to where the dream is leading. She is not a representation of herself, but of acquaintances within your profession (colleagues). She was enclosed within the security of the large station-wagon, indicating that they are sort of cocooned in their beliefs (the vehicle was surprisingly large and sturdy).

However, you become aware of a strange Eastern European man in your front room (the hub of your subconscious). This man is a representation of a part of your own character. He was watching television and therefore interested in an outside influence (the broadcast). This links nicely with the open window. Some sort of conflict could be indicated here between you and your colleagues, but the dream points in another direction.

The man had a beard and was in shirt-sleeves, which suggests a casual side of your character, perhaps the lazy side (which we all have). Now we are coming to the crux of the dream. You felt comfortable with this man until your friend turned up. This suggests that you feel the need to show a more professional side of yourself when colleagues are around. You wanted to be rid of him but he was ensconced; although you feel that the business approach is best, you cannot prevent your natural self from remaining just under the surface. You are sometimes torn between presenting a façade and being your natural self.

The dream begins to come together. Next, you were asleep, but wake up (in your dream). You are in the dark. This is a very illuminating statement, but let us proceed a little further. Although your female friend (your colleagues) has a bed (they are comfortable) – in other words, she is unaware of your struggle with your natural self – you are concerned about another man (the complete you). You picture him, fully clothed (ready to face the outside world), but he is uncomfortable, on the sofa without sheets and pillows (unhappy with the situation).

In short, this is a dream of divided loyalties, regarding not your friendly colleagues, but yourself. Your subconscious is trying to draw your attention, via the dream, to the fact that you need to respond in a more relaxed way in certain situations.

The message is clear. At the time of the dream, there was an alternative avenue of ideas you could pursue. However, you decided it would be too constraining and returned to

your usual mode of thinking, blending the new with the
established. However, there is a window or weak point on this
path (in your theory) which you have sealed with an
explanation that you do not fully understand. One side of you
advocates correctness, while the other insists on a more casual
approach. You were torn between the two. It would seem that
you are likely to find the permanent (real) answer by going
with the flow of your natural feelings, or following your
heart.

Cash Peters commented that, though not automatically opposed
to the idea of dream interpretation, he was slightly sceptical about
it and had always written off dreams as random flash-frames thrown
up by the subconscious as part of its job of assimilating the day's
events. For this reason, when he first read the interpretation of
his dream, he felt it was irrelevant and baffling. Later on, Cash reported:

> *However, after further study, hey presto! Everything fell into place
> and made perfect sense . . . there is an inevitable blurring in the
> analysis of what the problem actually is, but this is merely a matter
> of words and phrases. Once this interpretation is seen in the context
> of ongoing professional rivalry, it becomes an uncanny exposé of my
> darkest thoughts. I am astonished, not to say bowled over, by it.*

The characters in any fictional work, such as a novel, a play or
even a dream, very often portray, unwittingly, aspects of the person who created them. These separate features are unconsciously
projected on to the various participants and sometimes the traits
depicted are undesirable.

An unpleasant person seen in a dream who arouses feelings of an-
noyance and disturbance in the dreamer may represent part of the
dreamer's psychological make-up. In Cash's dream, therefore, the
large Eastern European man quite plausibly symbolized an indo-
lent side of his character.

The production of the golden corkscrew, immediately followed
by the sudden appearance of the large, and obviously metallic,

car, may have been the result of the scene-shift effect. The two objects have some visual and conceptual similarities. Every word in the written dream report must be examined to reveal a common thread. Here, for example, the theme of inflation – from the 'small' window to the 'enormous' vehicle and the 'overweight' man – may be significant.

In this case, the message seems to be that an unacceptable aspect of the dreamer's personality is over-developed. The dreamer's final recorded feeling was one of dissatisfaction at having given insufficient attention to something. Cash's dream alerts him to a conflict within himself. Action is necessary.

~18~

Barbara Garwell's Dream Interpreted

B ARBARA GARWELL, a famous psychic dreamer, kindly contributed the dream analysed in this chapter. It is an example of a seemingly simple dream which, at first glance, might appear straightforward to interpret. To a certain extent it is, but it includes aspects which had to be studied in minute detail before an accurate interpretation could be given.

BARBARA GARWELL'S DREAM

I was in an ordinary street, but didn't recognize anything familiar around me. Then I went and stood in the middle of the road. I saw my youngest daughter, Sandra Anne – who is married with three sons – coming round a bend on a toboggan, as if on ice. She looked so radiant and was dressed in a white bridal outfit, her blonde hair also outstanding. It was a sunshiny day and I smiled, and in my mind she was going to church. Then I awoke.

THE INTERPRETATION

To begin with, you are in an ordinary street (you are in a situation which you identify as normal). Nothing around you is familiar, though. Therefore the situation which you have identified as normal is not normal for you (although you recognize it as a street, you are unfamiliar with the surroundings). This indicates that you have found yourself in a new situation in your life, one which you readily accept exists for others, but until now hasn't applied to you. Then we see you stepping to the middle of the road. Under normal circumstances, the middle of the road might represent a hazard (exposing yourself to danger). However, in this instance, the road represents the mainstream of your new circumstances and it seems that you are readily prepared to venture into, and possibly allow yourself to be carried along on, the prevailing current (not once did you mention experiencing any fear). Therefore, you are willing to have a go in this new situation and see where it might lead you.

Next, you saw your youngest daughter, who was wearing a bridal gown. Here we are given the first clue which leads us to conclude that your daughter is a representation of part of you. Although dreams can relate messages in convoluted ways, we have to look for the simplest interpretation.

In this instance, we know that your daughter is already married with three children, so we must ask why she is wearing a bridal gown. When we address this question, we know that it does not make sense, so we have to look elsewhere. We decided to explore the symbolic meaning of a wedding dress. Apart from its obvious symbolism, a bridal gown could also represent an initiation ceremony or a new beginning. Straight away, this fits in neatly with the initial interpretation of the dream (that your daughter represents you in your new situation).

Sandra Anne is on a toboggan, as if on ice. This suggests that she is moving swiftly along the road with little or no resistance. As we have seen, it is you who are embarking on this new project or direction (you are the one who is standing in the middle of the road), so, again, it makes much more sense to accept that your daughter represents a facet of your character.

Here we have a clue as to what part of you has been aroused and is being stimulated by your new circumstances. You describe her blonde hair as 'outstanding'. Remember, you also used the word 'radiant' to describe your daughter. A toboggan represents speed and daring. All these things suggest youth, invigoration, bravery, new beginnings and a willingness to have a go. These are the facets of your character which have been stimulated.

Finally, it was 'a sunshiny day' (good omen), and you smiled (you were happy with the situation). This indicates that the outcome of your new circumstances will be favourable. This is reinforced by the fact that you knew Sandra Anne was going to church. As we know, Barbara, you live for your family and your faith in God. Therefore, the dream is telling you that, although you are embarking on something new (the unfamiliar road), you know that you will come to no harm because of your faith.

This is what Barbara said about the interpretation of her dream:

I found it to be sincere, true, and can see so clearly how it is relevant to my life now and forthcoming events that will surround me, especially the publication of my book. Yes, I am so full of hope and optimism over my future, as the interpretation shows. I found every line exciting; it was a joy to read.

The interpreter must always ask as a matter of course, whether one or more characters in a dream are really facets of the dreamer. In Barbara's dream, she saw her youngest daughter. Therefore, we had to decide whether her daughter represented herself, part of Barbara's own character, somebody else, or something else altogether. The entire contents of the dream were subjected to a detailed scrutiny in relation to the general message that demanded to be recognized. As soon as that message became clear, there was only one possibility: her daughter represented a part of Barbara's character, just as she is part of her mother in a biological sense.

Now let us interpret the same dream by means of various dream dictionaries and compare results. We shall use more than one in an attempt to match the circumstances of the dream as closely as possible. Any one dictionary would not cover all of the symbols. The dream begins with Barbara in an ordinary street, although she could not recognize anything familiar around her. The nearest dictionary entry we can find is 'Being on a street you've never been on before', which is interpreted to mean that the dreamer will do a lot of travelling. Then Barbara went and stood in the middle of the road. Not surprisingly, this brings us up against the first hurdle: we are unable to find any reference to being in the middle of a road in any of the dream dictionaries. Neither can we find any reference to a road with a bend. However, there are a plethora of meanings attributed to travelling on roads, from good health, happiness and fortune, to sorrow, losses and obstacles. The only meaning which comes anywhere near Barbara's description is 'The discovery of a secret'.

Then Barbara saw her youngest daughter, who is married with three sons, coming round a bend on a toboggan as if on ice. Here we hit further conflicting and opposing interpretations. Nevertheless, let us proceed by selecting the most favourable interpretations for these circumstances.

First, to dream of a daughter, according to one dream dictionary, will bring pleasure and harmony in the home. However, the same book translates the image of others riding on a toboggan as 'Death of an enemy'. Again, numerous meanings are attributed to ice, from financial ruin, losses and danger to fortune and a good omen. Trying to be as fair as possible, we have chosen one that reflects similar circumstances although it does not fit Barbara's description. This suggests that she will make a long journey.

Then Barbara sees her daughter looking radiant and dressed in a white bridal outfit, her blonde hair 'outstanding'. There is no mention in the dream dictionaries of looking radiant. The only instance we could find which relates to a bride looking happy in a wedding dress indicates that Barbara is going to have more children. Blonde hair, apparently, denotes friendships.

Finally, it was 'a sunshiny day' and Barbara smiled because she knew her daughter was going to church. According to one source, if a woman smiles on the street it means she has bad morals. However, the sunshine indicates that she will have a long and happy life. We cannot find any reference to watching one's daughter going to church clothed in a wedding gown, so we must choose at random from the multifarious meanings on offer, which include deceit, a spouse's unpleasant companions and difficulties to surmount.

It is tempting to have fun at this point and use the dream dictionaries to formulate a series of ridiculous assumptions. However, in an attempt to play fair, we will try to knit together the elements of Barbara's dream and make some sense out of the dictionaries' suggestions.

As a result, it would seem that Barbara is going to travel and that on her journey she will discover a secret which will somehow bring pleasure and harmony in the home. Presumably the secret is not the death of an enemy (one possible interpretation), as it is hard to believe that this would bring about such a happy atmosphere. It may be that this death will take her on another journey, this time, far away. Somehow this is going to result in Barbara having more children, which, in turn, will both lead to friendships and reveal low moral standards. Not surprisingly, all this will culminate in difficulties for Barbara to surmount.

Despite our sincere efforts to produce a sensible interpretation using dream dictionaries, it is blatantly obvious that this method of analysis is far from satisfactory.

~19~
Three Spiritual Dreams Interpreted

GAYNOR DAVIES, fiction editor of one of Britain's leading women's magazines, *Woman's Weekly*, supplied one of the dreams featured in this chapter.

Dream interpretation is always fascinating and from, time to time, something out of the ordinary crops up, which was precisely the case with Gaynor's dream. It bore an uncanny resemblance to two dreams which David Melbourne had interpreted for somebody else just a day or two earlier.

It seems remarkable that, out of the hundreds of dreams he interprets, out of the blue two subjects should report astonishingly similar dream material. Even more astonishingly, both these dreams were spiritual in nature, not the common types of dream we all experience on occasion, about falling, being pursued and so forth. The odds against this happening must be many thousands to one. Coincidence, one wonders? Or is there any such thing as coincidence?

Two further weird incidents occurred after David Melbourne had sent Gaynor her interpretation and they will be described later in this chapter.

The first two dreams were interpreted for a lady named Elizabeth. Unfortunately, Elizabeth has been confined to bed for many years suffering from multiple sclerosis. The severity of her condition means that she is now almost totally paralysed, unable even to turn the pages of a magazine, and finds it tiring to speak. Her asthmatic symptoms make her situation even more difficult.

Although, at the time of writing, the authors have never met Elizabeth, we feel privileged to know something about her. Since David Melbourne has been interpreting her dreams, he has come to feel very close to her. At the time MS was diagnosed, Elizabeth was teaching herself to play the piano, learning oil-painting and studying for a degree; she is proficient in many languages. These days, however, as she is unable to write, she dictates her dreams to her mother, Joan, who sends them to David Melbourne for interpretation.

Those who are fortunate enough to have met Elizabeth say that she is a very special person. She has tremendous strength of will, pours out love to others and accepts her situation without complaint.

Whether or not it is because of her illness, out of the many dreams interpreted for Elizabeth, a large proportion have been spiritual in nature. David has learned a lot from working on her dreams and feels that he owes her a debt of gratitude. She is a remarkable lady and he regards her with a great deal of affection.

ELIZABETH'S FIRST DREAM

Although I haven't passed my test, I was driving a car in France as a travelling chiropodist and got lost. Then I found myself in Germany and had to ask the way (speaking their tongue). Before I could get an answer, I woke up.

THE INTERPRETATION

Over the years, we have learned that sometimes when we dream of foreign countries this indicates a spiritual realm. When there is confusion as to the identity of an alien location, this reinforces the possibility.

A car is representative (in this instance) of a means of transport through a spiritual reality. This is reinforced by your references to being in a foreign country and becoming lost.

Therefore, you are travelling through unfamiliar – spiritual – territory, even though you can speak the language (communication is universal).

In this case, the chiropodist means someone who helps other people to tread the right path. The dream is telling you that, although you have developed spiritually to a considerable degree and, through your efforts and inner strength, you are (consciously and unconsciously) helping other people to develop themselves, you still have a little way to go yourself (you 'got lost'). However, you were not frightened to admit this (you asked the way). This indicates that you will indeed find the right path to tread.

ELIZABETH'S SECOND DREAM

I dreamed I was in Monaco. I saw a map in front of my eyes which was the shape of France, but it had 'Monaco' written across it.

I was in a large crowded room with a lot of people whom I felt were superior intellectually, not necessarily in rank or class. They were of different nationalities and one lady had some kind of headgear which gave me the impression she was a sort of princess.

I was conversing quite happily with various people, but everybody was speaking in German. I was talking to a small group of men dressed like German officers of Hitler's period. It was their tunics which gave me this impression. All the conversation was intelligent, not small talk, and I was very anxious to speak correct German.

Someone, I think it could have been the 'princess', said to me, 'Don't worry too much about the grammar. It's the words that count.' I tried to say something about remembering, but couldn't recall the word for 'remember' and hesitated. One of the German officers said, 'You know, even we Germans often can't remember the word for "remember".'

I woke up at this point, but the two phrases uttered by the 'princess' and the German stuck in my mind vividly.

THE INTERPRETATION

Rarely does one come across two dreams in succession which are shouting out similar messages in such a powerful way. In other words, we are dealing with another spiritual dream.

It is incredible that this dream bears almost the same message as the first, only this time, at first glance, it appears that there has been some sort of advancement in your spiritual awareness, which is amazing in such a short time.

There is another possibility, however, one which is more likely. Perhaps you were already advanced but subconsciously lacked some degree of confidence.

Again, you are in a foreign country and again, there is some confusion as to which country you are in. In this case the map says 'Monaco', but the country's shape is that of France. So you are once more in unfamiliar, and confusing, territory (the spiritual plane).

There is no doubt that this represents your spiritual subconscious. You are in a crowd of people who, you feel, are superior in intellect, not in rank or class. This confirms that the country represents a spiritual reality, because when we depart this world, we cannot take with us a single thing which is linked to materialism. Death has no respect for human greatness and reduces all of us to the same level.

The German uniforms and the princess indicate that you do feel subservient, lack confidence or regard yourself as intellectually inadequate compared to them (they are figures of authority). Here we come to the extraordinary difference between this dream and the last. In your first dream, you asked the way, yet here you are mixing with the inhabitants, albeit not quite on their level, you feel (mistakenly).

However, they are giving you a clear message, and that is: 'Do not feel inadequate – you have no reason to.' They are telling you that you are as advanced as they are (you were conversing and holding your own quite happily). It was only when it dawned on you that everyone was speaking German that you became unsure of yourself. You were preoccupied

with your accent, grammar and remembering certain words.
Until then, you were doing very well.

Now to the crux of the dream. The princess told you not to
worry about your grammar, because 'It's the words that
count.' Then one of the Germans reassured you that they
often can't remember the word for 'remember' (they are no
better than you). This conveys the clear message that you
have attained at least the same level of (subconscious) spiritual
awareness as these people possess.

The fact that the two phrases you quote stuck in your mind
upon waking is very significant indeed, because their message
is clear and should reassure you. After all, that is what the
dream is all about: reassurance. Perhaps you were too
concerned that you might still have a little way to go. We all
have some way to go.

The dream is telling you not to worry. You have already
travelled a great distance along the path of spiritual
development.

GAYNOR DAVIES' DREAM

*I was in Holland with a few people, probably my immediate family.
We were in the area of Amsterdam, though it didn't look like
Amsterdam. I didn't have a great deal of time, but I wanted to take
the family sightseeing. I couldn't decide whether to take them to
Edam or Gouda and was trying to find out from local people (in
authority, I think) which was the nearest place. I don't know in real
life where Edam and Gouda are in relation to Amsterdam, by the
way. As the dream went on I was driving and suddenly realized I
was driving on the left when I should have been driving on the
right. Then I woke up.*

We knew that Gaynor leads a busy life as fiction editor of a presti-
gious magazine. In addition, her accompanying letter contained
some important clues which made the interpretation of her dream
easier. She mentioned that she sometimes dreams in puns and spec-

ulated whether the word 'cheeses', descriptive of Edam and Gouda, might signify Jesus.

Gaynor told us that she is confused about what she feels about Jesus. She also stated that she is always conscious of the battle for dominance between the two sides of her brain. Finally, she revealed that she has psychic abilities.

It is amazing that, consciously, Gaynor had no idea what her dream meant, yet her subconscious knew exactly what it meant; it almost certainly prompted her to add the extra information in her accompanying letter. After obtaining Elizabeth's permission, David Melbourne sent Gaynor a copy of Elizabeth's dream accounts and their interpretation along with his analysis of her own dream.

THE INTERPRETATION

You will already have noticed, Gaynor, that your dream bears some striking similarities to those of Elizabeth. In addition, the extra information you gave us leaves us in no doubt that we are dealing with another spiritual dream. All that remains now is to piece it together.

In the dream, you were in a foreign country and, as in Elizabeth's dreams, there is some confusion about the location; you were 'in the area of Amsterdam, though it didn't look like Amsterdam'. Immediately, we are alerted to the possibility of a spiritual realm.

You were with a few other people, whom you suggest were probably members of your family. Again there is some uncertainty, which indicates that we are definitely dealing with matters of a spiritual nature; the people represent loved ones who already dwell in a higher plane.

You didn't have much time – dreams are often short-lived – and you wanted to take them sightseeing (your subconscious wanted them to accompany you on a journey of discovery within that realm). You sometimes dream in word puns, so you are correct to speculate that 'cheeses' could mean Jesus.

This indicates that you are searching for an answer which will put an end to your uncertainty in this matter.

Now we get closer to the crux of the analysis: you were not sure of the way to Edam or Gouda (Jesus?), so you tried to find out from local people (those in authority, you thought), again, souls who dwell in that realm, which place was nearer. So the dream is indicating a search for spiritual answers. Then we are given a strong clue to reinforce this interpretation, not in the dream material itself, but in your description of it. You mentioned that you didn't know in real life where Jesus (Edam and Gouda) is in relation to spirituality (Amsterdam).

Finally, the whole interpretation comes together very nicely indeed. You discover that you have been driving on the wrong side of the road. Knowing your confusion as to which side of your brain is predominant, we feel that the dream clearly indicates that you have been seeking the answers from the wrong perspective, the left brain, which is associated with abstract analysis, calculation, etc. This is certainly something you need to use regularly in your job. However, the right brain, which is allied to creativity and emotion, is the side of the road you should follow to reach your destination.

In short, your dream is acknowledging your confusion about matters relating to spirituality (which most of us share, incidentally). However, it also bears a powerful message. To find the answer you seek, don't be analytical or too critical of facts which appear to be contradictory. Rather, for the purpose of your search, use the right brain and follow your heart.

When Gaynor read this interpretation she commented:

I was excited by the dream analysis and it gave me a feeling of satisfaction. It was almost 'what I wanted to hear'. I'm always being told by psychics, healers and astrologers to follow my heart, to trust my feelings, to have confidence in my psychic abilities. And now it looks as if that's what I'm telling myself in my sleep! No wonder I wake up exhausted some mornings.

This remarkable story does not end here. About two days after he sent Gaynor her dream interpretation, David Melbourne received his first ever letter from Amsterdam, enquiring about his dream interpretation service. It arrived totally out of the blue.

Just four days after that, he received a letter from Elizabeth's mother, Joan, asking him to interpret two more of Elizabeth's dreams. Joan kindly gave us permission to reproduce the following passages from her letter:

> *The first dream was one she had a week or two before the last two dreams which you have already interpreted for her, but she thought it probably related to them.*
>
> *She dreamed she was driving in England, then – in a flash – she was driving in the US. She was on the left-hand side of a very busy road with three lanes each way, but she felt completely safe ... Liz stressed the fact that she felt so safe and her own idea about the dream was that her driving in the US on the wrong side of the road perhaps signified that she was going the wrong way in life, but the fact that she felt quite safe maybe meant that she was now going along some different lines? However, she's eager to know what you make of it.*

As David read the description of Elizabeth's dream, his jaw dropped in astonishment. Needless to say, except for a few obvious differences, his interpretation of Elizabeth's dream was strikingly similar to that of Gaynor's. David was left wondering whether this extraordinary sequence of events contained a message for him. It certainly reassured him that his interpretations were entirely accurate.

Now let us go over a few facts and examine the methodology behind these interpretations. First, Elizabeth's case illustrates the importance of knowing about the dreamer's situation. The MHQ form (see p.167) is invaluable in gathering essential background information about the dreamer. Elizabeth has a serious progressive disease which, naturally, is likely to figure prominently in her dreams, along with her thoughts about the future and her spiritual worth.

A distant 'other place', such as a foreign country, can represent a spiritual realm or an anticipated afterlife location which the dreamer may be travelling towards. It was curious that Elizabeth dreamed of being a travelling chiropodist in her first dream. It seems likely that this was a verbal pun linking feet/sole and soul. Elizabeth's soul was travelling, seeking the way, but the dream was not ready to provide further information at that point.

Things that are said, and stand out, in dreams are of great significance It seems that David Melbourne has expertly interpreted the spoken comments in Elizabeth's second dream, as were interpreted as encouragements given to her by her subconscious about her spiritual merit.

One possible set of associations for the word 'Monaco' includes the name 'Princess Grace' and it is interesting that a princess featured in the dream. Grace, of course, is a very spiritual quality and confirms the elevated theme of the dream.

Gaynor, being professionally involved with words, has recognized verbal puns in her own dreams. The phonetic association between 'cheeses' and 'Jesus' reveals that her dream is about spiritual matters rather than the mundane topic that is superficially presented to the dreamer.

The synchronicity of receiving these consecutive dreams on the same spiritual theme from two different people may also be significant to David Melbourne and his own spiritual development. Interpreting dreams can further the analyst's psychological and spiritual advancement, because the process involves constantly looking for signs and symbols that indicate a more profound meaning than the superficial one.

~20~
Mike Kenward's Dream Interpreted

S OME time ago, David Melbourne came up with the idea of interpreting dreams for the other contributors to *Horoscope*, to give the readers an opportunity to find out a little about the people involved in producing the magazine.

The editor, Mike Kenward, thought it was a good plan, until David suggested including him. He made it known, politely, that he had certain reservations about the validity of dream interpretation, and added, 'I never remember my dreams.'

However, he agreed that in the unlikely event that he had a dream which he could remember, he would pass it on to David for analysis. Some time later he did recall a vivid dream and, rather reluctantly, wrote it down and posted it off.

It proved to be a classic message-bearing dream, full of powerful symbolism, and painted a vivid picture. Relatively straightforward to analyse, it focused on one or both of Mike's children. It also appeared his subconscious was trying hard to bring him a lucid dream.

MIKE KENWARD'S DREAM

I was sleeping in my normal bed but it was in a forest; I was on the 'wrong' side of the bed with my wife on the other side. Both my children were in single beds either side of our bed, but they were about 10 and 12 years old (they are now 19 and 21). Our pet dog was asleep on our bed (this is not very unusual).

I was aware that there were some large tigers in the forest and, sure enough, one appeared, standing on our bed between my wife and me. It started nuzzling the back of my neck. Our dog had moved off the bed by then. I froze in fear and held my breath, but I realized that the tiger might sense this fear and kill me, so I forced myself to breathe normally and relax; at this the tiger licked my neck and I felt quite happy with the situation. After a while he moved off and my wife and I tried to turn on the bedside lights, which would not work. Nor would the overhead light, but we found a torch and used it to see if we could see any more tigers. We could not. We then left the overhead light on (it now worked), as we felt it would stop the tigers returning.

In his covering letter, Mike pointed out that he likes tigers in waking life and that the one in his dream was a very big one. He also said that he enjoys walking his dog through the woods.

THE INTERPRETATION

To begin with, we find you in your normal bed with your wife, your children (the family) either side, in a forest, (the outside world), but you are on the 'wrong' side (role reversal). Your pet dog (the one you have now) is also there, reinforcing the fact that this dream concerns your children as they are now.

Although the opening of your dream is quite short, it reveals a lot of information. The fact that you are in your own bed, albeit on the wrong side, with your children and dog, tells us straight away that we are dealing with your domestic situation.

We have strong clues which tell us that, over the years, roles have been reversed. The dream indicates this by showing your children at a younger age. However, your dog is the dog you have today, which suggests that, when your children were younger, your wife used to do most of the worrying about them.

However, you are now on the other side of the bed, indicating that it is you who now bear most of these anxieties. If you had dreamed of your children at their present age, with you still on the wrong side of the bed, we would have had to look for another meaning. As it is, there is little doubt that the dream centres on one or both of the children.

In the dream, you are aware that there are some large tigers in the forest (possible hazards in the outside world – 'possible' because you say that you like tigers). It would appear that the tiger represents something that you are afraid or wary of.

Next you find the tiger on the bed between you and your wife, which indicates that you suspect an outside influence might present a possible threat that might split your opinions. It starts nuzzling the back of your neck (getting threateningly close), perhaps too close for your liking (you are frightened and hold your breath). The dog has gone, which shows that he has served his purpose in this dream, helping to set the scene.

You realize that the tiger might sense your fear and kill you (you are worried that the outside influence could detrimentally encroach on your family). You force yourself to breathe normally and relax (you try to adapt to the situation). At this, the tiger licks your neck and you feel happy about it (you begin to warm to it). After a while the tiger moves off, indicating that this outside influence is no longer around.

At this point, your subconscious has almost finished conveying its message and it presents you with an anomaly so that you can initiate a lucid dream. It is a classic case of the light-switch effect. When the lights fail to function, your subconscious is saying, 'Come on, Mike, you know about this from reading David's articles. Recognize it and acknowledge it.' Unless you had gone to great lengths to program yourself during waking hours, this would be unlikely to succeed. However, it does show that your subconscious considers that you are ready to experience a lucid dream.

Next, you get a torch to see if there are any more tigers (threats in the outside world) and then turn on the overhead light. Normally a dreamer is unable to switch lights on within the dream, but in this case, to round off the dream and to make the light-switch effect blend in with the rest of it, your subconscious allows the lights to work. This is quite rare. You feel that the light will stop the tigers returning. This means that you have shared your concern with your wife (shed light on it) and are also on the look-out for similar outside influences which might appear in the future.

The dream has a clear message: you dealt with a problem correctly by not over-reacting to a situation, and showing a certain amount of tolerance. However, your subconscious is also telling you not to bear the burden of worry alone. Two heads are better than one.

In a covering letter, David Melbourne told Mike that his dream might be a warning, possibly alerting him to a similar threat looming on the horizon.

Some time after he had sent him the interpretation, David received the following comments from Mike Kenward:

> *I was rather sceptical about dream interpretations. I guess most of us are sceptical about new ideas about which we have no personal experience. I also found that I have very few dreams that I can recall the next day, so it was some time before I sent a dream for interpretation.*
>
> *Having written it down, it seemed to me to have no obvious meaning and I thought it might just be a bit odd and not carry any message. I was, therefore, surprised that, on receiving your interpretation, it matched exactly a situation that had occurred a few months previously. Quite uncanny. Furthermore, your warning also proved to be helpful, as a recurrence of a similar situation was later avoided.*
>
> *I suppose that I'm a born sceptic, but one who now sees there is something in dream interpretation.*

Mike's letter went on to say that the comments about the light-switch effect made him realize that he had learned about this phenomenon from one of David's previous articles but, as he deduced, he didn't remember it in the dream. 'Perhaps next time,' said Mike.

Situations in dreams that are not usual to the dreamer in wakefulness, and are therefore particularly noticed, tend to have a strong symbolic point to make. The reversal of a husband and wife's sleeping places in bed appears to be a straightforward statement from the subconscious that the dreamer is playing an inappropriate role. Similarly, an anomaly in the ages of the dreamer's children indicates circumstances that have continued over the years.

It is not surprising that the scene-shift effect transformed Mike's dog into a tiger. Dreams move along by the law of least effort and an animal can easily be changed into one of a different species. The position of the tiger 'between my wife and me' suggests an area of conflict.

When Mike 'froze in fear', this probably reflected the state of sleep paralysis that exists in REM sleep. Wisely, he responded by trying to relax and not over-react.

The next scene, where the light-switch would not work, was virtually a false awakening. This is not subject to interpretation, because it simply illustrates one of the natural limitations in the dream-producing process. However, Mike's subconscious may well have been telling him to initiate a lucid dream.

Mike and his wife then worked together to see if they could find any other tigers, so the dream ended on a note of harmony.

Judging from Mike's letter, the interpretation was accurate. However, if the dream had been analysed using dream dictionaries, the interpretation would have been entirely different and wildly inaccurate.

Because Mike's dream involves some powerful imagery and symbolism, it provides some excellent material to demonstrate the pitfalls inherent in dream analysis by means of dream dictionaries.

Starting with the bed, we find hundreds of possible meanings, but no mention of being on the wrong side, or the bed being outside. The nearest we can get is a bed used for camping outside, which apparently means that the dreamer will purchase real estate.

The location was a forest. Again, numerous meanings are given. However, the nearest suggests that dreaming of being in a forest with relatives indicates that the dreamer will be jilted by his lover. Next, we have a sleeping dog, which, according to one dictionary, means that Mike need have no fears. From the many interpretations for a tiger, the closest indicates that enemies will beset the dreamer's path. Then the tiger leaves, which apparently means that Mike will suffer a serious illness.

Mike froze in fear, which is translated to mean that he will receive news telling him that a wealthy relation has died and left him a considerable legacy.

Not one dream dictionary appears to be aware of the light-switch effect. Instead, it is suggested that being unable to turn on lights represents a danger in a love affair or even imprisonment and great misfortune to come.

Mike and his wife did eventually turn on a light. This is supposed to indicate that he can either expect success in business or yet another inheritance.

As we have seen, a Freudian analyst might suggest that the light refusing to come on indicates a fear of impotence. However, when the light did decide to work, it would imply that the problem had been solved, all in the space of a single dream. A Jungian might say that it reveals a fear of being exposed to, or by, something, again, a problem that would seem to have disappeared when the light came on.

All these suggestions add up to an entertaining, but incredible and ludicrous, interpretation. There is a more sinister side to this, of course. If the dreamer were somebody of a nervous disposition, it would be dangerous for them to take seriously a dream-dictionary analysis.

~21~
A Precognitive
Dream Interpreted

WHILE THIS BOOK was being written, David Melbourne unexpectedly received a further letter from Elizabeth (see Chapter 19), dictated to her mother, Joan. It described another dream, one which would reveal an astonishing message.

In an accompanying letter Joan said she was frightened about what the dream could mean, adding that Elizabeth already suspected it might foretell her own death. Joan made a point of explaining that Elizabeth had no fear of death, but Joan felt uncomfortable about the dream and both women clearly believed it was a precognitive one.

When he analysed the dream, David was stunned. It was precognitive, but it was not about Elizabeth's death. Its meaning is so extraordinary that David felt he must check the analysis thoroughly several times in case he had made a mistake. In fact, he sectionalized the dream about a dozen more times, just to be sure.

However many times he analysed the dream, the outcome was the same. Then he agonized about whether he should send Elizabeth the interpretation, because she predicts a remedy (not a cure) for multiple sclerosis that will eliminate the symptoms of paralysis from this dread disease.

David found himself in a dilemma. If his interpretation was wrong, it might give false hope to MS sufferers. Would he be able to live with himself? Should he continue writing this book?

After much soul-searching, he reasoned that, until this point, he had had no doubt that his methods worked and that the vast majority of his analyses were accurate. Moreover, he had never given any dream as much attention as this one. It simply had to be accurate.

Finally, David sent the interpretation to Elizabeth and asked her for permission to include it in this book. When she told him that she would be pleased, he felt as if a huge weight had been lifted from his shoulders.

ELIZABETH'S DREAM

I saw an open book which looked like a Bible. The text was even set out in little sections like verses, although it wasn't a Bible. What it said impressed me. One section was about me and the MS. The gist of it was that MS wasn't cured. The last bit I remembered reading was: 'Twenty-first century, no paralysis'. Then someone woke me up.

It is easy to understand why Joan was so concerned. The analyst must delve deep when interpreting such a dream. A superficial treatment could have devastating results. It is not unusual to dream about dying, but dreams of this kind often translate into something entirely different: the end of a relationship, a habit or a way of life, for example.

THE INTERPRETATION

For obvious reasons, I suspect strongly that this is a precognitive dream. The open book appears to speak for itself (your life is an open book). However, in this instance, the symbol is less straightforward. Libraries, bookshops and books themselves sometimes represent knowledge. The book refers to you and mentions MS twice. So here we have a dream which is dealing with either you, MS, or both. As you will see, the dream is simply using the symbol of the book to establish that it represents, primarily, MS.

The facts that the book resembled a Bible, and the text was presented in something akin to verse, are relevant. In other words, this book is for others to study and learn from. That is the purpose of the Bible. Therefore, it becomes clear that this dream is dealing with MS (there is still much to be learned from and about it). Alternatively, the message might be that people have a lot to learn from you, which is quite possible. However, it makes more sense and fits in with the rest of the interpretation if we accept that the dream is mainly about the disease itself.

It was crucial for me to understand this before I went any further. I had to ask myself why your dream chose this particular symbol and not just an ordinary open book. To start with, there is nothing ordinary about your life, especially now, but I do not think that this was the point of the dream. It could have chosen easier ways to put across that idea. Digging deeper, I came up with what I am certain is the right answer.

Could this dream be foretelling the time of your death? The thought crossed my mind and I am sure it occurred to you. However, within a short time, I dismissed this possibility. To understand why, we have to take a closer look at the text in the book. The last bit you remembered reading was: 'Twenty-first century, no paralysis'. This is too vague. Precognitive dreams are nearly always much more precise, especially about something as important the dreamer's own demise. Besides, if the dream were predicting a death, it would not go to the lengths of putting the text into verses. No, this dream translates as a message for others (there is much learning to be done concerning MS).

We and many others are going to meet our end before or during the next century, so such a prediction would be unremarkable. In what way is your dream precognitive, then? Too often people miss the point when they interpret dreams, either because they are looking for the worst, or because they complicate things too much. The answer here is simple and obvious and it makes much more sense: there will be a remedy which prevents paralysis in MS sufferers, but this advance will not come until the twenty-first century. It is not necessarily good news for those like yourself who are suffering now – or is it?

The deciding factor in this interpretation was that, in your dream, you read that 'MS wasn't cured'. This is what the dream is all about. There will not be a cure, but there will be a remedy which prevents the terrible disabling effect of MS.

Why should your subconscious have the audacity to tell you that your disease is not cured? You know that all too well. Rather than communicating what you know already, it is telling you something else. I find this particularly exciting, because I have never interpreted a precognitive dream where the prediction has such major implications.

Since he completed this analysis, David has studied Elizabeth's dream many more times and his conviction is stronger than ever that the interpretation is accurate. He has given a great deal of thought as to why the dream did not give a more precise date for the predicted medical breakthrough and came up with the following reasons.

Had the dream given a precise date, it might have served to confuse, leading him in another direction; Elizabeth's subconscious is well aware that he interprets many of her dreams. The more one ponders whether the message could have foretold her own demise, the less likely this seems. The prediction of a person's demise in the twenty-first century would be laughable. A great percentage of those who are alive today will die during the next century. Many of us may come to an unexpected end even before the millenium.

As to why the remedy should appear in the twenty-first century and not in the twenty-second, it seems reasonable to assume that there might be a breakthrough in the treatment of MS during the next 100 years. David believes that the answer is quite clear and that the dream is being precise in stating that MS is not cured, but there will be no more paralysis. He feels, judging from experience, that the breakthrough will occur before, during

or soon after the millenium, within the first few years, perhaps.
    Because the interpretation deals with such a sensitive subject, as soon as he had finished writing this chapter, David sent Elizabeth a copy and invited her comments. She dictated the following reply:

> *To all fellow* MS *sufferers:*
>
> *I have every faith in Dave's interpretation of this dream; I know he worked long and hard on it to be certain.*
>
> *Let's hope and pray that this will happen and certainly those who are stronger now will benefit fully.*
>
> *Hang on to hope.*

~22~

Perspectives and Prospects

IN THE RATHER rare lucid dream, where the dreamer suddenly becomes fully aware of dreaming, as though conscious in an artificial or illusory world, if you will something to happen, it happens, although perhaps not quite in the way you anticipated. Nevertheless, by some process, your thoughts are turned into visual images. Essentially, in a lucid dream, whatever you think, you will then dream. You can, for example, conjure up a dream companion simply by thinking about that person.

There is the same process in ordinary, non-lucid dreams, too, except that these dreams appear to be constructed from subconscious ideas about matters of current concern or interest to the dreamer instead of, or as well as, conscious thoughts. The dreams flow along, constantly calling attention to the underlying dream thoughts by means of both verbal and visual associations. It must therefore be possible for a dream to be unravelled once its original construction is understood.

The ancients adopted this straightforward approach. During the Roman period in particular, dream interpretation was very advanced. Unfortunately, in the West, the Christian Church regarded it as sorcery, so the ancient wisdoms were neglected and lost. Later, when interest in dreams revived, some extreme and narrow theories, such as those of Freud, were overly influential. Dreams are not necessarily sexual in nature or the result of elaborate disguising processes.

In the last few decades, however, the approach to dream interpretation has reverted, sensibly, to the simple, logical methods of the ancients. We now have the additional advantage of a clearer understanding of the construction of dreams. We are aware of such things as scene-shift effects and the presence of natural limitations in dreams, like the inability suddenly to increase the brightness of dream lighting.

The technique for dream interpretation outlined in this book has some similarities with ancient methods, such as the practice of obtaining background information about both the dream and the dreamer, but also includes relevant recent findings. Without advocating any particular theoretical framework for dream analysis.

The commonly employed method of attempting to understand a dream by looking up the meaning of dream images and themes in dream dictionaries has been shown to be crude and unsatisfactory in comparison with a systematic analysis.

Therefore, a standard, universal, dream-report form and questionnaire is a valuable tool in dream interpretation. The MHQ (Melbourne–Hearne Questionnaire – see p.167) gathers background information about the dreamer and specific data about the dream. As well as assisting in the process of interpretation, the data can be subjected to statistical analysis to find consistent patterns or even new dream phenomena.

By interpreting our own dreams we gain self-knowledge and insight. We begin to comprehend and appreciate the subtlety and complexity of parts of the mind to which we cannot normally gain access. The process opens up a channel of communication with, and puts us on better terms with, deeper levels of our psyche. As our self-understanding is enhanced, we become more balanced and integrated. Our dreams can also communicate useful, and even crucial, information to us once we have learned to decipher their unique language.

We spend six years of our life dreaming. Each night we steal away to another reality, with different people in different places. Is it not reasonable to try to gather information about this other life? It can become a compelling pursuit.

This book has, apart from expounding a technique for interpreting dreams, provided extensive information on many aspects of dreams and sleep. While it seems that dreaming sleep is not essential for well-being in adults, the remarkable characteristics of the dream state may be employed in many productive ways.

For example, many people can develop lucid dreaming, some simply by becoming aware of the concept and then being more alert to anomalies in dreams. Others are aided by cassette tapes which use the technique of psychological suggestion to trigger the lucid-dream state.

The lucid dream is a wonderful experience. The imagery is often extremely sharp, bright and vivid and the dreamer has the astonishing knowledge that absolutely everything is a totally internal construction, a product of the brain. Even more amazing is the ability to control events in the dream by thought alone. The dreamer is able to fly through the air like Superman, or walk through walls like a ghost.

Lucid dreams can provide an interesting and exciting recreation for the dreamer but they are probably of greatest benefit to creative and artistic people. In the lucid dream, almost any combination of sensory and conceptual element can be constructed. The dreamer can travel into the future or visit an alien civilization in the lucid-dream state and observe the costumes, buildings, furniture, art, etc. The lucid-dream state is an untapped resource that, we feel, will be increasingly employed for creative purposes in the future.

The impartial dreamer or dream-observer is likely to come to a far better understanding of what really happens in dreams than the conventionally trained scientist. People with no theoretical bias have the advantage of a greater insight into dreams. They are open-minded about telepathy and clairvoyance, for example, and their observations may reveal consistencies between, say, precognitive dreams, such as a regular latency period between the premonition and the event.

Many people report having dreams which seem to give flashes of past lives they have lived. During past-life regression therapy these scenes can be developed and often reveal a definite and significant link with the dreamer's problems in this life, as though the residue of past lives is affecting their present incarnation. Past-life dreams are characterized by strong emotion; people are wearing period costume and dreamers may see themselves in a different body.

The unbiased dream observer will not dismiss such dream images or force a superficial explanation on them, but will consider them in their own right and see if they tie in with other dream phenomena or experiences. The insightful person can entertain the idea that, despite the evidence of our senses, we may live in a mentalistic universe, a 'mind world'.

What of future developments concerning dreams? In 1975 Dr Hearne discovered that he could get subjects having lucid dreams to signal to the outside world by moving their eyes, and he realized that several technical developments involving dreams were theoretically possible.

One day we may actually be able to see what people are dreaming on a television screen. Tapping into dreams might feasibly be carried out by means of the microbiological monitoring and recording of parts of the brain (especially the visual cortex), using non-invasive techniques yet to be devised. Before we can view dreams as they occur, however, we shall probably be able to hear what is happening in another person's dream.

Such techniques would constitute an extreme invasion of privacy, but they would also provide clear and graphic insights into dreams. The dream could be exposed to truly scientific, objective analysis and psychology would advance in a great leap.

The technique of hypno-oneirography pioneered by Dr Hearne has shown that internal visual imagery can be externalized using an outline-tracing method. Maybe it will one day be possible to have a record library of people's dreams (and nightmares) so that anyone can experience them.

There will be corresponding development in virtual reality (VR) technology. You can now wear a VR helmet which produces computer-generated sensory information, particularly sounds and visual images. At present VR systems are crude but in a very few decades the equipment will be so sophisticated that the visual images, for example, will be indistinguishable from real vision. Perhaps televisionscreen contact lenses will replace the helmets, too. In the next century, most people will probably be experiencing VR all the time they are awake. The VR computer system will be able to modify perceptions to make everyone and everything look and sound wonderful. Non-existent but utterly convincing computer-generated people could be created.

We should consider the implications of the impending technological revolution. The social consequences will be enormous. For example, you would be able to live in a bare structure that looks, to any virtual realist, like a palace. People will not have to travel, because the universe (created by the massively powerful VR computer system) will come to them. Real social interaction will probably decline considerably. Dream monitoring and recording technology could be merged with VR so that the dreamer, when awake, could relive and alter a particular dream – and anyone else will be able to tune in, too.

Everyday life will increasingly resemble the dreams we now have only when asleep. Perhaps we are already in the ultimate VR system without realizing it.

Appendix

The Melbourne/Hearne Questionnaire (MHQ)
For Dream Interpretation

STRICTLY CONFIDENTIAL

Please give as much information as possible, using BLOCK CAPITALS.

A: THE DREAMER

NAME:

ADDRESS:

USUAL OCCUPATION:

SEX:

DATE OF BIRTH:*

TIME AND PLACE OF BIRTH:*

(*This information is useful for solar/planetary/lunar influence research into dreams and dreamers)

EDUCATION:

NATIONALITY:

MARITAL STATUS:

NUMBER OF CHILDREN:

RELIGION:

INTERESTS, HOBBIES:

WOULD YOU SAY THAT YOU ARE PSYCHIC?
(i.e. you experience telepathy, clairvoyance, premonitions, etc.)
☑Yes ☐Don't know ☐No (Tick)

HOW WOULD YOU OBJECTIVELY DESCRIBE YOUR
PERSONALITY?
(please underline one of the three categories for items a–g)

a. Extrovert – In-between – Introvert

b. Assertive – In-between – Mild

c. Emotional – In-between – Stable

d. Trusting – In-between – Suspicious

e. Serious – In-between – Carefree

f. Confident – In-between – Worrier

g. Independent – In-between – Need others

FIRST NAMES OF PEOPLE SIGNIFICANT TO YOU, E.G. PARTNER,
FAMILY, COLLEAGUES, FRIENDS. (These may be represented in
disguised form in the dream.)

LIST MATTERS THAT ARE PARTICULARLY ON YOUR MIND AT
THIS TIME – IN ORDER OF CONCERN (most important first), e.g.
concerning relationship problem, career, house, illness, money,
decisions to make. Give a brief summary:

a. _____

b. _____

c. _____

d. _____

e. _____

WAS/IS THERE SOMETHING SPECIAL DUE TO HAPPEN A DAY
OR TWO AFTER THE DREAM?

☐No ☐Yes (If so, give brief details)
_____

B: DREAM REPORT

PROVIDE A FULL ACCOUNT OF THE DREAM.
Spend some time thinking about your dream and writing the
report. Describe everything you can remember – even sketch
what you saw in some scenes – because sometimes items that
seem to be insignificant are, in fact, very important in the
dream analysis.

DATE OF DREAM:
_____

TIME OF DREAM:
_____

BED TIME:
_____

ESTIMATED SLEEP-ONSET TIME:
_____

DREAM REPORT:
_____

_____

(Continue on separate sheets if necessary)

C: ADDITIONAL INFORMATION

(Please provide as much information as possible. This categorized data is useful not only in the interpretation, but also for comparison purposes. Various patterns may be noticed between these items in the dreamer over time, or between different people.)

DID YOU TAKE ANY MEDICATION BEFORE SLEEP?

❏No ❏Yes (If so, give details)

WERE THE SLEEPING CONDITIONS UNUSUAL? (e.g. Different bed from usual)

❏No ❏Yes (If so, give details)

WHAT WERE YOUR THOUGHTS BEFORE SLEEP?
IN GENERAL, WERE THESE THOUGHTS: (Tick)

❏Very pleasant ❏Pleasant ☑Neutral

❏Unpleasant ❏Very unpleasant?

WOULD YOU DESCRIBE THE DREAM AS A NIGHTMARE?

❏No ❏Yes

WERE THE DREAM EVENTS POSSIBLE IN REALITY?

❏No ❏Yes

WERE THE EVENTS LAWFUL?

❏No ❏Yes

WERE THE EVENTS CUSTOMARY AND NORMAL FOR YOU?

❏No ❏Yes

WERE THERE LINKS TO EVENTS THAT HAPPENED IN THE DAY BEFORE?

☐No ☐Yes (If so, give details; continue on separate sheet)

WAS YOUR SLEEP MORE DISTURBED THAN USUAL THAT NIGHT?

☐More disturbed ☐Usual ☐Less disturbed

HAVE YOU HAD THE DREAM BEFORE?

☐No ☐Yes

HAVE YOU ANY IDEAS YOURSELF AS TO WHAT THE DREAM MEANS?

ANY OTHER RELEVANT BACKGROUND INFORMATION

YOUR ROLE IN THE DREAM: (Tick)

☐Observing ☐Taking part ☐Both

THE SETTING(S): ☐Indoor ☐Outdoor ☐Both

☐Familiar to me ☐Unfamiliar to me ☐Both

☐This country ☐Abroad ☐Both ☐Other

SENSES EXPERIENCED IN DREAM, APART FROM VISUAL: (Tick)

☐Hearing ☐Taste ☐Smell ☐Touch ☐Pain ☐Sexual

NUMBER OF PERSONS/CREATURES SEEN IN DREAM:
Briefly describe these persons/creatures: (Name, sex, age, clothing, behaviour, etc.)

1.

2. _____

3. _____

4. _____

5. _____

6. _____

(Continue on separate sheet if necessary)

SIGNIFICANT THINGS SAID BY DREAM CHARACTERS:
(Indicate who said them)
_____

_____

_____

DID YOU EXPERIENCE SLEEP PARALYSIS? ☐No ☐Yes

EMOTION(S) ON WAKING:
_____

_____

PSYCHOLOGICAL STATE ON WAKING:
☐Very unpleasant ☐Unpleasant ☐Neutral

☐Pleasant ☐Very pleasant

AMOUNT OF ACTIVITY IN DREAM:
☐Very much ☐Much ☐Some ☐Little ☐Very little

AMOUNT OF NOISE IN DREAM:
☐Very much ☐Much ☐Some ☐Little ☐Very little

COLOUR:
☐None ☐Some ☐Much ☐Not noticed

BRIGHTNESS OF DREAM IMAGES:
☐Very bright ☐Bright ☐In-between ☐Rather dark

☐Very Dark

WAS IT A LUCID DREAM? (i.e. where you are actually aware that it is a dream while you are still dreaming and can control the events)
☐No ☐Yes ☐Not sure

DID THE DREAM OCCUR ON AN ANNIVERSARY OF A SIGNIFICANT EVENT FOR YOU?
☐No ☐Yes ☐Don't know (If so, give details)

WHICH THINGS STUCK IN YOUR MIND MOST ON WAKING?

RATE THE STRESS IN YOUR LIFE CURRENTLY
☐None ☐Little ☐In-between ☐Much ☐Very much

WEATHER INFORMATION (that night):

BAROMETRIC PRESSURE IN MORNING (if known):

2 ADDITIONAL QUESTIONS FOR FEMALES:

HOW MANY DAYS AFTER THE 1st DAY OF YOUR LATEST CYCLE DID THE DREAM OCCUR?

IF YOU ARE PREGNANT, AFTER HOW MANY WEEKS INTO PREGNANCY DID THE DREAM OCCUR?

Bibliography

Aserinsky, E. & Kleitman, N. (1953) Regular periods of eye motility and concomitant phenomena during sleep. *Science*, 118, 273–4.

Aubrey, J. (1890: orig. 1696) *Miscellanies*. Library of Old Authors, Reeves & Turner, London.

Cattell, R. and Eber, J. (1969) *Sixteen personality factor questionnaire*. Institute for Personality & Ability Testing, Illinois, U.S.A.

Dodds, E.R. (1971) Supernormal phenomena in classical antiquity. *Proceedings of the Society for Psychical Research*, 55 (205), 189–237.

Evans, C. and Newman, E. (1964) Dreaming: an analogy from computers. *New Scientist*, 24, 577–9.

Evans-Wentz, W. (1960) *The Tibetan Book of the Dead*. Oxford University Press.

Faraday, A. (1972) *Dream Power*. Hodder & Stoughton, London.

Faraday, A. (1974) *Dream Game*. Hodder & Stoughton, London.

Fontana, D. (1993) *The Secret Language of Symbols*. Pavilion Books, London.

Fordham, F. (1953) *An Introduction to Jung's Psychology*. Pelican Books, London.

Fox, O. (1962) *Astral Projection*. University Books Inc., New York.

Freud, S. (1961; orig. 1900) *The Interpretation of Dreams*. George Allen & Unwin, London.

Garfield, P. (1974) *Creative Dreaming*. Ballantine Books, New York.

Garwell, B. (1996) *Dreams that Come True*. Thorsons, Wellingborough.

Graham, H. (1995) *A Picture of Health*. Piatkus Books, London.

Green, C. (1968) *Lucid Dreams*. Institute for Psychophysical Research, Oxford.

Gurney, E., Myers, F. and Podmore, F. (1918) *Phantasms of the Living*. Kegan Paul, Trench, Trubner & Co., London.

Hearne, K. (1973) Some investigations into hypnotic dreams using a new technique (B.Sc. project). University of Reading.

Hearne, K. (1975) *Visual imagery and evoked responses* (M.Sc. thesis). Dept. of Psychology, University of Hull.

Hearne, K. (1978) *Lucid dreams – an electrophysiological and psychological study* (Ph.D. thesis). Dept. of Psychology, University of Liverpool.

Hearne, K. (1981) A light-switch phenomenon in lucid dreams. *Journal of Mental Imagery*, 5 (2), 97–100.

Hearne, K. (1981) Lucid dreams and ESP. *Journal of the Society for Psychical Research*, 51 (787), 7–11.

Hearne, K. (1982) Effects of performing certain set tasks in the lucid dream state. *Perceptual and Motor Skills*, 54, 259–62.

Hearne, K. (1984) Lucid dreams and psi research. In *Current trends in Psi Research – Proceedings of an International Conference held in New Orleans, Louisiana, August 13–14*. Eds. B. Shapiro and L Coly, Parapsychology Foundation, Inc. New York, pp 192–218.

Hearne, K. (1986) An analysis of premonitions deposited over one year, from an apparently gifted subject. *Journal of the Society for Psychical Research*, 53 (804), 376–82.

Hearne, K. (1987) A new perspective in dream imagery. *Journal of Mental Imagery*, 11 (2), 75–82.

Hearne, K. (1989) *Visions of the Future*. Aquarian Press, Wellingborough.

Jones, E. (1949) *On the Nightmare*. Hogarth Press, London.

Jung, C. (1964) *Man and His symbols*. Aldus Books, London.

Price, H. (1949) Psychical research and human personality. *The Hibbert Journal*, 47, 105–13.

St Denys, Hervey de (1982; orig. 1867) *Dreams and How to Guide Them*. Trans. Nicholas Fry, ed. M. Schatzman. Duckworth, London.

Time–Life Books (1990) *Dreams and Dreaming and Psychic Voyages* (Mysteries of the Unknown). The Time Inc. Book Company, U.S.A.

Ullman, M., Krippner, S., and Vaughan, A. (1973) *Dream Telepathy*. MacMillan, New York.

van Eeden, F. (1913) A study of dreams. *Proceedings of the Society for Psychical Research*, XXVI (part LXVII), 431–61.

Index

Further Information

David Melbourne and Dr Keith Hearne put on occasional one or two-day seminar/workshops on dream interpretation. These are open to anyone who is interested in dreams.

Various tape cassettes on sleep and dream topics are also available.

For information please write to

42 Borden Avenue
Enfield
Middx.
EN1 2BY

Please mark the envelope 'Dreams'.